THE EAGLE
AND THE
COCKEREL

THE EAGLE
AND THE
COCKEREL

Alan Rhode

First published in the UK in 2023 by
Zinfandel Publishing, in partnership with whitefox publishing

www.wearewhitefox.com

ISBN 9781915635167
Also available as an ebook and an audiobook
ISBN 9781915635174 and 9781915635181

Edited by Emily Randle and Gemma Wain
Designed and typeset by seagulls.net
Cover design by Nathan Burton
Project management by whitefox
Printed and bound in Suffolk by Clays Ltd, Elcograf S.p.A.

This story is based on true historical facts that
They don't want people to know.

I

A Brand in Himself

'Boulevard Auguste-Blanqui au croisement avec la Rue Vulpian.'

Gliding away in silence, the self-driven Cabeille shared a notification from ROME, the ubiquitous social network of Europe.

Eleven days to the vote that will change history.

A prolonged glance in the mirror pleased Vincent d'Amont. No tell-tale sign of ageing yet. And if somebody had hinted at the traditional pride of a French politician past his prime, he would have responded that rear-view mirrors on driverless taxis could be of no other use than self-admiration. In truth, he had acquired a secret habit of searching for everlasting youth in all reflective surfaces.

Vincent d'Amont wasn't missing the rude manners of Parisian taxi drivers, their open frustration at short journeys, or the loud phone calls in disregard of passengers. Fortunately, riding in a taxi in Paris was much more enjoyable now, after he had ensured that every arrondissement included self-driving routes.

Shortly after entering Avenue Trudaine, Vincent lifted his head towards the white shape of the Basilique du Sacré-Coeur, nestled at the top of the Montmartre hill, sharp and glittering under the high sun of that spring morning.

Vincent had presided over many an official ceremony at the Sacré-Coeur. On each occasion, the then mayor of Paris had repeated his meticulously rehearsed script: that the Basilique, a symbol of national penance after France caused the doomed war with Prussia under Napoleon III, epitomised the atavistic passion and polarisation of French politics. Why had the Church of Paris selected the site of Montmartre, cradle of the revolutionary Commune, if not to chastise the Republicans? It had then taken four decades of predictable wrangling before the Sacré-Coeur was completed.

Yet whenever Vincent saw the imperious contour of the Basilique standing proud against the skies above Montmartre, his memory would draw him back less to stately functions and more to that midsummer-night incident when the Sacré-Coeur almost cost him the mayorship.

The night when his office had rung the Archdiocese of Paris at two a.m. to arrange an immediate visit to the Sacré-Coeur, the awkward time justified with a Mozambican dignitary wishing to visit the Basilique before his early departure. Within two hours, and with all the highest echelons of the Archdiocese up in a frenzy, the mayoral visit had taken place.

Was this a diplomatic visit or a date? Did Vincent d'Amont lie to the Church?

Amanda Arnaud, the doyenne of the French sensationalist press, had based her enquiry on poor images of a blurred lady entering the Basilique next to Vincent. The Mayor's Office had hastened to communicate that she was a member of the Mozambican delegation, but Arnaud's requests for comment from Maputo had yielded no response.

Despite the wide publicity, and the unavoidable petition for the mayor's resignation, the political brouhaha had quickly petered out. The episode had instead sparked further gossip about the persona of Vincent. His well-groomed appearance, impeccable attire and documented appreciation of the fairer sex hadn't gone unnoticed in national coverage of the Sacré-Coeur case.

Will the people vote to unify France and Germany? the Cabeille's news ticker kept scrolling.

Vincent had arrived. He was about to meet Amanda Arnaud for the first time. To his dismay, as a location for their interview Arnaud had chosen a lofty café very dear to a mature Parisian clientele – an age group that Vincent tried to elude, lest they infect him with their stiff elderliness.

When, once inside the café, he walked towards her, Arnaud had already taken her seat in a room reserved for the two of them. Her eyes lit up. She was sporting a bright orange suit, and heavy make-up covered her tanned face, topped off by voluminous, streaked blonde hair. He had always suspected that her bouffant owed a debt to some unidentified anchorwoman of a distant past.

'I'm glad you've agreed to meet me,' Arnaud said after quite a stilted handshake.

'This – and much more – for the last printed tabloid of France,' he replied.

'Bygones are bygones?'

'I'm here, no?'

As a rule, Vincent tried to preserve every relationship regardless of what might have gone on with the other person. He had never liked to burn bridges and, when he was tempted to do so, an adage always resonated with him: *A broken clock is right twice a day.*

Amanda Arnaud looked at Vincent with a blend of curiosity and amusement. Not only did he appear to lack any kind of rancour, he had even singled her out to concede a rare interview. Vincent d'Amont preferred to interact directly with people through live broadcasts on ROME rather than answering to journalists, probably because most media disliked him. Yet the man at the centre of European politics was now giving a tabloid interview to a female gossip columnist, to the chagrin – no doubt – of all male political commentators.

Arnaud glanced outside of their private room, which now seemed unnecessary. The sparse grey-haired customers of the spacious café, outnumbered by white-jacketed waiters, were obviously disinterested in their surroundings. The glacial ambience of the chic patisserie mirrored the rearward vibe permeating Paris, superbly nostalgic and suspended in time. Perhaps this lofty decadence was fertile ground for the next revolution.

'April the eighth will be a crucial day for Europe,' Arnaud began. 'No fewer than one hundred million netizens will vote on ROME to decide whether France and Germany should merge to create Charlemagny and leave the European Union.'

She paused, as if to stress the solemnity of her introduction, then resumed.

'Commentators raise concerns about the poll's reliability, suggesting that a social media vote is never safe from malfunctions or rigging. Aren't they right?'

'The referendum will run on blockchain, a safe technology used for e-voting in many countries.' Vincent addressed the expected question with no hesitation. 'Blockchain is trustworthy and hack-proof. People raising these doubts are ignorant, or manoeuvred by the old political establishment, spreading fake news for fear of losing power. But we are all tired of seeing the same elite making the decisions. People should be allowed to determine their own future, finally.'

Unimpressed by him deploying his populist ethos so early in the interview, Arnaud made a technical remark. 'Another concern is legal. Even if voters decide that France and Germany should unify, this will happen through a social media poll, not a binding referendum.'

Vincent nimbly retorted: 'Again, the fear of seeing politics changing makes some misinterpret reality. ROME is trusted in Europe more than political institutions are. Whatever decision the people take, the governments will not ignore it.'

'Assuming the new super-country you envisage comes to pass: why should Charlemagny abandon the European Union?'

'Because the Union is destined to break. And Charlemagny doesn't belong to a collapsing Europe.'

Aware that her readers were less interested in politics than in Vincent's controversial figure, Arnaud changed her angle. 'What's the role of Vincent d'Amont in this unprecedented campaign?'

'I'm representing the natural right of people to determine their independence in a free manner – nothing more.' A personal touch of his followed: 'I was born and bred in Alsace, a land that was pushed and pulled between France and Germany five times in the last two centuries. They trampled on the local people's dignity. Dreadful.'

Consummate in eye-contact strategies, Vincent looked straight at Arnaud.

'The European Community was created to appease France and Germany. We can say that Europe has served its purpose: the bond between France and Germany is now stronger than ever. So, there's no time like the present for moving to the next step: unification.'

'Do you see yourself as the first president of Charlemagny?' she asked.

'It's unimportant. Before anything else, we must focus on achieving Charlemagny. There are so many ways in which each of us can serve Charlemagny. Let's leave the gentlemen in Brussels to obsess about titles and roles.'

Arnaud was disappointed. Not in the least spontaneous, Vincent's prefabricated answers were falling flat, perhaps on purpose. This rare interview represented a great opportunity for her, and she wanted to wring a story out of it at all costs. Maybe an unsettling remark would help to crack his phlegmatic armour.

'You're accused of being narcissistic ... of dragging Europe into deep waters for your own reasons but not to admitting your own mistakes ...'

'That's bitchy. There's no need to make it so personal. The future of Europe and possibly of the entire world is at stake here. That's much more important than any considerations of my persona.'

For all he had just said, Vincent liked talking about himself and, at times, he referred to his dream of Charlemagny in such terms as to imply that the entire project represented, in the end, a facet of his own person.

'You're currently the celebrity with the highest number of ROME followers in all of Europe. Millions and millions. One year ago, you were barely ranked among the hundred thousand most-followed people. What's the secret behind your success?'

Arnaud's question reflected the incredulity within the social media industry at Vincent's impressive feat on ROME. His surge in the last year seemed to defy all algorithms. Too good to be true, whispered – perhaps out of envy – more than one SEO expert. Just as a financial miracle often hides a Ponzi scheme, this unprecedented popularity had to conceal some chicanery.

'I must have explained well why Europe failed. People aren't stupid,' was his dismissive answer.

'Miss Cliché would argue that you're playing on the people's worst feelings …'

Vincent tensed. A most popular investigative vlogger, and deeply in love with Europe, Miss Cliché had relentlessly teased him from the start of the whole Charlemagny idea. But what irked Vincent was less her vlog's antagonism than the incessant, methodical fact-checking Miss Cliché always carried out on every syllable he uttered. She wouldn't let anything less-than-true slide with him: a cumbersome task, given the range of inaccuracies that followed Vincent's quoting of historical facts or statistical data to his advantage. Recently, he had come out with a theory whereby Charlemagne had been born in Alsace, his homeland, but without much evidence to substantiate it. A son of the post-truth age, after all.

Resourceful as he was, Vincent had proudly devised a faultless solution to address the frequent cases where Miss Cliché unveiled one of his imprecisions: he would throw another untruth on top of the first to make his opponent's work even tougher, or change topic altogether. Like former lovers bearing mutual rancour, they constantly poked and provoked each other in over-the-top tones on social media, their friction appearing genuinely harsh, not some acted pantomime.

Arnaud had on purpose made that annoying reference to Miss Cliché's criticism of Vincent, hoping that by lashing his ego she would prompt some spicy answer on his part. Her public deserved more than ready-made assertions.

'I should file a complaint against Miss Cliché for stalking,' he said, the irony barely covering his irritation. 'She spends all her time talking about me. Doesn't she have a life of her own?'

'Miss Cliché accuses you of minding your own interests more than those of Europeans …'

'Listen – I've received death threats for my views on Europe. If I was as selfish as she claims, I would've stayed silent instead of putting my life at risk.'

'Miss Cliché says you're all sizzle and no steak …'

'Miss Cliché is a vegan; she doesn't know what she's talking about …'

Arnaud chuckled at the soft pun. Considered Miss Cliché's greatest competitor, here she was now, waving her rival's remarks to goad Vincent into an unguarded response.

'And let me add one thing, Amanda: she pontificates about Europe, but Miss Cliché left Italy for the United Kingdom. That's not very patriotic. She keeps slandering me, and there's one reason why I've not brought her before a judge: I dislike dealing with lawyers. I sent her a text last week: *Let's have a public face-to-face on ROME – you and me – instead of chasing each other through the media*. She hasn't even come back to me. Miss Cliché is all bluff and bluster.'

'Do you know each other personally? That's news to me,' asked Arnaud, glimpsing the embryo of a possible story.

'Yes – Miss Cliché worked in Brussels as the assistant of a fellow MEP when I was at the European Parliament.'

'Ah.'

'You should write that: I openly challenge Miss Cliché to a debate on ROME. There's still some time before the vote. We'll talk, and the people will ultimately decide who's right and who's wrong. What does she fear?'

* * *

Late afternoon had arrived by the time Vincent left the café. The Cabeille was waiting outside. Next stop: a small community outside of Paris, in one of those frequent never-ending days. The car smoothly accelerated along Rue Vergnaud, turned right onto Place Pierre-Riboulet and passed close by Parc Kellermann, a wide expanse of lawns and playgrounds that bordered Boulevard Périphérique, the large ring road enveloping the city. '*Quel plaisir, Marquis de Sade,*' he whispered as the Cabeille sped past the Bicêtre Hospital.

Will Charlemagny ever see the light? the news ticker added.

The Cabeille was entering the large highway connecting Paris to Lyon when Vincent received a call.

'How did it go?' the other asked.

'She tried to make it personal, to distract me from the referendum, but I managed to bring the discussion back to Charlemagny. I also said that I want to face Miss Cliché on ROME.'

'Mm,' said the caller, unconvinced. 'I already told you that it's not a good idea. We're ahead in most polls – why invite her to challenge us?'

'I'm not someone who shies away from a debate,' replied Vincent, piqued at being questioned. The call didn't last long.

After traversing suburban Moissy-Cramayel, the Cabeille entered a nondescript industrial park, replete with predictable rows of warehouses, parking lots and wide patches of brown-field. Clusters of tower blocks, with their neutral lights, dotted the dark hills around.

Vincent left the Cabeille at the first empty spot, and walked through the gloomy compound. Worrying that his coat might drag in the dirt, he moved quickly, but not enough to prevent a swirl of grit from dusting his outfit.

Large trucks were parked by most units, but no human action could be seen. Vincent wandered clueless for five minutes in search of his destination, then spotted a weathered wooden gate. After pressing the grey button on an unlabelled intercom, a squeaking voice said: 'Please come up, second floor, we're on-air!'

The flaking gate opened with a soft vibration. Surprised by the place's shabbiness, Vincent climbed three sets of stairs to reach a doorway, where a steel metal sign stood high.

RADIO GALLIQUE

A girl with a bright floral jacket – which Vincent identified as cheap on the spot – welcomed him into a minuscule lounge. Flustered, she kept darting glances at him. They stood there alone, apparently waiting for someone. He smiled, then looked in other directions.

After operating in sizeable obscurity for years, Radio Gallique had recently grown into an unexpected French media phenomenon. This underground digital channel allowed anyone to call and have their once-in-a-lifetime experience as a guest of a wild show without protocol.

The founder – a burly man known as Dijon – had started broadcasting music from his own living room many years earlier. To this day, Dijon was the main host, spending day and night on the waves, to the point – they said – that he even slept in a cramped room next to the studio.

Music now played a very minor part in the programmes of Radio Gallique. Calling them 'programmes' wasn't entirely accurate, as the schedule lacked any kind of separation between shows. A renowned French media critic had once written: *The broadcast of Radio Gallique mostly consists of a constant, endless stream of statements, rants, irrational and utopistic ideas bounced back and forth. People just talk and talk: it's anarchy on the airwaves.*

The ideological *trait d'union* linking the motley audience of Radio Gallique was a thunderous, although patchy, idea of patriotism. The mantra of French self-defence had established itself so deeply among Dijon's followers that it now prevailed over any other value.

'Monsieur d'Amont! Have you come here all by yourself?' Dijon welcomed the most popular guest ever to grace that grubby floor. 'I'd expected to see a squad of bodyguards after all those death threats!'

'The honour is mine. I'm followed all day long, in one way or the other. It doesn't hurt to be all by myself, sometimes.'

'We've thousands of messages for you. Honestly, I didn't believe you would accept our invitation. And so close to Charlemagny day – you must be so busy, right?' asked Dijon, who had a tic, that of tilting his neck to the right, whose frequency was apparently linked to his state of mind.

'I wouldn't have missed this invitation for any reason. What you've done all these years – rekindling radio – deserves recognition. You know, when I was twenty, I adored playing at the discos around Colmar.'

'I didn't know you were a DJ,' replied Dijon, delighted.

'Yes. After skiing, I'd meet up with my friends and mix some records. Music has always been an important part of my life. Music gives a soul to the universe, wings to the mind, flight to the imagination, a charm to sadness, and life to everything – as Plato said.'

'You had a classical education, I recall!'

'Yes. It's a shame that now all schools, even primary schools, are fixated on computer programming and engineering. They neglect classical studies, which build the brain and give order to pupils. This is a period of time when we need order.'

Dijon's colleague was still staring at Vincent.

'This is my colleague Marguerite,' said Dijon. 'She's my assistant.' 'Marguerite, nice to make your acquaintance,' Vincent said with a penetrating glance. Marguerite blushed and smiled up at him.

'Listen, Vincent. I can call you Vincent, right?' asked Dijon, with hesitance and excitement blended in his voice. 'We're about to go live. As you know, our shows are audio only. This is our strict policy; even if it costs us money and visibility – because ROME penalises us for not posting videos – we've always stuck to it.'

He paused, then added in a guilty tone: 'ROME ... she can be dictatorial ... please don't report me, I know you're close to ROME. Mind you, at least Marlene Gäch has broken the American monopoly on communication.'

Vincent nodded, a little uncomfortable with Dijon's blunt comments about ROME laying down the law. Comments that he couldn't challenge, though.

Radio Gallique allowed listeners to submit audio messages with a maximum length of thirty seconds. Dijon called these messages 'droplets'. A monthly cap of a single droplet for each listener applied. A limit that was easily enforced, given that a user could only send droplets to Radio Gallique through their ROME account. There was scarcely any need for human filtering of the droplets; an algorithm was constantly at work. Dijon had never disclosed the criteria by which droplets were prioritised.

Vincent was just sitting down when Dijon began his show.

'Today's guest is the most discussed man in Europe! He who understood well before others that France and Germany are better than all other European countries ... and so we need to act ... you will soon be able to vote on uniting these two wonderful countries and leave the European Union.'

The stance of Radio Gallique on Charlemagny was unequivocal.

Vincent was still expressing his gratitude for the warm introduction when Dijon interrupted: 'Droplet!'

'I've been a carpenter all my life,' the first dropleter said. 'But getting decent work has become impossible. How can we compete with Poles and Bulgarians selling their families off for a bowl of soup? *Merde.* Charlemagny must protect us!'

Vincent, who experienced a dense adrenaline rush every time he was live on radio, looked at Dijon. The latter gave him the go-ahead.

'Immigration is Europe's biggest issue. But let's say it – nobody has the balls to stop it. Years ago, a German Chancellor even opened the gates to more than half a million refugees, but she regretted that idea when they flooded the country. The moral is: you cannot bypass your people to open the gates of your land; you need to hear first what your country wants. Charlemagny will be different. We'll close the borders to empty-handed foreigners – I'm sorry to all the politically correct.'

Deafening artificial applause erupted in the studio. Vincent was adding a few words, but Dijon cut him off.

'Droplet!'

'I don't see why we keep paying money to those poor countries in Eastern Europe,' another began. 'We can barely take care of ourselves – why help countries that waste our money?'

'Very true,' Vincent observed. 'France and Germany together contribute more than half of the European budget. Absurd—'

'Droplet!'

'We French work hard and pay taxes here. We should be preferred over immigrants … if things stay the way they are … people will kick the shit out of politicians … just a matter of time.'

Vincent was poised to address the droplet, but Dijon, putting his microphone on mute, leaned over and whispered: 'Please let me send another droplet … we've a great rhythm going … what a shame it'd be to spoil it.'

'We're being played by bureaucrats in Brussels,' began the fourth dropleter, more articulate than the previous ones. 'I want to talk to and understand the politicians who make decisions about my life. Some of these people in Brussels don't even speak French. Should I accept being ruled by a Lithuanian politician? At best, they speak English, the language of the country that first decided to leave Europe. Are we protecting the French language? It is considered one of the noblest languages on earth, but we are not doing enough to protect it—'

The droplet ended. The thirty-second allowance had elapsed. The open principle of Radio Gallique was clear: say less, so that everybody may have their say, regardless of how well spoken they are.

As Dijon glanced over at him with anxiety, worried perhaps that he might do something not entirely in tune with the draconian policies of their set-up, Vincent found room to speak.

'The language of a nation is a large part of its identity. Our language represents so much of our people's history, culture, feelings. It's like a musical instrument – and I love music – it says a lot about the player. French is a wonderful language, and Frenchmen used to call it an *affaire d'État*—'

'Another droplet!' Dijon shouted, twisting his neck to the right. The intensity of his spasms was increasing. The thirty-second rule applied to Vincent d'Amont, too. This time the studio hadn't resounded with enthusiastic applause.

A sequence of droplets followed.

'... If you've lived an entire life in an African hut, you'll never know how to live in a modern city ...'

'... The US and China are threatening Europe. Let's fight back ... !'

'... What's this "non-binary" bullshit ... ?'

'... Spaniards don't respect rules. It's their nature ...'

'... Why're you allowing that Italian bitch to mock you, Vincent ... ?'

Droplet, droplet, droplet!

Gradually, as if in a musical crescendo, the harshness of the words, the chaos of the concepts, the manifestations of self-pity all grew in parallel. To the ears of the rational listener, these messages blended into a cacophony, a chorus of whining voices, each one boosting the other and all making the same point. With his constant, frenetic pressing of buttons to play droplets or activate bursts of applause, Dijon, whose sweat-soaked neck now regularly swung left and right like a pendulum, was akin to a demonic pianist. An algorithm directed the orchestra.

Vincent knew how, at times, the united voice of people could act barbarically, difficult to tame and deaf to any reasoning. He had learned to nod when it happened, to listen, to accommodate the enraged speakers in the same way a child, lost in the wild, would seek safety from an approaching bear by playing dead.

When, in his thirty precious seconds, a caller contested that Germany wasn't a good fit for France – for it was Germany that had made life impossible in Europe – Vincent began to craft a response, explaining that France and Germany had been the closest allies in Europe for a long period. So if the Union had failed to deliver what was expected, that was due to other countries.

This was when Dijon ad-libbed: 'I hope we don't end up being German subjects ...'

Vincent frowned. He hadn't expected the founder of Radio Gallique to contradict him in public. As his quivering lips struggled to find an incisive rejoinder, Dijon called forth the next droplet.

'France needs to leave the European Union ... but merging with Germany can be very dangerous ... there are more of them than us, their economy is stronger ... are you sure you are leading us in the right direction ... ?'

Vincent was enraged. What unsettled him was not so much the fact that any comment against Germany, at this stage, might threaten Charlemagny's unity, but rather the heretical idea that he was being questioned on Radio Gallique, a supposed anti-European stronghold from which he would have expected unequivocal support.

Not that Vincent wasn't equipped to be challenged. In fact, he liked engaging in fierce arguments with his opponents. It had recently happened at a conference with the European Central Bank, a most notorious lion's den for any Eurosceptic, and Vincent had enjoyed the praise of the media for his courage. He fed on confrontation. What was harder to tolerate was to receive friendly fire.

Vincent found it increasingly difficult to address the incessant whirlwind of droplets. Expected as a triumphant appearance centred around him – the mastermind of Charlemagny – the show was instead proving to be an act dominated by Dijon, who now looked less a friend than a rival. Vincent knew that his eloquence was failing him this evening, and attributed his dazed performance to the anarchy reigning at Radio Gallique. He strangely missed the gossipy but, ultimately, more elevated atmosphere of his earlier vis-à-vis with Amanda Arnaud.

With Charlemagny approaching so fast, poor approval ratings weren't allowed. A lacklustre performance at Radio Gallique wouldn't go unnoticed. Miss Cliché would for sure highlight it, with all the other vloggers following. He had lost his touch, people would say, or they would claim that he was unable to deliver Charlemagny. It was like one of those doomed poker games, he thought, recalling the many all-night games

he had played while still in Colmar. He was loath to surren-
der, though. He asked himself what the young Vincent would
have done to make a derailing poker night a success. He would
have bluffed, was the answer. So when someone expressed in
his droplet a less-than-expected enthusiasm for Charlemagny,
Vincent reacted.

'Your hesitation does you no honour,' he chided the dropleter. 'You're clueless. I'm not going to give up. You must trust
me. A strong man makes a strong country. I'm talking to all
of you who are listening: I want you to get mad. I want you to
protest. You must get mad. So, get up now, all of you get up
from your chairs, go outside and … paint!'

Dijon looked at him, puzzled.

Vincent quieted, his eyes still expressing anger. He
now seemed a very different person from the man who had
chatted amicably in the lobby earlier on. Standing up under
Dijon's mesmerised stare, he yelled: 'You need to graffiti
Charlemagny on the walls of your house, on the side of a
bridge, on top of a roof – wherever you want. Let the world
know how much Charlemagny means to you. Do it now!
Don't waste any more time!'

Marguerite, biting her upper lip, gazed at him from behind
the glass screen of the studio. From his stool, Dijon looked up
at Vincent. He couldn't work out where his celebrity guest was
heading. But no further droplets for the day.

'Words, words – people are tired of them. Talk is cheap.
What you *see* is what matters. So, we need to give a face, a
shape, to Charlemagny. Only then will the people of France
and Germany take Charlemagny seriously. Get out and paint!
Graffiti is art!'

During his shows, Dijon's eyes occasionally fell on the dashboard to check the audience's live reaction. On average, the approval rating stood between 50 and 70 per cent. It seldom went higher. After Vincent, a staggering 95 per cent pulsed on the dashboard – nobody had ever achieved something like that.

There was no longer any sign of confusion on Dijon's face. He finally understood. More effective than thousands of droplets, Vincent d'Amont had stolen the show. Dijon knew he had to set aside his own ego, this time, for the great cause of Charlemagny. People would absolutely get behind Vincent's appeal. Charlemagny was ever closer.

'Go out and paint! Go out and paint!' Dijon shouted too.

II

A Lady on the Move

'*De donde eres?*'

The cabbie boasted a thick West Midlands accent even in a foreign tongue.

'I'm not Spanish. I'm Italian,' Lucìa Morè replied.

He saw her amiable smile and burst into genuine laughter.

'Apologies … I always mix up the accents!'

'Don't worry, I love Spain! But I'm from the north of Italy. I grew up in a small town that you surely don't know. Close to Milan, where all the fun is.'

Lucìa's resigned tone was a humorous one, but it reflected the undeniable fact that young people's lives in Vigevano revolved around Milan – less because Milan necessarily fulfilled a lifetime ambition and more because Milan was an unavoidable destination for many.

Their earliest encounter with the city was when, as adolescents, they hopped on a local train to spend weekends at the permanently air-conditioned shopping malls by the Duomo. The journey's first leg involved a ride on the two-coach train to Pavia, with the unmistakable squealing of the tired locomotive as it jerkily pulled out of the station. This was exactly when the well-to-do Milanese fled Milan to bask on the Genoese

coast in summer or traverse the Dolomites in winter. And if
forced to spend a weekend in town, they would rather stay
home secluded than mingle with the suburban *maranze*.

Later, as college freshmen in Milan, with the relatively short trip not justifying a room away from home, the
Vigevanese engaged in a testing daily commute. On Monday
morning, the 7.30 regional train was late because the 6.30 was
also behind schedule. On Tuesday, it was running late due to
some glitch. The Wednesday delay was linked to a longer-than-
expected carriage-cleaning time. On Thursday, the train had
to make an emergency stop to let a ticketless passenger alight.
The commuter finally accepted a lift in a car on Friday, only to
wind up jammed on the *tangenziale*.

Commuting was like living suspended in an alienating no
man's land: having to get back home before the sun set, they
failed to create any personal ties in Milan, while the stressful everyday journeying slowly eroded them and their bond to
Vigevano. So, many eventually moved to Milan. But, priced
out of the centre by gentrification, a flat in the ever-expanding
hinterland often became the only option for fledgling families,
whose parents were destined to see their kids spending weekends at the Milanese malls.

Lucìa Morè hadn't made that choice. Never feeling drawn
to Milan, she had completed her international law studies
at the University of Pavia, sharing a flat with other students
in the nearby campus. After graduation, she had joined the
department of European Union Law as a junior lecturer under
Professor Liam Sherwood, a Briton authentically passionate
about Italy and Italians. When the professor was elected to
the European Parliament in an Italian constituency, Lucìa had

promptly joined his team in Brussels with the specific role of reviewing pending bills. And when after the Brussels tenure Professor Sherwood had joined the University of Birmingham, Lucìa had followed him there too. Many Italians at that stage would have gone for London, but just as she had always avoided the Milanese glitter, so it had come naturally to stage the next bit of her life far from the sparkle of the Thames.

'How long have you lived in Birmingham?' asked the driver.

Lucìa had reached a quasi-celebrity status in continental Europe, but British people very seldom recognised her – and the Birmingham cab drivers even less, despite her years in Brum.

When she didn't jog or use her bike, Lucìa enjoyed chatting with cabbies. Not just practical to while away the time, these exchanges allowed her to feel the people's pulse on everyday issues. A very useful tool for a news vlogger on the rise.

'What do you think of the poll in France and Germany?' Lucìa asked the driver nonchalantly.

'That we did it right to leg it from Europe. They keep rowing … Trust me, France and Germany will do the same!'

'Let's first wait for the outcome. The people haven't spoken yet. And it's different from Brexit: this isn't an official referendum, just a social media consultation.'

'Are you a journalist?' he asked, eyeing her in amusement. 'You talk like one.'

Lucìa chuckled.

The taxi stopped at its destination, Edgbaston Park. She got out and walked the short distance to a two-storey building located next to the Birmingham Rowheath Athletics Club. This narrow construction at the heart of Birmingham University hosted Miss Cliché, the popular news vlog that

Lucìa had set up, almost single-handedly, right after arriving in Birmingham.

Unlike those vlogging as a pastime, Lucìa had launched Miss Cliché with gusto, set on challenging the biggest deception perpetrated online: fake news. Fact-checking – a skill she'd developed in Brussels by enduring innumerable nights at her office in Espace Léopold – had come in very handy to make the enterprise a success.

Brussels seemed far away now. Miss Cliché absorbed all Lucìa's energies, with endless work to take care of, resulting in a very slim private life. Unlike in Brussels, though, she wasn't working in the shadow of Professor Sherwood. Lucìa was now a protagonist.

'Morning, Lucìa. Somebody's waiting in your office,' a colleague winked.

Miss Cliché's newsroom occupied the second floor of the refurbished warehouse. The architecture of the building was in origin very austere, but the old brick façade now featured glass walls that allowed tradition to blend with modernity. One of the few survivors of the renovation was a metal-grate lift – formerly an industrial elevator – shrouded by an iron stairwell recently painted pink.

The newsroom's inner décor mirrored the style of most modern co-working spaces. Open-plan, replete with large rectangular mahogany tables for contributors and their laptops, it featured a tiny cafeteria at the far end, while an often-busy pool table filled the opposite corner. There was also room for two large replicas of red London phone boxes for conference calls, and a set of reclining chairs – much needed by contributors after their writing marathons.

Lucìa had a personal office in which she spent very little time, preferring to share a large table with the others. Moreover, as the only available meeting room had been sublet to a start-up fashion company, her office was often used by others for catch-ups.

When she entered her office, Rachel was sitting on Lucìa's chair.

'You're the only one who could ever drag me to this desolate part of the UK!' Rachel said, after standing up to hug her friend, not caring who was listening.

Rachel wore an orange silk skirt, well suited to the dark tone of her long legs and a clever match to her avorio La DoubleJ sweater. Very attentive to her appearance, Rachel invested a lot in haute couture, cosmetics, jewellery and accessories, not permitting a single aspect of her countenance to be neglected. A pair of jeans and sneakers were fine for Lucìa, who liked defining herself as a countryside girl.

'You should stop thinking so badly of Birmingham,' Lucìa remarked, laughing. In normal circumstances, the open space would have been peaceful at this time but, with Charlemagny getting closer, the newsroom was teeming with people. They moved to the quieter coffee corner. 'It's nearly evening already, and knowing our passion for Venice, I thought I'd surprise you,' Lucìa said, pointing at a cupboard. She then pulled out a vintage-looking bottle, setting it with a proud gesture on the counter. A bright orange liquid glowed inside. The label, too, was orange, and portrayed an ecstatic female dancer swaying seductively. One glance at the *aperitivo* was enough to remind Lucìa of the much-needed freshness that cold drinks brought to the hot Venetian summers.

Lucìa poured the *aperitivo* into two large tumblers, added prosecco, a spurt of soda water and, with a final sleight of hand, dropped two thick orange wedges in each glass, causing the drinks to fizz intensely. She handed a tumbler to her friend. '*Et voilà*. Bevvy is ready. Canal Grande for you!'

Rachel had just flown in from New York. Usually focused on domestic politics, the American public had this time shown a particular interest in European affairs. The idea that a social media vote could usher in the unification of France and Germany had aroused a wild curiosity there.

'So ... I read on the plane that Vincent d'Amont is challenging you to a live debate on ROME.'

'Mmm ... I'm actually planning to turn down his proposal.'

'How come? It's a great opportunity.'

'I don't want to validate the cause of Charlemagny by debating with him. I'm not even sure ROME has ever moved on from what the professor and I did in Brussels. What if Marlene Gäch—'

'The Lucìa I know is too ballsy not to say yes. I hope you'll change your mind. It'd make for a relaxed couple of hours with popcorn in hand.'

'Yes, you'd watch me doing all the tough work from your comfy sofa.'

'I'm not the one who's chosen to be a celebrity vlogger ...'

'Rachel, there's no mercy when you debate live before millions of people ... it's not like posting a video ...'

'I'm sure you would get on top of it ... the camera loves you, Luci.' Rachel looked through the glass wall at the buzzing open space. 'I've heard that Vincent d'Amont doesn't have a real office.'

'He's constantly on the move,' Lucìa commented. 'He spends half his time on ROME, and the remaining part visiting all possible endorsers: journalists, politicians, CEOs, artists, whoever can help him.'

'Marco Polo,' Rachel commented ironically. 'Am I wrong, or is this quite a unique situation? You and Vincent d'Amont are leading the two opposing camps, but neither of you is in a party or holds an institutional role. Vincent d'Amont is the former mayor of Paris, rising to fame after a fall into disgrace; you a teaching assistant in international law who turned into the most famous news vlogger in Europe.'

Lucìa was amused by Rachel's journalistic depiction of the circumstances.

'I'm not a leader,' she contended. 'Governments weren't attaching enough importance to what's happening, so I decided to throw my small weight against this whole Charlemagny idea; but I'm not the leader of the "No" camp.'

'Does the "No" camp have a leader at all?' Rachel enquired.

Lucìa gave her a wistful glance.

After some apparent hesitation, Rachel said: 'I've a shameless request.'

Lucìa raised her eyebrows. She didn't know what to expect.

'Anything we can nibble on?'

Lucìa rolled her eyes in mock reproach and giggled. 'I've missed you!'

She opened the cupboard and the fridge, unpacked a box of breadsticks, unwrapped some Italian bresaola, poured out loads of olive oil and gave a ceramic plate of the Italian tapas to Rachel.

'I can't believe I'm allowing myself the luxury of an aperitif. I've been working around the clock for months,'

Lucìa complained. Rachel smiled; she remembered from Brussels her friend's inclination to lament the fact of being over-busy.

A moment of silence, and Lucìa's mind went to the time she'd first crossed paths with ROME. It had been a wintry Brussels morning when the news broke that two hundred digital businesses were asking the Commission to veto ROME's proposed acquisition of TellMe, a popular chat service. Already a leading social media platform in Europe, ROME wasn't yet the peerless giant that she would soon become, but her competitors wanted to stop an acquisition that, they feared, could turn ROME into a dangerous monopoly.

Marlene Gäch, an elusive software programmer, was the creator of ROME. The merits of her founder aside, the lightning-fast growth of ROME was indebted to a string of unprecedented tax breaks granted by the Federal Republic of Germany. Despite many arguing that the incentives represented a form of illegitimate state aid, the European Commission had never taken any serious action against Germany.

It didn't take much for ROME's bid for TellMe to come onto Lucìa's radar. With good foresight, Professor Sherwood explained the implications in his usual technical lingo. 'A social network that also operates a search engine and a marketplace targets a popular chat app: it's a cross-industry concentration of incredible importance,' he said. 'With this acquisition, ROME will have an additional arrow in her quiver to gain further market power and make it harder for others to even enter the market, let alone compete. The risk of a monopoly is clear, but I'm not sure the Commission sees it.'

'They'll kill competition.' Lucìa's sentence captured all.

For the first time, the professor invited her to release a press statement under their joint names, and even to give an interview in his place. She was already starting to garner visibility in a male-dominated Brussels, and to establish a reputation for herself as a troublemaker. That some didn't appreciate her efforts in Brussels would be proved by more than one episode – including when, after she had just spoken at a debate, a male co-panellist whispered to another condescendingly: 'Here she is – Miss Cliché.' The microphone was nasty enough to deliver to a full audience the mansplaining brickbat that, despite her initial anger, Lucìa would later weaponize as a self-ironic name for her new vlog.

The European Commission ended up approving the buyout. Lucìa was baffled. Less so Professor Sherwood, knowing that two factors had served ROME well: Germany's rooting for the merger, and Europe's ambition of competing with Chinese social media.

The professor's shadowy predictions materialised quickly. Within months, ROME grew into an escapeless destination in the digital journey of Europeans. The multifaceted platform kept expanding at a dramatic speed – not only did the number of users skyrocket, but the array of features offered increased above even the wildest forecasts. What ROME was unable to develop internally, she took from others through incorporations. Fulfilling the aspirations of Marlene Gäch, ROME was soon the place where people could find anything.

The search engine results were never casual – surgically influenced by user activities on the social network or the marketplace. If a specific interest emerged from a search engine query, the social network would show related content.

Similarly, marketplace shopping patterns were used to shape social network pushes, or to create custom-fit search results. Owing to her sophisticated, never-resting algorithm, ROME learned more about her people, steered their choices, moulded their opinions, homogenised the behaviour of a vast community, developed itself into a real home for users. ROME influenced the daily lives of hundreds of millions. A circular, incessant sharing of data flowed between the various tools of the platform, which mutually bolstered their individual efficiency and capacity of penetration. It was an enticing spiral that drew users deeper and deeper into a vortex of consumerism, numbness and, in the end, isolation.

Hugh, the closest of Lucìa's colleagues, entered the kitchenette.

'Lucìa – something important. You know when, yesterday, Vincent d'Amont incited the public to graffiti walls in the name of Charlemagny … ?'

Lucìa and Rachel stared at him.

'People are following his battle cry. The French Minister of the Interior reports that, last night alone, three hundred and twenty-one walls in Paris were Charlemagnised. Other cities are following suit.'

Hugh pointed at his tablet, which displayed a skilful drawing portraying the flags of France and Germany merged into one. He scrolled down in search of other graffiti. Some weren't much more than scribbles, but others were remarkable, like one showing an eagle and a rooster poised over the word Charlemagny. Someone had even painted a portrait of Vincent d'Amont.

'He might well have commissioned it,' Lucìa said wryly.

'He's raising the stakes,' commented Rachel, who knew from her own country's experience how this communication strategy – namely, stirring people's emotions for the purpose of power – could be very dangerous.

'What's the people's pulse on Charlemagny?' Rachel, still sipping her Venetian Spritz, asked Hugh. The two had only met a couple of times, but enough to know they didn't like each other much.

'Over two hundred polls were recently carried out in both France and Germany,' said Hugh, who had a thing for maths, as he browsed his tablet. 'Charlemagny is slightly ahead, it seems …' He coughed up some figures. 'Eighty polls reported a slight majority for Charlemagny. By "slight", I mean a gap between "Yes" and "No" equal to or less than four per cent of votes. In another sixty-five polls, a tiny majority is for Europe; but then there are ten polls where Charlemagny has a lead of more than four per cent and another five polls going the other way. In all the other polls, the share of undecided people interviewed was more than forty per cent, so we didn't really consider those ones useful.'

'Gimme a break, number monkey,' Rachel sighed.

'The ground isn't completely level,' Lucìa observed. 'When unhappy, people tend to vote for change, and the media put Charlemagny at the centre. It makes it very difficult for us to build a case for Europe.'

A young woman shyly approached the group to inform Lucìa that the Arakan Army had just conquered Sittwe. The Arakan Army, a guerrilla group based in north-west Myanmar, belonged to an ethnic minority, the Rakhines, who had long waged a war of independence against the Bamar majority. The seizing of Sittwe, a state capital, marked an escalation of local warfare that had never received much attention from international media.

'Alaula, can you please publish a five-hundred-word video, ASAP?' asked Lucìa. 'Any chance we can plus it up with real-time mobile footage directly from Sittwe? Footage must already be available somewhere. Perhaps you can ask Belch to crawl through social media.'

Alaula nodded, then headed to the other side of the newsroom. Her family was originally from Myanmar, and she often focused on news from the Far East.

'The world isn't standing still as we wait for Charlemagny,' Rachel pointed out.

'True,' agreed Lucìa. 'Europe and America tend to be self-centred, but there is so much imbalance in other areas that impact on our future, without us even realising it. And it's often overlooked. That's why Miss Cliché tries to give visibility to distant situations – those that aren't under everybody's eyes.'

Miss Cliché, indeed, stood out in the media arena for posting non-stop news videos created by vloggers from around the world. The team at Edgbaston Park worked hard to ensure that a brand-new quality video was uploaded at least every ten minutes, night or day. The clips, subject to rigorous fact-checking but, as a norm, published with no changes imposed by Lucìa or Hugh, had been fundamental in driving the rapid rise of Miss Cliché.

Acclaimed internationally as a champion of investigative vlogging, Miss Cliché had unveiled dozens of scandals, financial frauds and other wrongdoings of public interest everywhere. Be it a video from Uganda denouncing threats to opposition candidates or a case of water contamination in California, freelancers found in Miss Cliché a courage and receptivity to projects that was lacking in most other media outlets. And for those vloggers from the many countries that still thwarted freedom of expression, Miss Cliché was the only gateway to the net without censorship of any sort.

Lucìa was popular with contributors for another reason. Unlike most vlogs, Miss Cliché ensured a fair economic reward for creators. Lucìa hadn't forgotten the hours she'd devoted to the role of teaching assistant at the University of Pavia, nor the draining experiences of Italians with unpaid internships. She had created Miss Cliché as the place where she would have liked to be at the start of her career.

'Why do you think Miss Cliché is so successful?' Rachel asked, suddenly plunging into interview mode.

'Because people feel that we aren't looking for sensational news at the price of being inaccurate or ruining somebody's reputation. We triple-check all information. You'll never find clickbait on Miss Cliché … we aren't Amanda Arnaud.'

'Naming and shaming,' commented Rachel, who knew well the long-standing rivalry between Lucìa and Amanda Arnaud – an antagonism that hinged on their opposite attitudes to news-making. Arnaud would do anything for a story, even infringing the rules: 'the end justifies the means' was her favourite quote from Machiavelli. She asserted that only an audience could judge what was acceptable journalism and what was not. So the high click-rate of an article was capable, in her pragmatic view, of sanitising any wrongdoing on the author's part. Lucìa believed, instead, that journalism should be based on ethics and on respect for others, with no imaginable exception. For her, there were moral boundaries that should never be crossed, and popularity didn't necessarily go hand in hand with quality.

Noticing that, at the simple mention of her journalistic foe, Lucìa's face had clouded over, Rachel shifted. 'How's Professor Sherwood? I've fantastic memories of him – an authentic mensch. Is he in?'

Lucìa brightened. 'The professor is a very authoritative columnist, but not actively involved. He's helped us from the start, yes, but at a distance. He doesn't want us to look politically biased.'

'I guess he doesn't want you to feel overshadowed.'

'Who knows?' Lucìa lowered her eyes.

'Remember, even if it was the professor who took all the accolades, everyone in Brussels knew that you were the one hewing wood and drawing water behind the scenes,' Rachel pointed out.

A sudden call from the newsroom broke their conversation. Lucìa was to record her daily video in ten minutes' time. Since the beginning of Miss Cliché, she had never failed to publish a video every day. It didn't matter whether she was feeling well or ill, blissful or sad, curious or aloof: she had never missed one. The clips were filmed in her personal office, with Lucìa sitting at the desk, behind her the refreshing greenery of Edgbaston Park. When she travelled, her team ensured that filming facilities were available at her destination.

When Lucìa came back to the kitchenette, complaining once again about her lack of spare time, Rachel couldn't help asking: 'So, it seems there isn't much room for a private life. Are you seeing anyone?'

'No. I've no time. Is this an official interview, by the way?'

Rachel chuckled. She was entitled to ask Lucìa this genre of question. They had grown so close in Belgium that, even though they had not seen each other for a couple of years – not since Rachel had moved back to New York with the *Wall Street Journal* – the chemistry was still there. It wasn't an issue that they were different in personality: Rachel extrovert and loud, Lucìa warier and on the scrupulous side. Rachel could still recall with hysterical laughter the meticulous fashion in which Lucìa had introduced herself the first time: 'Hi, I'm Lucìa. The accent goes on the *ì* and you should pronounce the *c* as in *cheetah*.'

'You broke a few hearts in Brussels, didn't you?'

It was, indeed, not only due to her temperament that Lucìa was still remembered in Brussels. Her Mediterranean complexion, black hair and hazel eyes, the generous cleavage, velvety cheeks and naturally white smile were uncommon traits in European civil servants. Her seeming oblivious to her charms only made her even more attractive.

'How long are you staying with us?' asked Lucìa, eager to change the subject.

'I'm leaving tomorrow evening. Destination Paris.'

'Ah ... shame ... it's short ... then tonight we need to party ...'

'Yabadabadoo!' Rachel yelled. 'Girls will be girls.'

'Let me have a quick end-of-day briefing with Hugh. I promise, ten minutes tops. Then we'll run away.'

Lucìa's promise was met. Shortly after, the reunited duo started off with brio on their walk to central Birmingham. They would first skirt the edge of Edgbaston Park, shadowed by a sweep of oaks and redwoods, then pass through the city's leafy fringes with their stately Georgian houses, and finally to their destination, the Gay Village, where a good share of Birmingham's social life was. They had so much to chat about on the way.

'You wouldn't believe it, but this is the first time I've been out in a year. Friday pints with my colleagues in the pub under the newsroom don't count.'

'That's because you work too hard. After the vote, you should come to New York and rest. You can stay with me. I'm renting a flat in Chelsea – not a mansion, but cosy.'

'That'd be so nice. I miss our evenings in Belgium.'

'Me too.'

'But what Miss Cliché is doing is worth my sacrifice. Now more than ever. I don't know how you see it from America, but the situation here in Europe is serious: fascism is in fashion, the Union is crumbling and, on top of it, Vincent d'Amont has come out with his brilliant idea of Charlemagny.'

'We're taking it very seriously in the US, Lucìa,' Rachel assured her. 'That's why the *Journal* has sent me to Europe.'

'It's all already written, he believes,' Lucìa said, appreciating her friend's full attention. 'People will vote on every issue in real time, and the era of a bunch of privileged politicians deciding on behalf of a powerless population will come to an end – so he claims.'

Rachel recognised the populist tone.

'Unsurprisingly, ROME has found all these ideas enticing,' Lucìa continued. 'She sees more power and profits available for her if she's allowed to manipulate people's lives. If we're not careful, we'll soon find a barcode printed on our skin. Technology should bring people together, not establish a tyranny by brainwashing people with fake news. If we don't stop them, they'll succeed, and ROME will become their digital army.'

'It gives me goosebumps,' Rachel said.

'They're starting with France and Germany. Then they'll move on to Austria, Belgium, Denmark, Italy, Luxembourg, Switzerland … I can already picture the waiting list of countries wishing to hop on Charlemagny. Eventually, they'll also incorporate Eastern Europe and look down at it like it's the province of an empire.'

'The US will rescue Europe for a third time, then.'

Rachel's ironic mode won her a smile from Lucìa.

'But it's our evening together, Rachel … so, let's try to unwind … no more Charlemagny for the day!'

They stopped to grab a bite, as Rachel hadn't eaten since the plane, and then moved to the venue that Lucìa had chosen for their night. The place stood out jauntily on a converted glass roof terrace. Its bustling could be heard from the ground. As they walked out of the lift into the main room, Rachel glimpsed two shirtless men swaying wildly at the far side of the crowd, in a corner reserved for dancing. Loud music strengthened the already-thrumming ambience.

'If we can't unwind here, we can't unwind anywhere!' Lucìa had to raise her voice as they found a less crammed spot by the bar. A set of well-crafted metal prints with drag-show images was lined above the counter.

'It's my first time here,' Lucìa said. 'But I know Ash, the owner. Ash is non-binary and has an enlarged family: two partners, both non-binary, and a child who hasn't yet chosen their gender. I interviewed Ash two months ago and they keep inviting me to the club. I thought that tonight, with you, was the right time.'

Lucìa had recently mentioned this interview to her father in Italy over a zoom call. 'What do you mean, *chosen their gender?*' Her father had screwed up his face.

'It's quite a unique family, Dad. They've decided to be gender-neutral parents. They don't impose on their child any clothing or toy linked to a specific gender. And they use the pronoun *they* instead of *he* or *she* for the child.'

'A bit dense, don't you think?'

'Unconventional, for sure … but why stupid?'

'I mean – you know I'm the most liberal of all, darling,' her father said. 'I'm fed up with Vigevano's rural thinking. But the idea that you shouldn't treat a boy like a boy and a girl like a girl …'

'Wait. Perhaps I didn't explain myself properly. Ash isn't trying to make their child genderless. Ash explained this to me. They're just making sure their child is free to be who they really are.'

'You're giving me a headache with all these pronouns. Is the child a boy or a girl?'

'That's the point. They wouldn't tell. Gender-neutral parents believe that anatomy doesn't necessarily match with gender.'

'Is Ash a woman or a man?'

'That's another good question.'

Rachel laughed at hearing about Mr Morè's reaction.

'Your dad's not entirely wrong,' she said. 'Why force a boy or a girl not to act as a boy or girl? I know that you're the Taliban when it comes to protecting LGBTQ rights, but this whole idea of gender-neutral parenting doesn't make much sense to me.'

The Taliban reference snatched a laugh. 'You can tell all this to Ash. They should be here soon.'

Lucìa's announcement was timely. A slender figure endued with androgynous traits walked through the crowd. Square smooth cheeks, short black hair with a mohawk-like top, dark piercing eyes – this person exuded self-confidence and pride. They smiled at Lucìa.

'Ash!'

'Miss Cliché – finally! In our humble club!'

'Not true. It's fancy.'

The two hugged.

'Who is this I have the pleasure of meeting?' asked Ash in a vibrant and husky voice.

'She's Rachel. A close friend who happens to work for the *Wall Street Journal* in New York.'

'Beautiful plus intelligent, then …' observed Ash, almost causing Rachel to blush. 'Rachel, you're very fortunate to be Miss Cliché's friend. Not only am I selfishly grateful because she interviewed me without bias, but I reckon that Miss Cliché is our lifeline against digital fascism. We don't treasure freedom enough. Charlemagny would ban our place.'

'You're too generous,' replied Lucìa.

A young man with shaved blond hair and gold-rimmed round glasses was standing next to Ash, looking trepidatious. He kept a wide-open hand pressed against his bare chest.

'Pardon, I should have introduced you,' Ash apologised. 'Miss Cliché and Rachel, please meet my dear friend Roger.'

An ecstatic Roger stammered out all his enthusiasm to Lucìa. 'I'm so happy … that you're here tonight … I'm a big fan of yours … you're so cool … can we please get a selfie together … ?'

Something that had already happened a couple of times in Paris or Berlin, this was the first time Lucìa had been asked for a selfie in Birmingham. She got herself under Roger's sweaty arm right away.

'A gay icon!' yelled Rachel, regaining some space. She wasn't joking – four or five people were already in line for a selfie with Miss Cliché. Besides valuing Lucìa's open-minded interview with Ash, the local LGBTQ community had been keenly observing her fight against Charlemagny. They liked her.

'Go and get Vincent d'Amont!' someone shouted.

The others queueing to meet her expressed similar concepts: that Miss Cliché was a great example for them, that they wanted the scalp of Vincent d'Amont. She didn't have the heart to reveal to the new, unexpected fans her intention of turning the debate down.

The club's five projectors, normally used to spewing out music videos, were now beaming the name of Miss Cliché against a rainbow background. As more people flowed towards the corner of the club where Lucìa stood, the throng around her expanded. With joy the revellers clashed one against the other in a tribal dance, magnifying the force of the exuberant crowd. For precaution, Ash had two more bouncers come upstairs. They recommended Miss Cliché jump behind the counter before she got hurt. She did so, and Rachel followed.

Ten, twenty, thirty people, and then the entire club, began chanting amidst a sea of waving hands: 'Miss Cliché-tcha-tcha-tcha! Miss Cliché-tcha-tcha-tcha!'

The shrewd Ash thrust a mic into Lucìa's hands.

'The people want to hear you.'

Lucìa took it hesitatingly and glanced at Rachel.

'C'mon, attagirl!' her friend shouted.

Lucìa was galvanised and – if it hadn't been too blasphe-
mous – would have likened her condition to that of a newly
elected pope saluting the faithful from the balcony of St
Peter's. The DJ had lowered the music, but the dancing and
revelling still echoed in the room when Lucìa, now standing
on the counter, spoke.

'You're all too generous!' she yelled.

A lanky girl with purple-green hair and red spectacles
interrupted: 'God save Miss Cliché!'

The crowd howled.

'Friends, we're in danger! Somebody is scheming to create
a massified society in the hands of greedy social media, where
the main role of people will be to consume, stay silent and die.
They'll outlaw diversity, because diversity unavoidably gener-
ates the critical thinking that all authoritarian regimes fear.
They want us to spend our days clicking and buying!'

The crowd booed at the dreadful prospect.

'Somebody is scheming for a world based on conflict
– always in need of finding a new enemy. One day the
Americans, another the Chinese or the Russians, so that they
can keep us in check and use fear of the enemy as an excuse
to destroy our rights!'

Many in the crowd gasped at the idea of a threat to the
rights for which gay people had fought hard. Coloured paper
cups started to fly around in a sign of peaceful protest.

Miss Cliché spoke for a good ten minutes, repeating the
messages already promoted in abundance on her vlog. Yet the
club's spirited atmosphere made her ideas sound even spicier
and more compelling. Ash nodded approvingly. Rachel was

amused to see Lucìa rallying like a rising political leader. On purpose, Lucìa omitted to quote the name of Charlemagny. She didn't need to – the audience knew what the threat was.

When Ash told them that at least two hundred people downstairs were trying to get inside, and that not all of them were necessarily fans, Lucìa and Rachel knew that their night out couldn't resume as if nothing had happened. Ash arranged for a courtesy limousine to pick them up by a secondary exit. As they hurried through the back of the club, pursued by the sound of the full room still calling Miss Cliché's name, staff members kept stopping Lucìa. It'd been a joy listening to her, they said.

'So much for a night without thinking of Charlemagny,' sighed a smiling Rachel, once they were slouched in the back seat of the limo.

They both laughed.

'At least we've gained a limo all to ourselves,' Lucìa smiled cheekily.

Rachel chuckled, rummaging through the minibar.

'We should celebrate your performance at the club. And you still believe you shouldn't do the debate with d'Amont? C'mon!'

Lucìa rolled her eyes emphatically. She didn't want to go there again.

'Is everything comfortable, ladies?' asked the composed driver.

'Yes, it's wonderful, thank you,' replied Lucìa, grateful that he had interrupted the conversation.

'How far are you allowed to take us?' Lucìa asked.

'Anywhere from Orkney to Cornwall, madam.'

'Okay. Please take us to Stonehenge!'

The driver raised an eyebrow, then nodded.

Lucìa knew from their time in Brussels how Rachel longed to see the famed ring of bulky stones in Wiltshire.

'Are you crazy, Lucìa?'

'It's now or never, Rachel. Stonehenge will inspire us, and perhaps bring us some luck.'

'Schweet!' Rachel yelled before clinking her miniature gin against Lucìa's nip vodka bottle.

'I've a proposal for you,' Lucìa said, turning serious again. 'A ticket to Berlin.'

Rachel squinted her eyes. 'What?'

'It seems that the very first developer hired by Marlene Gäch has been missing for weeks. He's known as Employee Zero. You should go there and sniff around. We must find him. I suspect that Employee Zero knows something that they don't want people to find out. I don't trust ROME.'

'I suspect my boss in New York wouldn't like me changing itinerary,' Rachel replied.

'Your boss doesn't have to learn about this detour. The ticket is on us – it's already booked. We reserved a room for you at the Matesanz Hotel. It's in the hotel cafeteria that the founders of ROME used to work in the platform's early days. We should start our investigation from the very beginning of ROME. We must find Employee Zero.'

'We sure do know each other well!' Rachel burst out. She did find Lucìa's proposal intriguing. They hugged. It was like being back in Brussels.

III

Flâneurs

'*O Pátio das Cantigas …*'

With exaggerated effort, Vincent d'Amont repeated the melodic title pronounced by his dining companion.

'One of the most popular Portuguese *filmss* ever released,' replied the other, who had a dark complexion, large black eyes and a sleek hairstyle.

'And you produced it?'

'Yes, co-produced it.'

For all the homework he had done on the man, Vincent acted as if he was learning these facts in that very moment.

Bernardo Madeira was a renowned producer. Starting as an assistant on the set of Portuguese series, he had climbed to executive producer, overseeing in that role all possible stages of various European productions – from casting and location scouting to editing and post-production – before accepting an irrefutable offer: Chief Executive Officer at Metropolis, the entertainment streaming arm of ROME.

'I'd like to understand your proposal better,' Vincent added, after giving his own image a quick check in the glass of a nearby wine cooler.

'It's rather *sstraightforward*,' replied Madeira, who spoke a heavily accented but grammatically correct English. He had a lisp that often produced a somehow-endearing slushy *ess*.

'You are one of the most popular men in Europe these *dayss*. Charlemagny is the biggest news story, and it will remain so for months, even years. We intend to release a short *seriess* on Charlemagny for Metropolis. No more than three episodes, and you should be in it.'

'I've no acting experience.'

'Nobody would be better than you to interpret the events of these weeks. You are used to cameras, anyway. Please don't believe in the 10,000-hour bullshit. Do you know how many movie stars lack any kind of acting *skillss*? I've done some homework on you,' Madeira added. 'You like your *shirtss* slim, well fitted. You were an admirer of a family couture house in Caudry but left it immediately when an American group bought the atelier. To this day, a fragrance by Tiziana Terenzi is your one and only *concesssion* to a foreign brand. Once, a lifestyle expert observed you were "a brand in yourself". You even declined a hefty advertising endorsement, but only because the legal department at the Hôtel de Ville dissuaded you. I want you in the *seriess*.'

Vincent, flattered, listened to Madeira's reasoning with his full attention. Regardless of the outcome with Charlemagny, he had rebuffed the idea of resuming a career in politics. So it wouldn't be that inappropriate for him to ponder this opportunity. Moreover, he was unenthusiastic at the prospect of living on his mayor's pension alone. Another upside: Metropolis would be compensating him for a series that would also serve to promote his political project.

'If I decide to accept, will I have free rein with the story?'

'There will be no conditions attached. You can draft an account of these vibrant *dayss* together with one of our experienced writers. Once the screenplay is ready, I will be the one to sign it off. That's all. No round table of executives scrutinising the story. No pressures from above. Freedom.'

'It seems a win-win.'

'No doubt about it, Monsieur.'

Vincent d'Amont was excited yet unsure about this proposal. Would he lose his credibility as a political ideologist by wearing the second hat of an actor? Trump, Schwarzenegger, Zelenskyy, they had switched from one role to the other – true – but in the opposite direction: first show business, then public office. Would it work this way around?

It nonetheless occurred to him that Vincent d'Amont was more than just a former public officer; Vincent d'Amont was also a marketer, a writer, an influencer, a disc jockey – maybe a little narcissistic, but there was no limit to what he could achieve. A modern-day Andy Kaufman on the political stage; a chameleon able to nonchalantly shed his skin, to arouse bold feelings, but without ever reducing himself to a Zelig. Because he was the one to blaze the trail, not follow it.

'You deserve to know what you would receive in return,' added Madeira. He then mumbled a long figure. Vincent looked at him, poker-faced.

'But we expect *revelationss*, behind-the-scenes insights, never-heard-of stuff, you follow me? The story must be spicy.'

'I've so much spicy *stuff* in store that I could open an Indian deli. But if I ever decide to go with your project, it'll mean that my new memoir must be ditched. All the royalties will be gone. Your offer doesn't make up for the loss of revenue.'

Unmoved, Madeira observed: 'A *seriess* can generate higher royalties than a book. Sales of books have fallen for ages.'

'Yes, but I could publish the book and then sell the rights for a movie.'

'You've a problem with timing, though: interest in the referendum will fade at some point. How long will it take you to write the book? *Monthss*. Then you will need to publish it, sell the movie rights, and then the picture will have to be produced. We are talking about years, not months. With our project, we'd start preproduction immediately after the referendum, the morning of the ninth.'

'How can you do it so quickly?'

'We've already done most of the casting. The *locationss* are ready. We're just waiting for you.'

'How will you structure the series?'

'I should have you sign an NDA before disclosing anything. But it's a series on you, anyway, so I'll keep no secrets. The mini-series is made of three episodes: the first to show why Europe isn't working, and how those who dissent are called *populistss* by the media. Remember, I'm Portuguese, I know what I'm talking about. The second episode should focus on your incredible life: your fall from power and resurrection. And, finally, the last episode – Charlemagny ... boom!'

The idea of a series on him made Vincent feel a tingle, a pleasant sensation at the nape of his neck he'd often experienced in his past – particularly when he was still in advertising and he'd known a great idea was in the making. He hadn't felt that tingling for a long time, not even in the last few months with all the public curiosity. Vincent thought with remarkable ease of a dozen ideas, at least, to improve Madeira's concept. He didn't say

anything, though. Madeira's words had emboldened his resolution not to let the opportunity to capitalise on Charlemagny pass.
However, he still didn't know whether they would be part of the
same team. So he changed tack: he made the other talk more.

'How will you fund all this?'

'Metropolis is profitable. We have plenty of *fundss* available. It isn't so easy, nowadays, to have a budget like ours.
We want the best actors, the most advanced special effects,
and a comprehensive promotion schedule. You don't want
your achievements told in an indie movie, do you?' Madeira
asked Vincent, as if he suspected that the latter might consider
producing the series all by himself.

Madeira hinting at a lavish budget gave Vincent food for
thought, and it wasn't positive. If people learned about these
negotiations, they would think he was not really focused on
Charlemagny. He would appear distracted, a money-grabber
who put personal economic interests before a ground-breaking
political project for Europe – somebody unworthy of trust. If
Miss Cliché disclosed the mere fact that he had found time to
discuss a television series so close to the referendum day, he
might even risk losing the vote. For all he knew, this lunch
with Madeira might even be a set-up.

Vincent backtracked. 'This is a key moment for us all, and
I cannot make any decisions right now,' he said. 'You think,
like many others, that I am just a born entertainer; but I've
actually devoted most of my life to politics, and I can't have
any distractions in the final week of this campaign.'

'I'm not trying to hurry you. But *pleasse* remember that
time is of the essence here,' Madeira warned him.

* * *

That same day, ROME launched the official streaming presentation of the Charlemagny poll.

A digital emcee explained how the 8/4 vote would work: *'The eighth of April: you will decide whether France and Germany should unite into a single country outside the European Union. You will be entitled to vote if you are registered to ROME and have lived in France or Germany for the majority of the last twelve months. A person will be deemed to have lived in France or Germany for the majority of the last twelve months if, during that period, sixty per cent or more of their sessions on ROME have taken place on devices located in France and Germany.'*

The presentation ended with a disclaimer the governments of France and Germany had insisted upon: *The vote is not legally binding.* But the digital emcee hastened to add that *'the governments of France and Germany will nonetheless take into deep consideration the will of their people.'*

It felt a lifetime ago, but the path towards Charlemagny had started just one year earlier, with Vincent d'Amont stirring controversy all around Europe with his proposal to establish Charlemagny.

Born and bred in Alsace, a land fought over by France and Germany throughout history, Vincent d'Amont believed that this long-term rivalry hid a bittersweet rapport of brotherhood – a tight-knit relationship bound to lead to a union between the two nations.

The new adventure had given Vincent d'Amont a strong boost in popularity. Many French politicians, intellectuals and journalists, even outside the conservative milieu, had proclaimed enthusiasm for the idea of an unprecedented axis between France and Germany. People had increasingly shared

Vincent's incisive words and, within months, his fandom on ROME had reached a record number.

Dodging the temptation to create a party, he had single-handedly promoted the unification of France and Germany under Charlemagny. His courage in moving away from all traditional schemes, the strong – albeit charming at times – language used, and his independence from any apparatus, had all helped the fast resurgence of Vincent d'Amont.

A flurry of videos of him commenting on all the latest news reports ran constantly on ROME, often accusing Europe of misbehaviour – for the words *European Union* and *Europe* were equals in his eyes – and the inadequacy of Europe to meet the challenges posed by China, relentlessly depicted as an imperialist threat to Western culture.

Owing to Vincent's patriotic words, French people were sharing a heart-warming renewed sense of camaraderie. Frenchmen had spent decades enduring the apparent threat posed by migrants in the *banlieues*, while powerlessly watching the growth of non-European powers. It was time for revenge. Somebody had finally arrived to instil a sense of pride and togetherness in the French nation, even at the cost of appearing politically reckless. The idea of a stronger fellowship with the Germans – so successful in governing their country – didn't scare Charlemagniers: in fact, it was the opposite. Vincent's language was now much more brazen and aggressive than it had been during his time as mayor of Paris, this switch of attitude contributing to his reputation as a chameleonic politician.

The media showed a peculiar interest in his personal life. As he had always felt unsuited to marriage, his portrayal as a committed bachelor was well deserved. Online tabloids were nonetheless wrong in depicting him as a womaniser, for he had always been rather selective in flirting.

It was in politics that Vincent d'Amont was a real loner. Although his self-reliance had so far rewarded him, he had reached a stage where this strategy might no longer prove sufficient to further the ambitious design of Charlemagny. Having established a wide and stable followership in France, but still reluctant to aim for any institutional role, Vincent d'Amont would soon need to find a way to capitalise on his popularity, lest he should reach a stalemate. He had to decide what he wanted to do once his movement had grown up.

* * *

Bernardo Madeira looked up, baulking at the three hundred or so stairs. *That damn French tripe: I haven't digested it,* he complained to himself. *Or maybe it's just that I can't stand d'Amont.*

Madeira began his solitary ascent towards the Basilique du Sacré-Coeur. *It looked whiter in pictures,* he noticed with a shade of disappointment. *But it was damn beautiful,* he conceded. Madeira liked the majestic outline, the elegant design, the weight of history behind the Basilique. *It would make a great set for a spy story,* he thought.

Vincent d'Amont had arrived at the brasserie one hour late. *He has no manners,* Madeira thought, shaking his head. *Does he really believe that I'd ever make a series on him, arrogant bastard? No way.* But Madeira had needed a good excuse to be in Paris. Otherwise, ROME wouldn't have allowed him to travel.

Madeira had never liked ROME either. When he told people of the irrefutable offer received to join her, he meant it literally.

Madeira had had to accept. Not only for the awful lot of money at stake, but also because it had been clear to him that ROME would have made his life a misery if he'd refused. For a starter, no investor would have ever backed one of his series against ROME's will. And even the most desperate of actors would've refused to deal with him had he ended up on ROME's blacklist.

For sure, they're geolocating me right now, Madeira guessed. Once back in Berlin, I'll have to invent a reason for me visiting here, possibly something better than a tour with a Mozambican dignitary. He chuckled.

The steep stairway was busy. Madeira had to dodge large groups of tourists descending quickly while, step by step, his feet kept raising mechanically towards the Sacré-Coeur. The view of the nearing Basilique didn't distract him from the secret purpose of his visit to Paris, though.

He was my only real friend in Berlin, Madeira thought. I couldn't say no to him. And he's taking a huge risk to meet me today.

Madeira's first period in ROME had been fine. The unprecedented funds, the adulation of the European elite – who, for all the claim of independence, were in awe of ROME's media might – a large penthouse in central Berlin; they had all seemed the crowning achievements of a brilliant career.

A clause in the contract allowed Madeira full creative control over the series. At least, this had been his belief until the evening when, as he was flying privately back to Berlin, Metropolis had sent a notification to his user account: *Bloody Red Dragon is coming!*

It was a production Madeira had never heard of, let alone approved. After watching the trailer, he made a frenetic round of furious calls to his team. All his assistants hid behind a wall of silence, pretending not to know anything about this new series, but Madeira insisted until he made one talk. Reluctantly, the stuttering assistant revealed there was a secret team in Metropolis engaged in sensitive projects that was accountable only to Marlene Gäch.

Bloody Red Dragon was one of these sensitive projects. A series on a fictional Chinese leader whose ambition was to wreak havoc on the world so that his country could emerge as an undisturbed leading power, it showed China orchestrating wars, disseminating pandemics, causing famines, and plotting every other conceivable crime against humanity.

Madeira was livid. *Bloody Red Dragon* had been kept a secret from him because he would never approve it, he was sure. Gratuitous anti-Chinese propaganda when the invasion of Taiwan was still fresh in people's minds? Were they mad?

With three out of four European households watching its shows, Metropolis could easily stir public opinion towards any direction, good or evil, and ROME knew it. The scheming behind his back only exacerbated Madeira's fury.

He had barely ended yelling at his assistant when Madeira received a call whose timeliness hit him as eerie. He had never talked to Marlene Gäch, so he learnt with surprise that she could speak perfect Portuguese, even with a moderate Lisbon accent. It wasn't a gentle call, though. When he tried to express his anger, she cut him off abruptly. Madeira was told that ROME was working for a bigger cause, and that he shouldn't try to interfere with something so beyond him, but to just work hard and enjoy the generous salary. Madeira bit his tongue so tightly not to retaliate that he feared his lisp might worsen; but he knew too well that a wrong word could compromise his career – or even his existence.

The humiliating conversation with Marlene Gäch was still resonating in him when Bernardo Madeira reached the cramped parvis of the Basilique du Sacré-Coeur. Hundreds of people were walking in all directions. He felt a bit uneasy with his double-breasted suit, strikingly in contrast to the synthetic outfits of the tourists around; yet, he was aware that there was something more important to think of than his attire.

Looking at the people surrounding him, for one instant he had the impression that a man with a baseball cap and sunglasses walking at a distance might be his friend, but a couple of closer glances proved his guess wrong.

Where the devil is he? Madeira asked himself. He's German, he should be punctual. It would be impossible to find him with all these people if he didn't come out.

Madeira paced through the alley left of the Sacré-Coeur, separating the Basilique from Saint-Pierre de Montmartre – a less crowded walkway than the opposing belvedere. Halfway along the alley, he spotted a mime standing still by the wall. Perhaps because of the white make-up, Madeira had always found mimes and clowns extremely creepy. It was almost a phobia. When the mime winked at him, Madeira hinted at a smile, then walked away fast.

He kept scanning with his eyes, almost frantically, all the people around in search of his friend or any possible hint of where to find him, but in vain.

What the hell am I doing here? He's probably changed his mind, Madeira thought with apprehension.

After circling the Sacré-Coeur three or four times, he decided to enter the Basilique. There were fewer people inside. After having peeped inside all the confessionals to check if his friend was hiding there, he took a seat on a central bench, bent forward as if in the act of praying.

Why have I come here? Madeira asked himself again. Maybe because I don't like ROME inserting subliminal messages in kids' videos so that children pester their parents to get junk food? Or that they want to keep people glued to their devices all the time?

Madeira looked up at the magnificent mosaic of Christ over the choir and, while not a fervent believer in God, still he tried to find a celestial validation of his decision to come to the Sacré-Coeur, an action that he otherwise found irrational and reckless. Also, he liked to believe that no harm could ever happen to him inside a church.

Hoping for his friend to somehow approach him, Madeira waited on the bench for two interminable hours. Then he stood up, wiped his sweat-soaked hands with a linen handkerchief and – disappointed – left the Basilique.

There was no longer any crowd outside, just isolated tourists. He noticed that the eerie mime had changed position and was now standing in the middle of the parvis. To his annoyance, Madeira had to walk close to him in order to take the stairs towards Montmartre.

When Madeira approached the mime, the latter winked twice. This time, Madeira didn't even pretend to smile, and hurried away.

But, ten paces later, as if struck by lightning, he stopped, turned and moved back towards the mime. He got very close, stared at his painted face, then melted into a smile.

'Guten Tag, Employee Zero,' he whispered. 'What a nice *disguisse*!'

* * *

Vincent rented a large flat in the Latin Quarter, a penthouse on top of a narrow triangular building that reminded Americans of the Flatiron in NYC. When he arrived home after his lunch with Madeira, Emmanuelle was there.

She had been his assistant since the end of her studies in philosophy and art at the Sorbonne. At their first meeting, her unflinching gaze and faultless beauty had enchanted Vincent. That was in the months after his painful decision to leave politics, at a time when Vincent had felt trapped in a frustrating ennui and the ceaseless insinuations of his detractors had resonated strongly. He had continued to release statements in rejection of all allegations. It was a dangerous spiral, though: the more he spoke, the more his opponents questioned his past tenure.

Emmanuelle had understood the situation at once.

'Every time you deny something, it reinforces the lie, helping it to stick,' she told him. 'You're playing along with their games and harming yourself.'

Her words of wisdom had made him realise the necessity of taking a break from the near past. She was right. Once Vincent ceased addressing the rumours and allegations, they died away.

Emmanuelle was also the one who, hearing of his dream of France and Germany united, had encouraged Vincent to share his aspirations on ROME. It hadn't taken long for Vincent to work out her greatest talent – that of solving problems.

Emmanuelle was thrifty with words. This was the reason why her insights were so valuable, perhaps, because she invested so much of her energy in observing. Emmanuelle was a source of inspiration, a constant well of ideas to his benefit, and she wasn't ambitious for herself – appearing to experience fulfilment just from being by his side.

'You should take a look at Miss Cliché,' Emmanuelle – in the tone of a child making an innocent remark to an adult – suggested when he entered the flat.

Shrugging, for he knew that it couldn't be anything good, Vincent switched on the large screen hanging in his lounge. Miss Cliché had just published a news video titled 'Charlemagny in French court'. Hugh appeared on the screen.

'*This morning, France Souveraine, Vincent d'Amont's former political party, filed a petition against ROME and Vincent d'Amont with the Criminal Court of Paris on the grounds that the 8/4 e-poll would represent – and I quote – a "direct incitement to jeopardise the institutions of the French Republic and violate the integrity of the national territory", punishable under the French Criminal Code. France Souveraine claims that ROME's e-poll puts in danger the integrity of France by promoting the incorporation of France into Germany.*'

The clip showed stock images of Vincent together with members of his erstwhile party. He shuddered.

'*France Souveraine argues that, given the inertia from both the French government and parliament to take appropriate action against this extremely dangerous initiative, the Court has become the last resort to protect French sovereignty. The petitioners ask the Court to issue an interim decree to suspend the e-poll while investigations are pending. Given the timing of the case, the Court*

*of Paris has already announced that a decision on the suspension
is planned to be taken within forty-eight hours.'*

Seeing his former party comrades on the screen, Vincent
felt a stinging resentment – the same he'd felt during his political hiatus. He had since learned how to overcome this feeling:
by focusing on the today, trying to enjoy life for what it had to
offer, and not allowing issues to mar it.

He had never owed anything to France Souveraine, after
all, but only to its founder, Dom Natale, a sturdy entrepreneur-
turned-politician who had the merit of having immediately
grasped Vincent's world-class gift of the gab.

The unprecedented, zigzag journey propelling Vincent
d'Amont to the main stage of international politics had started
when Vincent was still an account executive at a major advertising agency in Paris. Ambitious, hard-working, endowed with
a fair amount of creativity and – even more – business nous,
Vincent had quickly moved up through the agency's ranks.
Undeterred by his colleagues' jealousy, with a newcomer's
enthusiasm Vincent brought a fresh twist to large marketing
campaigns. Once, for instance, the agency called him to save
a campaign for a male contraceptive: an uneasy and delicate
task, even in France. They needed someone outside the box.
After a sleepless night, Vincent ended up minting an eloquent
slogan: *When it rains, wear a raincoat!* The tagline became the
core of a very successful, although controversial, campaign that
contributed to a 30 per cent surge in product sales, earning the
agency an award at the Grand Prix de la Publicité in Menton.

Enjoying a boost in popularity, the agency soon won
another major client: France Souveraine, a recently founded
political platform whose existential aim was to challenge the

ratification of the European Constitution in a national referendum the following year.

Dom Natale had liked Vincent's fresh intellect immediately. Also, he found the chasm between Vincent's youthful appearance and his already prominent role at the agency amusing.

Once, in the making of the campaign against the European Constitution, Natale asked him: '*Mon enfant prodige*, which motto would you suggest for our efforts?'

After giving himself time to ponder, Vincent replied: 'I remember Valéry Giscard d'Estaing's slogan to define his ties with Gaullism: *Yes, but* … Public opinion read his hesitation between the lines – an attempt to have it both ways. It didn't work. People want leadership from their leaders. So our answer to the referendum will be: *No, but … no!*'

'That's a good one,' said Natale, not having expected a young marketer to draw inspiration from post-Gaullism for a slogan. He indeed harboured low expectations of the younger generations, thinking them overly spoilt and dull. He and Vincent often engaged in animated conversations, stirring up jealousy among Vincent's colleagues. With Natale lacking any offspring of his own, and Vincent very seldom speaking to his father in Colmar, it shouldn't have come as a surprise that they complemented each other.

The referendum repaid the agency's efforts: the 'No' camp won, and the French parliament refused to ratify the European Constitution. France Souveraine thus gained visibility in the country, achieving promising performances at local elections. What happened next was predictable, at least in comfortable hindsight: Natale asked Vincent to join France Souveraine as head of communications. The party apparatus didn't take well what they considered an arbitrary designation, and from then on they inexorably perceived Vincent as a bothersome outsider.

Vincent's uncommon path from party spin doctor to member of the European Parliament in Brussels didn't take long, but even more astonishing was his subsequent success as a candidate for Paris mayor. These remarkable achievements – impossible if not for Natale's unbending endorsement – had alienated the sympathy of his associates even further. Now, after all these years, they were still getting back at him, trying to put paid to his renewed political ambitions.

Barely a minute after the end of Hugh's video, Vincent received a call.

'Have you heard?'

'I've just learned about this crap from Miss Cliché. Quite ironic, considering that I'm the one called into question. Absurd.'

'Our French lawyers are already working to stop it. We've hired a major firm in Paris who say the criminal action is unfounded. Your former pals are just aiming at stopping the referendum – but if they succeed, it may take years before the case is resolved. And Charlemagny will be lost.'

A thick pause ensued.

'If the suspension is granted,' the caller resumed, 'the loss will be unimaginable. A fortune has been booked in advertising. If the court blocks Charlemagny, all advertisers will pull out.'

'I should immediately post a video,' Vincent suggested. 'Nothing in Charlemagny can jeopardize French sovereignty.'

'No. We must let our expensive French lawyers earn their bread – or brioche, as you prefer. I suspect that your inciting people to cover walls with graffiti will not help us on our day in court. Another slip-up from your side could be fatal.'

Vincent made a strong effort to control himself. *Do you really think you can lecture me on how to address the French people? I've a twenty-year career behind me, you arrogant witch.* The camera was disabled, so the caller couldn't see Vincent's tension. The call, again, didn't last long.

Emmanuelle, who had overheard bits of the conversation, came back to him expecting the worst, for Vincent tended to throw tantrums when antagonised. Instead, he seemed calm as he watched her entering the lounge.

'Would you join me for a stroll by the Seine? It's a wonderful evening out there.'

'Ah, *très bien* ...' Emmanuelle said below her breath. She went to the cloakroom to reach for her white trench.

The tiny Rue Lagrange, where Vincent lived, merged into Quai de Montebello, a street touching the Seine's left bank. As they walked, the twilight stillness made it easy for them to enjoy the wide view of the cathedral to their left.

'You're too young to remember how it looked before the fire,' he said, glancing at Notre-Dame. 'Had I been the mayor when they rebuilt, I would have done something very different, not tried to recreate the roof exactly as it had been before.'

Emmanuelle nodded. She appreciated the privilege of strolling through Paris with a former mayor, not a commoner.

Save the sporadic passers-by and the occasional Cabeille darting up the road, the bank was quiet.

'I'd like you to come to Colmar with me next weekend,' he proposed.

'I would be happy to,' Emmanuelle replied, her tender profile softening further.

'An old friend of mine, Léon, will join us for dinner at the hotel restaurant. I haven't seen him for ages.'

'I would be happy to meet your childhood friends,' she said.

Vincent smiled. It hadn't happened that often, recently.

He failed to tell her of an old episode concerning his friend Léon. They'd both been seventeen. At the time, the d'Amonts owned a chalet in Lac Blanc, a mountain resort. Skiing not being among Vincent's passions, he'd spent his holidays, and earned some monies, by playing music during the après-ski evenings fuelled by mulled wine.

The long winter nights occasionally ended with a stretch of poker between friends. Then something remarkable had occurred at the end of a seemingly lacklustre poker night. Vincent drew four cards to find himself with the unexpected godsend of four jacks. His cards had gone against all the odds, and he felt a sudden, intense shudder of excitement. Only two players were still in the game with him: Léon, who had drawn two cards, and another one, who had opened the round by doubling the pot but without swapping any card.

Vincent knew that nobody expected him to hold a poker after a four-card draw. As two four-of-a-kinds in the same game were extremely rare, the player who had not swapped cards could have, at best, a straight or a full house. It was an ideal situation for Vincent to add further fuel. So he did – betting the full pot. A noticeable sum now on the table, a thick silence fell on the room. But the third player made an unexpected move: not only did he check Vincent's bet, he also re-raised the entire pot. Vincent's confidence now began to flake. The amount of cash at stake was too much for his limited teenage means.

The other man didn't have the *physique du rôle* of the bluffer, Vincent believed. He had to have powerful cards. Then came the turn of Léon. He lit a cigarette, gazed at his cards, glanced sideways at Vincent. He seemed to him as ruthless as ever. The table didn't have a rule on the amount of time a player could take before announcing his next move. Léon took ten minutes, feeling an eternity to Vincent, who had by then lost all assurance. It was part of his nature to feel the chaotic helter-skelter between extreme sentiments, from pleasure to pain in a matter of seconds.

'Full pot,' announced Léon.

Vincent felt like he was dying. While sure to have the best cards, he also knew he couldn't go on at this level. He was caged. Léon's money bag seemed bottomless; Vincent's was not. They had very loose rules at the table. In theory, they could have gone on forever raising the stakes, one after the other. But Vincent took the game – and his money – seriously. So he folded, aware that it would take him the entire season to repay that single hand.

Splashing his face with ice-cold water in the host's bathroom, his legs still shaking with incredulity, Vincent made several guilt-spurred resolutions to soothe his conscience, among which were to never re-raise a full pot again and never, ever drink before poker.

He hadn't yet questioned the game when, on his way back to the living room, he heard: 'What a sucker! We had him all the way.' It was Léon. Vincent now saw the night in an entirely different light. He stood in the hall alone for a minute to regain control, before going back to the others.

Vincent had known Léon since childhood. He had always got along well with Léon, who was cold yet impulsive, moderately smug because of his status – his father owned the local disco – but essentially a good person. Vincent had always thought they were friends.

When he reached the living room, Vincent had to pretend everything was fine. They had swindled him. He would even learn, years later, that 'merry-go-round' was the name of that night's trick. More than any other, that episode taught him to be wary of people always – especially when they were close. Yet, for all that had happened, Vincent still cherished his memories of youthful bravado with Léon. So he didn't dislike the idea of their upcoming dinner in Colmar.

Emmanuelle and Vincent had reached Pont de la Tournelle. Perched on top of a very tall pillar on the bridge was a statue of a young woman laying her hands maternally on a child's shoulders.

'Sainte Geneviève. She rescued us,' Vincent said. 'When Attila the Hun invaded France and moved in the direction of Paris, Geneviève persuaded Parisians not to flee. She was right: Attila went to Orléans. Paris was safe. We should all fight and resist as much as Saint Geneviève did. She's inspiring.'

As he escorted Emmanuelle along the Seine, Vincent remembered the last time he had shown a lady around Paris – that night at the Basilique du Sacré-Coeur. It all seemed a past life, now that he felt free from the duties of politics.

'You will now meet the man making our dream possible,' he said with a hint of mystery as they walked along Rue des Deux Ponts, on Île Saint-Louis, the tiny island amid the Seine.

Emmanuelle looked at him, her eyes widening imperceptibly. They turned onto Quai d'Anjou. The precise geometry of the stone path skirting the river, the orderly sequence of birches by the bank, the compact row of two-storey houses on the inner side of the road, all helped to convey calm and harmony to the fortunate strollers.

A carved gate had been left ajar. Vincent opened it fully. Emmanuelle followed him through. They found themselves inside a wide cobbled courtyard. No one was in sight.

Vincent had to be acquainted with the place, thought Emmanuelle, as he moved confidently towards a wrought-iron door to their right. Inside, a narrow wooden staircase took them upstairs, into a large hall, whose opulence astonished her. As soon as she stepped inside, Emmanuelle was indeed overwhelmed by the surrounding wealth of gilded woodwork, wide landscape paintings and tall mirrors.

Her eyes were immediately dragged towards the high ceiling, richly painted with broad images of Venus set in nature, an unequivocal homage to Italian Renaissance art. She felt in awe of such beauty.

A resounding man's voice, drawing closer from an adjacent room, welcomed them in. 'Vincent – please, come in … Oh, I see you've brought some lovely company.'

An impeccably attired man walked with confidence towards his guests. He was rather short, and his sunken blue eyes presided over a beaky nose and pointy ears. The intricacy of his features, mirroring the craftsmanship of the surrounding décor, lent a peculiar intrigue to his persona.

'Emmanuelle, please make the acquaintance of a dear friend, the brilliant Auguste Destouches,' said Vincent in a thespian tone.

Emmanuelle was surprised. Vincent had never mentioned this friend.

'A friend and an admirer of Vincent d'Amont,' Destouches added.

'Your home is wonderful,' Emmanuelle complimented him.

'Home must be a bastion of orderliness and virtue amid the urban inferno, they say. But this house would have never become my abode if not for Mayor d'Amont,' Destouches said with a satisfied glance at Vincent.

'The city of Paris was – bluntly speaking – in dire need of funds. I knew that Auguste would treat his home with the respect it deserved. So, I approved the sale,' Vincent clarified.

'May I offer you a drink?' the host asked his guests, swiftly moving on from the subject of his property.

'Yes, please. I've had a difficult day; there's a chance that a local court will suspend Charlemagny because of an insane criminal action against me. Absurd.'

'I've just heard about this idiocy myself,' commented Destouches, waving his hands in feigned desperation as he left the room for the drinks.

Shortly after, a green spirit in reservoir glasses stood on a silver tray placed by a nearby velvety sofa. On top of each vessel rested a sugar cube on a perforated spoon. With surgical precision, Destouches poured water on the sugar cubes, so that they quickly melted into the drinks.

He passed the first glass to Emmanuelle.

'Absinthe.'

'Am I wrong, or does this house have a reputation for past indulgences with absinthe?' Vincent asked.

'Bau-de-lai-re,' Destouches enunciated the name – addressing Emmanuelle, as Vincent knew the story. 'He used to rent a small attic room upstairs, where he met with a club of friends to enjoy absinthe and hashish during a monthly seance. The circle included Delacroix, Dumas, and many others that today we would call celebrities. But it didn't last long.'

'What happened?' Emmanuelle asked.

'At first, Baudelaire praised the role of hashish in enhancing creativity, but he then realised the sadness of using substances to create art. He understood that every user of drugs would succumb to them. So he left the Club des Hashischins.'

Emmanuelle sipped the absinthe. The spirit tasted of aniseed and fennel, but the strong alcohol content rapidly overcame any other flavour in the mouth. She sensed a concomitant flow of adrenaline and relaxation, and an early sense of elation.

While he cradled his absinthe, Vincent gazed at a painting that had never failed to capture his full attention since his very first visit to Destouches. The canvas portrayed three naked women in evening conversation by a natural pool. A light shone on the women and on the tall trees behind the pool, allowing the viewer to see a group of ancient buildings in the background. The scene gave Vincent some degree of inner peace, pairing perfectly with the absinthe-induced sense of alienation.

'How did the two of you meet?' Emmanuelle asked.

Destouches cast a conspiratorial glance at Vincent, who reciprocated it.

'I think I met Vincent at a vernissage, but I'm not sure.' Destouches was the swiftest to reply. 'What I remember very well is our first conversation, about my great-grandfather, whose name I share with pride: Louis-Ferdinand August Destouches.'

'Emmanuelle, you'll know Auguste's great-grandfather by his *nom de plume* – Céline,' Vincent said.

Being the descendant of one of the most brilliant but controversial writers in French history had marked the life of Auguste Destouches. As a vacillating youth, the sharing of his blood with a man that had supported the Nazis during their occupation of France had generated more insecurity than pride. However, his feelings towards his forefather had changed in later years, when Destouches had resolved to idolise Céline no matter what, even at the cost of forgetting the fierce antisemitic pamphlets whose language even some Nazi officers had found too brutal during the war.

'I'm no antisemite,' Destouches warned. 'But we need to understand the context: it was a much more fractious era in Europe than it has been for a long time now. There were fascist regimes in power in Germany, Italy, Portugal and Spain. Stalin strangled Russia. France was still in tatters. Violence, even in words, was common.'

Destouches continued to speak, gesturing with excitement; the absinthe had served its purpose. Vincent kept nodding. He hoped his friend wouldn't share with Emmanuelle his thoughts on eugenics. But Destouches was now fixated on Céline.

'We shouldn't forget the contribution my forefather made to French literature,' he added. 'Someone even said that he changed the French language forever. And for what – years ago, when the publishing company that owned the rights to his work tried to republish his essays, a fierce row erupted in France. They had to cancel everything. Fortunately, the copyright on his works has now expired. Whoever wants it can now print it.'

'Why did such an intelligent man make those mistakes?' Emmanuelle asked her host in a most sincere tone. The remark amused Destouches. Vincent found it appropriate to join the dialogue.

'Auguste, I remember our first conversation, the one that sparked our friendship. Antisemitism wasn't even a topic. We agreed about one of Céline's greatest qualities: he recognised the natural symbiosis between France and Germany. Céline didn't like the Nazis. He even teased German officials with jokes about Hitler that left him on the verge of suffering serious retaliation. He knew that France and Germany had to join forces. It just happened in the wrong way.'

Destouches smiled at him, his deep-rooted conviction that Vincent d'Amont was a born politician reinforced. His forefather's legacy was indeed a question of extreme sensitivity to him, and he acknowledged that his friend Vincent always addressed the matter with the appropriate delicacy.

Although Destouches treasured his being a descendant of Céline, and that he was living in Charles Baudelaire's home, he hadn't attained his wealth by producing art. Destouches was a self-taught programmer who had created an empire in the online betting industry. Learning coding in his youth on solid foundations – for his father was a physicist with an interest in computing – the young Auguste had spent many hours watching his father type. Imitation is the best form of learning, as they say, and Destouches was living proof of it.

Destouches had begun his entrepreneurial journey at an early age, with a rather rudimentary platform allowing gaming sites to advertise more efficiently. After reaping the first substantial fruits, he started dedicating less time to programming and more to business development, strategy, networking – preferring a quick pitch in a blazer to long coding nights in a baggy jumper.

The somersault from online advertising to the betting industry had been quick. Exploiting his ties with the world of online gaming, Destouches had managed to raise abundant capital for a new political betting app. Another successful venture for him, and not the last. Coming close to billionaire status, he had earned the media moniker 'King Midas'.

'My friend, I have new, valuable info on Charlemagny,' King Midas told Vincent quite abruptly. 'I assume I can speak freely before Emmanuelle, right?'

'Yes, sure – Emmanuelle is my muse.'

'A most attractive muse, may I say,' Destouches couldn't help observing with a piercing stare. 'As you know, Charlemagny is the most popular political betting event of all time on our apps; people have placed over four million bets in the last three months alone.'

'Yes, I know,' replied Vincent with a hint of a smile. Destouches had been one of the earliest contributors to his Charlemagny campaign, and Vincent still believed that his financial contribution had mostly been driven by a political passion – but now the surge of bets over Charlemagny on his apps was repaying Destouches with profit. King Midas had ensured to monetise his beliefs.

Destouches rolled out some numbers. 'From the very start, most bets were placed on the "Yes". The odds are now at roughly 1.45, giving a probability of around sixty-nine per cent that people will vote for the birth of a great new country.'

Vincent looked at him with a pained expression on his face, as if waiting to hear something he didn't know yet.

'Please look at this ...' Destouches then said, as he widened his eyes to convey playful suspense. He passed Vincent a tablet whose screen showed a list of some forty names. Vincent recognised many of them: French journalists, artists and other well-known people. He also knew a couple of foreign names. One was that of the current Foreign Minister of Germany. A multi-digit number was written next to the name.

'Kickbacks?'

'No ...' replied Destouches. 'Online bets these guys have made on Charlemagny. Even when they use proxies or unorthodox payment methods so as not to be traced, we're still able to identify them. We have a system to crossmatch IP addresses and device IDs with other data to find out who placed the bet. We're required to do so by anti-money-laundering rules.'

'You know the life and death of your gamblers.'

'It's called *due diligence.*'

Emmanuelle was savouring the moment. It had taken just minutes for her to conclude that Destouches was a resourceful man and that his success had to be deserved. With the rhythm of the conversation bouncing back and forth easily, the two friends appeared to her to be quite close.

Vincent knew where Destouches wanted to lead him. But, as often happened, he let the other speak first.

'Vincent, if the Foreign Minister of Germany has invested money in Charlemagny, even under disguise, it means he believes that people will vote for us. Maybe he believes in Charlemagny himself. We need to persuade the minister to start diplomatic meetings with France ASAP. He's a senior member of the Cabinet and, for all his passion for claret, an authoritative figure.'

'It will be tough,' replied Vincent. 'We might have some room with the Germans, but the biggest obstacle is France, especially with this damned leftist government. They hit us hard from the start, even though France has as much to gain as Germany from Charlemagny.'

'It means they're scared,' Destouches contended. 'But if Germany calls France to the table, they will not shy away.'

Vincent had always recognised the capacity of Destouches to see positives in any situation, and the absinthe was not impairing that skill tonight – the opposite, in fact.

'I need to ponder this move,' Vincent replied. 'One of the reasons so many people trust me is because I'm not part of the establishment. If I tried to lure the Germans into negotiations, Charlemagniers would think I am compromised by old politics.'

'It can be done in a subtler way. But, please, I haven't invited you just to talk about politics,' the melodramatic Destouches said. He poured them another glass of absinthe. 'This is a product you'll never find in stores. I have it made for me by a renowned distillery in Pontarlier. The same value of thujone that Toulouse-Lautrec enjoyed in his Tremblement de Terre. I suspect the police would have a case to argue if they checked my liqueur cabinet.'

They laughed.

Destouches then looked at Emmanuelle. 'Please, tell me more about you,' he asked.

Destouches learned that Emmanuelle was born in Vietnam, had studied at the Sorbonne, possessed a flair for painting, and that an entire room at Rue Lagrange was now her art studio. Although she had lived in central Paris from an early age with an adoptive family, it had felt natural to Emmanuelle to dedicate her creativity to Vietnamese silk painting. She had travelled many times to her country of birth to refine her art, learning from artists in Hanoi keen to revive this ancient form of painting.

As she spoke, Emmanuelle gently moved her hands. Destouches listened with careful attention, then spoke of himself.

'I started as a man of numbers,' he said. 'But soon an interest in art began to build in me; perhaps a subconscious influence of my forefather. I acquired this residence because of my love for art. While I'm aware that it was heavily influenced by French art in modern times, I regret to say I possess little knowledge of Vietnamese art.'

After uttering these words, he realised how any reference, even implied, to the past French colonialism in Vietnam might sound unbecoming to Emmanuelle. She seemed unmoved, though. 'The Orient also inspired French art for centuries,' she observed. 'Delacroix painted the violence between Turks and Greeks. Gérôme illustrated the old practice of slavery in the Middle East. Chassériau showed life inside harems. They all depicted foreign territories as places where, let us say, exotic people engaged in wrongdoing, savagery, and inequality – as if all lands outside France were uncivilised. Perhaps they even smoked opium and drank absinthe in this room, at one time.'

Vincent raised one eyebrow, fearing that an argument over French nationalistic pride might start. A consideration reassured him, though: they were both too clever.

'True,' Destouches agreed. 'I'm impressed. However, the next generation of great French artists took a different path. Renoir made an incredible tribute to the beauty of women in Algeria. The ladies he portrayed very often were self-aware women, at least to the extent allowed in the country at that time, with deep and sensitive eyes, exuding a mischievous playfulness. Aublet created a wonderful depiction of a woman baring her glistening body at a Turkish bath. I even made an offer for it. These are authentic celebrations of femininity, and there is no sense conveyed of women being accessories to men.'

Emmanuelle was watching Destouches, her velvety lips broken into an admiring smile. She liked the idea of a man so passionate, who clearly enjoyed repartee with women on an equal footing. As for her, she loved to pamper men, finding their soft spots and playing up to them – listening with all her senses, allowing his intellect to overwhelm her.

The calm atmosphere of twilight moving into darkness accentuated the confidence of Emmanuelle and Destouches, conversing about art as if they had known each other for quite some time. Vincent was listening with pleasure, but part of him was looking at the challenges of the forthcoming days. He was in one of the most ancient dwellings of Paris to talk about the destiny of Europe. Past was meeting future.

When he left Quai d'Anjou, the absinthe shrouded Vincent from the nightly chill on the embankment. Emmanuelle was still with Destouches. She was an independent spirit and knew that Vincent would be fine with her choice.

As Vincent walked with his hands in the pockets of his coat, someone from a crowded car shouted at him: '*Victoire!*'

The other passengers cheered and whooped. Vincent raised half an arm to salute the merry band.

IV

Berlin Days

'*Was darf's denn sein?*'

'A beer, please.'

Rachel had just taken a seat at the lounge bar of the Matesanz Hotel. The tiny spot, carved out from the corridor between the hall and the ground rooms, was furnished with only six or seven tables, from which people could order by raising their voices. Behind the counter was a young man with a greyish t-shirt and skinny tattooed arms. With nobody else in sight, Rachel allowed herself to answer a call.

'How's Berlin?'

'Not as cold as I expected, Lucìa. Spring has arrived.'

'And the hotel?'

'This place is amazing. More your style than mine, I know, but I like the vibe.'

In spotting the high shelves crammed with vintage books and magazines that lined the wide hall, Rachel – more a fan of boutique hotels – had indeed thought of Lucìa.

A rather unique establishment inside a converted factory in trendy Friedrichshain, the Matesanz Hotel gaily opened its lounge to a multitude of programmers, developers, artists, musicians, writers, advertisers and whoever wanted to be creative non-stop in a productive-but-chilled atmosphere. The fresh energy of those lounging around the sofas and tables, bent over their laptops or chatting by the coffee machine, had cheered Rachel up.

In the early days, ROME's founding team had similarly spent endless nights in this lounge to launch the new platform. An occasional beer or coffee, then back to their joyful coding sprints, dreaming of moving fast and breaking big.

Berlin was the most fertile hub in Europe for high-tech start-ups. The city had supported many successful ventures and was now thriving with well-funded incubators and accelerators. Life was less expensive than in other European capitals, and the nightlife was sparkling enough for people to fulfil the *work hard, play hard* philosophy.

'So, I met up with a former colleague of mine here in Berlin,' Rachel said. 'A very knowledgeable acquaintance. A year ago, he did a story on ROME. Well, there are gaps, things that don't add up.'

'Meaning?'

'Marlene Gäch – she spends her time secluded on the eighty-ninth floor of the Drexler Steinmetz, the headquarters of ROME. She rarely appears on the other floors, let alone at social events or in the media.'

'Any idea why she's so reclusive?'

'Maybe she's ill. Self-made digital tycoons – they work day and night for years and then fall sick. But there's something else that doesn't convince me …'

Rachel paused and looked around with circumspection. After ascertaining that the tattooed barman wasn't listening, she resumed.

'Marlene Gäch holds a fifteen per cent share of ROME. Considering that the other shareholders – mostly German banks or investment funds – don't own more than two or three per cent of the company each, Gäch still has enough shares to guarantee herself decision-making power. The strange thing is that her stake in ROME is held through a bearer share company in the United Kingdom.'

'You're getting too technical now. I'm losing you. I've never worked for the *Wall Street Journal* … c'mon!'

'You're right. Sorry.' Rachel laughed. 'Bearer shares are shares not registered in the company's books. Basically, the person holding the paper shares is the one entitled to make decisions and distribute the profits of the company.'

'Is this normal?'

'Not really. Bearer shares are meant to hide the owner's identity. So, they're used very often to hide tax evasion or launder money. You keep the shares in your lawyer's safe and take them out only to sell the company or if you need to prove ownership. Because of their lack of transparency, most countries have banned bearer shares, but the UK reintroduced them soon after leaving the European Union.'

Lucìa groaned softly, perplexed.

Rachel added: 'My contact wonders why the German Financial Supervisory Authority allows this opacity. It's true that ROME isn't listed on any stock exchange, so the disclosure requirements for listed companies don't apply here; but, still, ROME is the largest conglomerate in Europe. Why are they using a medieval corporate structure? It wouldn't be allowed in America. And you Europeans still complain about us keeping our check-the-box regulations!'

Despite struggling to grasp Rachel's jargon, Lucìa urged her to continue the enquiry. 'We need to keep not one eye but two on ROME.'

'Will do,' replied Rachel.

'But now you should relax,' Lucìa encouraged her. 'I believe we booked you one of those wonderful rooms with the en-suite sauna.'

'Yep!' confirmed Rachel with a burst of her contagious laughter. The momentarily empty-handed barman glanced up from his mobile. He then lowered his eyes, smiling.

Lucìa was positive that Rachel could find other useful information in Berlin. ROME maintained its impartiality about Charlemagny, but she had learned from experience that social media was hardly unbiased. *A pensar male degli altri si fa peccato, ma spesso s'indovina*, a famous Italian politician had once said: you sin in thinking bad about people, but often your guess is right.

After her call to Berlin, Lucìa took the short walk to the University of Birmingham's Faculty of Law. Professor Sherwood sat in his office. The professor's desk was walled in by the customary towers of thick books. A deluge of coloured post-its, torn notepad pages and other makeshift reminders were scattered everywhere – hanging precariously from the wall behind the desk, falling temptingly out of books, firmly pressed under a mug, or long forgotten in a drawer.

'Hi, Prof,' Lucìa said after knocking on the open door.

'Good afternoon, Lucìa,' he said, raising his head from the desk and smiling at her.

'It seems someone is finally considering stopping the e-poll,' she announced with relief. 'The Criminal Court of Paris will rule in a couple of days. It has taken an unbelievable amount of time for someone to take the initiative, though.'

'I heard the news from Miss Cliché. Please, don't get too excited, Lucìa,' the professor warned. 'I doubt they'll grant the suspension. And if they did, it would be unfair: are they really considering preventing people from expressing their views?'

Lucìa was disappointed with the professor's words.

'Prof, the problem here is not the people's right to self-determination, of course,' she said. 'But votes can be manipulated, especially online. And with the complete lack of transparency of social media, we should doubt that ROME can guarantee fair play.'

The professor entwined his hands behind his neck. He seemed to quickly gather his thoughts before asking: 'Have you decided whether to attend the debate with Vincent d'Amont?'

She didn't answer. Everybody around her seemed obsessed with Vincent d'Amont.

'The debate would be quite an opportunity to show the merits of Europe and the reasons why we should support it again and again,' he continued, observing her lack of reply. 'You're a brilliant journalist. If you believe that ROME's behaviour is shady, you must investigate further. The war on Charlemagny shouldn't be pursued in a court of law. We live in a country, the UK, that attributes importance to the principle that regardless of who wins or loses, each side can walk off the stage with dignity and mutual respect. You can beat Vincent d'Amont at the debate and make a great case against Charlemagny.'

As often happened, the intrinsic coherence of the professor's arguments made a reply difficult. Lucìa never ceased to be surprised at his avuncular ability to inspire her. He had a flair for detecting priorities in knotty situations, reducing reality to its essential facts, rationalising even the most human feelings. Unsurprisingly, the professor was proving a crucial mentor to Lucìa in the Charlemagny campaign.

Lucìa felt a heavy responsibility resting on her shoulders, a responsibility she didn't want – that of being the greatest champion for the cause of Europe. In fact, Lucìa had always tried to be an unbiased vlogger, but that was no longer possible. Even if she didn't like the idea of being too self-centred, the media in Europe were mentioning her name every other hour. It was easy to fall – she recognised – into the trap of focusing on Miss Cliché alone. So Lucìa had devised a solution to avoid being trapped in the bubble of her new popularity: enquiring into the lives of others.

'How's your book on political relativism going, Prof?'

'Magnificently, Lucìa. Today I'm trying to express in writing the concept whereby two very antithetical political positions can both find solid and logical foundations, thus neutralising each other. For most individuals, choosing a position tends to be a subjective decision, often dictated by transient and irrational facts: family traditions, self-interest, fears, even our state of mind ...'

'All very current.'

'Very much so. Especially in an era where most politicians pander to people's desires, and are so afraid to take unpopular decisions. You can see a prime minister endorsing two conflicting stances within a couple of days because, in the meantime, the wind has changed direction.'

The professor had been deeply invested in his book on political relativism for two years. With his research, he was

applying to modern political science a very ancient philosophical doctrine, developed as early as the fifth century BC by the
Greek sophist Protagoras, who was credited with saying that
there are two mutually opposed arguments on any subject.

A debate between French presidential candidates, in which
the two kept trading ideological positions at their own whim,
had sparked the book idea. This vignette had confirmed the
professor's long-standing belief that politics had become so
aqueous that electors were deprived of any fixed point to follow.
It was all a constant reshuffle of cards, a kaleidoscope of changing slogans, a restless quest for consensus. Or, perhaps, these
were inherited features always present in politics, yet more
manifest in some periods than others: and this was exactly the
hypothesis the professor wanted to test.

'Vincent d'Amont has a nose for seeking out consensus,'
Lucìa pointed out.

'He knows where public opinion is going,' the professor
agreed. 'He played a blinder with Charlemagny – mastering
a quick comeback without a party behind him. He must be
careful, though: the momentum that has built him up so
quickly could also send him veering off the road at any point
– and us with him. History is in the hands of a small club of
egocentric politicians who can be rather economical with the
truth, I loathe to say.'

Ten minutes into her visit, Lucìa received a text. Three
different buzzing tones were set on her device: a very calm,
almost-imperceptible humming for messages with low priority;
a faster vibration for messages deemed of standard importance;
finally, a wild rhythmic drum solo was dedicated to those
messages that had to be read sooner than now. This time, the

bongos were coming from Hugh: *Miss Cliché is down. Please get here ASAP!*

Lucìa excused herself, dashing back to Miss Cliché, where the team were huddled around a dimly lit room like anxious fathers outside the maternity ward. Lucìa jostled through the small throng and reached the IT cave. As soon as he spotted her, Hugh came forward in haste.

'What happened?' she asked him, nervously.

'We still don't know. Right after you left, everything crashed. The backup of the vlog is safe – Belch has reassured me – but we still can't go back live.'

Belch was the chief technological officer at Miss Cliché. With his oversized jumpers, ill-fitting jeans, and a spotty pale face hidden beneath a straggly beard, Belch matched with perfection the stereotype of the digital boffin. He avoided any form of socialisation and, at the age of thirty-eight, was a proud collector of Korean webtoons. His nickname originated with a well-established habit he apparently practised often in the dark room. Fortunately for his teammates, he had quit picking his nose years before.

'Do you have any idea what's going on?' Lucìa questioned Belch. He sat slouched on his chair before a long row of greasy monitors.

'Hackers,' Belch replied. He didn't add much else.

'Why do we always need to drag words out of you?' Hugh chided him. He couldn't accept Belch's lack of tidiness, so any occasion to reprimand him was welcomed.

'I don't know how, but they passed four of our five layers of security,' Belch said, paying little attention to Hugh's remark. 'We'd be in much hotter water if they had got through the fifth layer as well, *ya know.*'

'How's Pandora?' Lucìa asked.

'Temporarily out of order,' replied Belch.

'*Ship* … !' she gasped.

Lucìa glanced absent-mindedly around the tech team's room. Empty bottles, dirty napkins and other forgotten items lay scattered on all the desks. Old notes and doodles were collecting dust on the whiteboard. The vibe was dirty and untidy, a feeling of seclusion permeating the entire room. This was the main reason why everyone at Miss Cliché tended to avoid the tech department, not minding that the constantly dim light in the IT cave meant nobody could see what happened behind its glassy walls.

Lucìa, Belch and Hugh headed to her office. They passed through the cafeteria, where just a couple of days earlier Rachel and Lucìa had shared their cheerful *aperitivo*. The atmosphere couldn't have been more different now – those relaxed times a distant memory.

'Are we completely cut off from the net?' Lucìa asked Belch.

'We can still exchange messages with our followers.'

'That's good – we can inform the community of what's going on. We need to do it as quickly as possible.'

'I will contact the police and the National Crime Agency, in the meantime,' said Hugh, who always wanted to show his resourcefulness.

Lucìa took a seat at her desk to write an effective message to the millions of followers of Miss Cliché. Having concentrated most of her energy on supervising the team or preparing her daily videos – where she spoke impromptu – Lucìa had not put pen to paper much of late. While preparing the message, she realised how much she liked the challenge of writing.

Lucìa jotted down words frantically for about an hour. Then she called Hugh in to share the result and finalise the message, which they planned to send out in a matter of minutes. Hugh made some observations, tweaking the statement. Her deputy in daily operations at Miss Cliché, and a far-from-impulsive soul, Hugh often added clarity to her decisions.

'Lucìa, your wording seems to imply that the hacking attack has come from outside Europe,' he said. 'But we are not sure. Yes, it may be China, Russia, even the US, but perhaps not. One of Vincent d'Amont's biggest backers is Destouches, who runs a large network of gambling sites in Europe. If I remember well, one of his sites was once accused of hacking competitors. So, Destouches has the resources to do what's being done to us today.'

Lucìa accepted Hugh's point of view; they couldn't point the finger at anyone. 'So many are scared that we can influence the e-vote against Charlemagny,' she observed as she deleted that bit.

They agreed on a final version of the statement, centred on a list of reasons for which people should treasure the Union's past achievements and future goals.

Friends!

Miss Cliché is temporarily down. This afternoon, ruthless hackers attacked us. Please don't worry: we will be back soon ;)

Still, we don't want this assault to stop us from making our humble contribution to the cause of Europe. So, this is the right occasion to remind ourselves, in very few words, why we should treasure the Union's past achievements and future goals:

1. Europe had never enjoyed a long period of peace such as the one started when the Union began to take shape after the Second World War. The Union has guaranteed peace and prosperity for many decades. We should never forget how the soil of our continent was stained by bloody wars for thousands of years. The secession of France and Germany would waste all the precious efforts made to maintain harmony in Europe!

2. *European citizens are free to move, live, work, trade and do many – I say, many – other things throughout Europe, without real boundaries between countries. We should NOT give up this liberty!*

3. *In Europe we enjoy very elevated standards of food, environmental and consumer protection … a real safety net against the greed of some businesses and a net of welfare provisions that must be protected!*

4. *The Union has funded many projects in the less economically developed territories. Not all, especially in the largest contributing countries, are glad about this form of redistribution. Yet, it is without doubt fair for the wealthiest nations to reach out to the less well-off!*

Lucìa abruptly stopped reading the draft. She wasn't persuaded.

'Hugh, something is wrong.'

'What?'

'A letter highlighting the efficacy of the European Union … too dry … I think we'll lose our followers. I've a better idea.'

'Being?'

'When Rachel and I went out the other evening … I did a little "speech" in a club. Don't look me that way, please; I simply said everything we believe in. This morning, Ash, the club owner, sent me a video. It's my quick speech, all edited, basically a medley of the footage taken that night. It looks so spontaneous, so homemade. It hasn't been released yet. We should send our followers an email with a short message plus the video. Period.'

They watched the clip together. Hugh was unsure about the idea of a video with a tipsy Lucìa speaking in a noisy bar. Yet Lucìa had the final say, and shortly after, the clip was sent to Miss Cliché's followers.

It had been out for less than ten minutes when Hugh walked back in. Both enthusiasm and exhaustion filled his voice. 'Lucìa, our message has stirred things up. Most news sites have already picked up the story. Followers are sending us thousands of messages of encouragement!'

Lucìa raised her eyes in sheer delight. An initiative pursued mostly out of desperation was apparently bearing fruit.

'The click-rate of the message is very high,' Hugh continued, 'and many are sharing our statement on their personal blogs or posting it to their accounts on ROME. Even the hashtag #JeSuisMissCliche is getting more popular by the minute.'

Lucìa chuckled, flattered, even though that hashtag did sound ominous. Italians can be rather superstitious.

The team shared some selected messages with her.

Miss Cliché: don't give up, please. My father's Polish, my mother's from Estonia. They both made a great life possible for us here in Germany. It wouldn't have been possible with walls or borders!

Miss Cliché: I'm a medical scientist in Budapest. We're carrying out a research project to develop a novel biosensor using acoustic

waves to detect tumour DNA. The research has produced promis-
ing findings. We owe everything to the Union's support.

There was also room for some old-fashioned feminism.

Miss Cliché: they're going after you only because you're a woman!
Please fight them, up to the very end!

After going through the messages, Lucìa spent the rest of the
day zooming with vloggers from everywhere. Not only did
they ask for comment, but also expressed what appeared to be
genuine sympathy. Even those who didn't share her views, or
who competed with Miss Cliché on breaking the news, knew
that something above any rivalry was at stake this time: the
freedom to express an opinion.

Midnight was approaching, and Miss Cliché was still
down, when Lucìa's device began to play bongos for a
top-priority call. Her tired eyes glanced at the screen. The
caller ID said: *Ten.*

She sighed inside; then, answered the call with an
unsure voice.

'Hello?'

'Miss Cliché: how are you?' the caller asked with the sooth-
ing, baritone timbre of the self-assured.

'I'm fine. Actually, it's been a tough day, sir.'

'I just heard about the attack. I'm calling to give you my
word that the Home Secretary and I are doing everything in
our power to help you.'

Astonished, Lucìa struggled to find a proper reply. After
stammering for a few moments, she said, 'I certainly feel

reassured to learn that the Prime Minister of the United Kingdom of Great Britain is with us, sir.'

'A duty and an honour for me, Miss Cliché,' the Prime Minister said. 'Too often hackers, crawlers and bots have influenced politics. We shouldn't underestimate the value of the Charlemagny vote; it's not just a social media poll, but much more. And, clearly, today's attack is meant to silence a voice for Europe.'

'Yes, sir. We believe that, if Charlemagny wins the e-poll, the result will shake Europe, triggering separatist sentiments everywhere.'

After a short silence, the other side spoke again.

'Based on our intelligence – and I trust you will not divulge this confidential information – a secret meeting between the French and German foreign ministers on the topic of Charlemagny is scheduled to happen very soon. It means they are both taking the poll very seriously.'

Lucìa wasn't surprised at hearing this: politicians always followed the popular mood, she believed, never the other way around.

'Your vlog is doing an astonishing job of defending Europe,' the Prime Minister praised. 'You are perhaps too young to remember the Brexit campaign well. I wish we'd had a voice like yours among Remainers at the time. Perhaps things would have turned out differently.'

A couple of years earlier, the Prime Minister had won the national elections owing to a manifesto that included a referendum on the UK re-joining the European Union. However, as his own party had not achieved an absolute majority in Westminster, he had reluctantly created a governing coalition with other parties, who were not at all keen to promote a new accession of Britain to the Union. So, his hands were tied on the topic of Europe, for the moment.

The PM felt his coalition allies wanted to impose too many conditions for the UK to be part of Europe again. They argued that, if the country went back into the EU, Britain should retain the rights that all the members had transferred to the Union in the distant past. A deal-breaker.

'It's the wrong mindset,' he told Lucìa with exasperation. 'The decision to join Europe for a second time should be made with a real sense of belonging. Either Europe moves forward, or it will collapse. There is no way to shape what some call a "two-speed" Europe.'

The PM paused, then resumed. 'The Tory government made a major mistake during the Brexit campaign: they told our people that we should remain in Europe – yes – but less integrated with the other countries. Nonsense. You can't keep a foot inside and a foot outside Europe. And our people didn't buy into this.'

Lucìa, wishing to express her sincere attachment towards a country that had given much to her, intervened: 'Sir, many of us wish that the United Kingdom was still part of Europe. However, this is still a great and welcoming country even outside Europe. Furthermore, the economy is going very well ...'

'Yes, Miss Cliché, but we have lost Northern Ireland,' the PM interrupted. 'And Scotland is always on the verge of threatening a secession. We have ended up losing our unity as a country after putting in danger our relationships in Europe.'

How right this assessment seemed to Lucìa. Perhaps it was her fate to cross paths often with savvy political thinkers, endowed with uncommonly strong minds that stood above the rest. The Prime Minister was one.

Miss Cliché had first met him for an interview while he was engaged in his eventually successful election campaign. His eloquence had immediately struck her. A candidate still relatively unknown to the public at large, the then-aspiring prime minister had revealed quite a unique political vision of Britain, and a fearlessness about swimming against the tide. For his part, he had appreciated Lucìa's blunt and fact-based way of conducting the interview. This call was their second conversation ever, yet they seemed to understand each other well.

The Prime Minister couldn't help observing how British history was often conveniently misread to show Europe in a bad light. 'Take Winston, my famed predecessor,' he said. (Fellow prime ministers refer to each other by their first name.) 'Brexiteers kept twisting his words during that bloody referendum. It is true that early on he said he believed that Britain was with Europe, but didn't belong to it. But this was when we were still at the core of an empire, and the conflict with Hitler was far away: his view changed after the war, when he said publicly that we should build the United States of Europe. Churchill's ambivalence towards Europe is often exaggerated. That's why fact-checking is fundamental; and I should say that you master this noble craft sublimely, Miss Cliché.'

His attestation of esteem sent a quiver of pride through Lucìa, knowing that a man so candid and upright would never pay anyone that type of compliment unless fully heartfelt.

Brexit was still an open wound for many in Britain. It really escaped the millions of Remainers why a majority of voters had made the masochistic choice of leaving Europe. They felt, even more bitterly, that they themselves had over-looked the implications of the referendum – that they could have done more to prevent this outcome. The news of the approaching Charlemagny vote had rekindled the Brexit grief in all its might. For those willing to see them, like Miss Cliché, the similarities between the path chosen by the UK many years earlier and the possible unfolding of Charlemagny were clear.

The warm conversation with the Prime Minister succeeded in invigorating Lucìa and giving a sense of further purpose to her mission. So, it was with renewed energy that she went straight back to the tech cavern. There, Lucìa learned from a surprised Hugh that the director of the Digital Crime Agency had called to say that he would deploy the best resources to help them.

'I've just received an unexpected call as well,' Lucìa chuckled.

The Cybercrime Team was already in action. Operating remotely from London, the officers had tried to unblock the vlog, but without success. Belch, quite aloof by nature, this time appeared shaken by the day's events – or, perhaps, by the unforeseen night shift. He tried to explain to Lucìa in layman's terms what the Cybercrime Team was engaged with. 'They're scanning the network, *ya know*. They've got this customised software, a powerful one, *ya know*. We don't know what happened: maybe our network was swamped with bogus requests, or they just hijacked us, *ya know*.'

Lucìa found Belch's lingo unintelligible, even worse than Rachel's financial jargon. Despite owing much of her popu-larity to a successful vlog, she saw herself more as a woman of letters than a tech girl. But she trusted Belch's skills, and this aspect was what mattered to her.

* * *

As Lucìa struggled with the hackers, Rachel was still at the lounge bar. After her second beer, she had begun chatting with the tattooed barman, the conversation turning quite naturally to the early days of ROME.

'I'd just begun working here when the guys launched the platform,' the barman told her. 'They were a nice bunch of people. Much more down to earth than the kids I see around now. Berlin has become too trendy.'

Rachel nodded. A similar evolution had taken place in Silicon Valley, her older colleagues at the *WSJ* had often told her: enthusiastic and naive tech-geeks slowly turning into self-aware capitalists after their first stream of revenue from once-unapproachable investors.

'Not that the guys missed any fun,' the barman added with a cheeky grin. 'They smoked an awful lot of pot. Not here, but in the back garden, of course. Sometimes I joined them. "Weed helps us code better. We concentrate more," they told me. I don't need to tell you what happened with girls in the laundry room upstairs ...'

'And the one guy that disappeared? I read something online,' said Rachel, who couldn't believe her luck at finding almost an insider.

'Employee Zero? A bit reserved, with his bald head. He enjoyed partying, but less than the others. He was not that carefree.'

'Did you ever talk to him?'

'A couple of times. He sat here, where you are now, alone for ten minutes. Didn't want to be bothered. Then he started talking. It could be things like "I know where I see myself in five years. If you can't see where you will be in five years … you've got a problem." The last time I saw him was ages ago. They all stopped coming here when ROME hit the big time.'

A couple came into the bar and sat at a table. The barman politely warned them there was only enough time for one drink. They nodded and ordered a glass of red wine for him, white for her. After serving the couple, the barman came back to Rachel.

'What brings you to Berlin, by the way?'

'I'm a journalist. I've come here from New York to do a piece on Charlemagny.'

'Ah! That's why you're so curious about ROME!' he exclaimed. 'But, look, I'm closing. Shall we grab a drink some-where? There's lots of nice spots around.'

The suggestion caught Rachel by surprise. She was quite his senior. In New York, Rachel wouldn't have accepted this type of invite, but it was her first night in Berlin.

When ready, the tattooed barman – whose name was Holger – took a black jumper from under the counter and switched the lights off. They left the hotel from the main lobby where four or five people were lying on the sofas, typing on tablets or drawing on sketchbooks.

Outside, the cobbled streets of Friedrichshain weren't particularly crowded. Occasional groups still moved from one bar to another or simply went home.

Rachel and Holger must have appeared an odd couple. Holger fully observed the signature Berliner clothing style: dark, casual, comfy. His pale cheeks were intentionally stubbly, which paired well with the long hair and thin moustache. An attentive listener with a calm tone, Holger gave out a chilled aura.

Rachel wore a smart red skirt suit and long black boots to keep out the cold. Her designer work bag, never left unattended, represented an attempt to mix professional ambition with personal care. Her beautifully manicured hands reflected her keenness to detail. Despite having grown up in a tight-knit family, Rachel had so far dedicated her life to journalism above everything else. Unlike Lucìa, she didn't feel the slightest bit of guilt for not having started a family of her own yet.

As they walked through Friedrichshain, Rachel spotted a huge slogan on a wall. *Charlemagny.* She wondered whether this was an omen of some sort.

Holger took his new acquaintance to a low-ceilinged bar in Simon-Dach-Straße. Quite popular in the area, this narrow establishment stretched through four long rooms, the last of which resembled a cave with its damp, flaking stone walls and candle-lit wooden tables. Holger suggested they should sit there. If the Matesanz was hippie, this place was more on the grungy side. Rachel giggled to herself, enjoying the idea of an unplanned night out.

When, after taking her time, a young waitress lazily joined them, Rachel ordered a Venetian Spritz. The waitress squinted at her in bored bewilderment. Holger chuckled. 'If I were still behind the bar, I'd do it for you. But I doubt they even have any prosecco here.'

Rachel had to go for a third beer.

'How often do you work at the bar?' Rachel asked Holger.

'Every evening except Sundays. I started when I was twenty and I'm still there. The managers are nice, and I get to meet a lot of people.'

'Don't you have any other ambitions?' asked Rachel, who immediately felt like a mother trying to stir up a son's aspirations without denting his pride. After all, she came from America, the land of competition.

'I want to open my own bar. I'm working on it with some friends,' he replied.

It'd be an improvement, she thought.

Holger felt obliged to elaborate: 'I like to enjoy life. Growing up was tough but I'm now happy where I am: renting an apartment all by myself, saving some money, feeling respected at the bar.'

'I understand,' Rachel replied, appreciating that Holger's happiness with his life was a good thing.

'What will you vote for on Charlemagny day?' she asked, changing the subject.

'I won't vote.'

'How come?'

'I'm tired of ROME.'

'Meaning?'

'ROME is already everywhere. I don't want her to mingle with politics, too.'

It seemed very concise, but sensible, reasoning to Rachel.

'But if forced to vote, I would vote for Europe.'

The waitress served their drinks. Holger continued: 'I closed my ROME account a year ago. The problem is that without ROME it's more difficult to reach blogs, watch movies or order at restaurants; there are even banks that won't give you a loan unless you're on ROME ... and I suspect it'll get even worse.'

Rachel thought of the irony: Europeans had long blamed the US for giving birth to the FANGs. Americans had been accused of introducing excessive deregulation on the net, being careless about people's digital privacy and too lax about fake news and hate speech. The roles were now dramatically reversed: a German social media platform had reached a monopolistic position in Europe in a way still unknown on the other side of the ocean. ROME connected, informed, entertained, influenced, fed, financed, and did countless other things to a huge multitude of people. Not content with that – it would seem – the biggest European conglomerate was now trying to influence politics with a poll that, regardless of its outcome, had been on everybody's lips for months. If an upside of Brexit existed, Rachel conceded, it was that it had saved the UK from ROME – at least for the moment. The platform, in fact, had never caught on in Britain.

Rachel decided to open up. 'I happen to know Miss Cliché very well. We worked together in Brussels. I met up with her in the UK right before coming here.'

'Wow ...' Holger said. 'I've a lot of respect for Miss Cliché. She's a free spirit.'

Rachel smiled in approval.

'I heard about today's hack attack,' Holger added. 'I feel sorry for her.'

'What ... ?'

Rachel sighed. While Holger had learned about the attack hours before while at the bar, she had stayed in the dark the whole time. Rachel rushed to Miss Cliché's homepage:

We are back!
The dangerous smurf attack has just been blocked!

* * *

While Lucìa succeeded in restoring Miss Cliché, Vincent d'Amont remained absorbed by his legal ordeal in Paris.

The highly efficient ROME had arranged an emergency meeting for him with the lawyers at Moulini Gambardella Dreyfus Avocats, the top Parisian firm with peerless expertise in criminal cases. ROME was determined to ensure that this legal hiccup did not stand in the way of the referendum.

So, early in the morning, Vincent took a Cabeille to the offices of Moulini Gambardella Dreyfus on the Avenue de l'Opéra, not far from the Louvre. He would normally have made the fifteen-minute walk to relieve the potential stress of the situation. Today, though, after spotting two vloggers lurking around the corner just as he was leaving home, he had opted for a Cabeille.

Vincent considered lawyers one of the least productive guilds of the modern economy, second only to politicians. Consequently, he attended legal meetings with the utmost reluctance. This time, however, he appreciated that the fate of his once-in-a-lifetime political dream might be compromised by judicial technicalities; and Vincent d'Amont would do anything to prevent some legal detail from stripping Charlemagny from him – even mingling with lawyers.

Moulini Gambardella Dreyfus occupied three storeys of a grand Haussmann building. The firm's spacious hall must have been refurbished in recent times, but still retained complete harmony with the building's sophisticated architecture. The surrounding grandiosity made Vincent wonder what extortionate hourly rates Messrs Moulini Gambardella Dreyfus might apply. A uniformed lady at the reception asked him to take a seat in the conference room. The high-ceilinged space was elegant but neutral, as was the set of branded sharp pencils in a velvet box on the large round table.

Before long a stubby, balding man, accompanied by a tall, slender and much younger woman, walked in with firm steps.

'Nice to make your acquaintance, Monsieur d'Amont. I am Paul Moulini, founding partner of the firm. My colleague is Cécile Moulini, junior partner and my daughter.'

Vincent d'Amont cast them a smile as he shook their hands.

'ROME instructed us to assist both their group and you individually in this delicate situation,' Paul Moulini, after inviting Vincent to take a seat, began. 'We would like to assign the Charlemagny case to the team headed by Cécile. Please note that this is not a nepotistic choice: Cécile is a talented and dedicated lawyer, with an impressive track record despite her young age. She has asked to work with you. We take motivation very seriously at Moulini Gambardella Dreyfus.'

Vincent took a prolonged look at Cécile Moulini, and she smiled in return. He had to admit that she was the most pleasant legal practitioner he had ever crossed paths with. Clever blue eyes, a button nose, a smooth neck. Vincent had been on the verge of simply letting the lawyers do their work, but her unforeseen appearance was now tempting him to help them with the case more proactively.

'I'm only interested in the outcome,' Vincent said. 'I've been told that ROME hasn't capped the budget for legal expenses, so I expect Moulini Gambardella Dreyfus to spare no effort.'

Moulini Sr looked at him, stone-faced, confirming what Vincent had already learned from experience – that all lawyers shared a complete lack of humour on the subject of billable hours.

His daughter broke the silence.

'Mr d'Amont, speaking bluntly – as you seem to prefer – let's say that your case is of interest to our firm less for the retainer than for the visibility.'

Vincent enjoyed being challenged by an attractive woman almost as much as he liked teasing bald overweight lawyers. The mother must be very beautiful, he thought.

'The purpose of today's meeting,' Cécile Moulini added, 'is to prepare a statement together for submission to the judge, who will decide on the suspension of the 8/4 referendum. Time is of the essence.'

She glanced at her father. Moulini Sr hesitated a second, then announced: 'I should let the two of you review the case together and finalise the statement.'

He stood up and offered his hand to Vincent, who concluded that Cécile's old man had attended the meeting solely to justify the final bill. After the father had left, Ms Moulini began to explain the legal implications of Vincent's situation.

'We cannot yet say whether a trial against you on the charge of threatening our national security will ever start. It will only happen if the prosecutors indict you, and the court upholds their request.'

Vincent already knew he would never be sentenced. As his new lawyer pointed out, the issue was different. 'Our focus is to avoid the suspension of the referendum,' she continued. 'If the suspension is granted with an interim order, there will be no Charlemagny vote for years.'

Vincent shivered at the prospect of his dreams shattered by legal paperwork. If that ever happened, Vincent swore to himself, he would incite Charlemagniers to rebellion.

'We should consider ourselves lucky.' She tried to cast things in a positive light. 'The judge could well have suspended the vote after receiving the petition. He hasn't. The judge will order the suspension of the referendum only if he sees clear evidence of an imminent crime. It's the law.'

Moulini then made a request to her client that she was uncomfortable with.

'Before we start reviewing your draft statement for tomorrow ... I am loath to ask you ... but I must delve into the case that involved you years ago. It may have an impact in court.'

Vincent had seen it coming, reluctant as he was to dwell on his difficult past. The assumption that nothing good could ever come out of a meeting with a lawyer was reinforced. They had to go through the scandal that had brought his political experience to a halt.

The turmoil had started with a police officer telling a colleague in a wiretapped call that Cabeille had tipped Mayor d'Amont to open the Paris streets to self-driving transport. Somehow, the press got hold of the recording and published it, causing a polarisation of public opinion between detractors and supporters of Vincent d'Amont. The officer never substantiated his allegations and, lacking any other evidence, the investigation soon folded. Without a criminal record, but with his reputation tainted, Mayor d'Amont had believed his career over.

'It must have been very painful,' Cécile acknowledged sympathetically. They had seen many clients with similar cases at Moulini Gambardella Dreyfus: politicians inculpated by newspaper headlines, then acquitted at the bottom of an inside page.

'A very dark period,' he confirmed. 'But also an opportunity for a clean slate. A rebirth, I can say with hindsight. No party expecting me to follow its rules, no anxiety about blunders in front of the camera, no more lengthy election campaigns. I'm actually wrong about that last one: the Charlemagny campaign has been even more trying than most elections.'

She smiled. The initial tension of the meeting had now eased. Client and lawyer, side by side, prepared the statement for the court. The likelihood that the document would be leaked to the media made its drafting even trickier. They had to be careful. For instance, if they argued that the Charlemagny vote couldn't possibly threaten the fabric of French society because the result was not legally binding, the significance of the referendum in the public's eyes would diminish.

They worked tirelessly from morning until past midnight to read, amend, adjust, tweak and reread the statement, to demonstrate that all charges were unfounded. Early the following day, Cécile Moulini submitted it to the Criminal Court of Paris:

To the Honourable Court:

Sirs,

I would like to set out some facts that clearly confute the unfounded allegations of the criminal complaint lodged against me.

The complaint states that I would be trying to undermine state institutions and threaten our Constitution by promoting the vote on Charlemagny. The complainants claim that our proposal to unite the sovereignties of France and Germany is designed to de-stabilise our country. This is untrue.

From a strictly legal standpoint, we should remember how French criminal law stipulates that, apart from negligence, a crime only exists when someone unequivocally intends to commit that crime. This is not true in my case.

The complainants argue that I ultimately aim to cause wide-spread political unrest to threaten our democracy. Utterly false. There is no reason to believe that the referendum may ever cause political unrest.

The referendum is intended to generate 'food for political thought' for French people. You often hear complaints about our people no longer being interested in politics. This is an opportunity to start a debate about where we are, as French people, and where we want to go.

I believe that, after the vote, many people around France will peacefully discuss the result, drinking a glass of our great Burgundy. Where is the political fallout in that?

Again: I have no intention of destroying our foundations or the Constitution, of which I am very fond, as my personal and public experiences clearly testify.

This unfounded criminal complaint is no more than a disguised attempt to deny people their right to express a politi-cal opinion. The claimants are afraid that French people will no longer trail behind the old-school wishes of politicians. The world has changed, as has the way people express their political ideas. Nowadays, people can share their views on social media. It is normal and acceptable.

We are not under some authoritarian regime. France is not China.

Freedom of expression is protected by the Declaration of Human and Civic Rights of 1789 and by our Constitution of 1958. The Declaration of Human and Civic Rights, in particular, states: 'The free communication of ideas and of opinions is one of the most precious rights of man. Any citizen may therefore speak, write and publish freely, except what is tantamount to the abuse of this liberty in the cases determined by law.'

This ludicrous case has been triggered by my former political party, France Souveraine, which is trying to abuse the system to settle an old score.

My detractors are ignominiously attempting to 'drag' the Paris Criminal Court into the grounds of 'active politics'. But we are a nation that knows that the role of judiciary power is not to steer the political direction of the country. Baron de Montesquieu has taught us that legislative, executive and judiciary powers should always be separate and independent agencies. Furthermore, a criminal court should not decide whether it is fair (or not) to explore the feelings of our people on the matter of Charlemagny.

We should allow the French people to exercise their freedom of expression on the net without any unfair restriction.

Thank you for your time and consideration.

Vincent d'Amont

V

The Sherwoods

When the noise of the binmen ushered her into a hazy awakening, Lucìa reached an early-morning epiphany: she would do the debate.

Professor Sherwood's inciting words, her itinerant night out with Rachel and the Prime Minister's epochal call, concluded with his best wishes for the debate, had all contributed to spurring her turnaround.

The threat of Charlemagny existed, irrespective of whether she accepted or refused the debate. Lucìa hadn't much to lose. Conversely, if Charlemagny won after her failure to confront Vincent d'Amont, it would take years for her to shrug off the guilt. Accepting his challenge was a sensible thing to do.

Still flat in bed, Lucìa texted her opponent: *I'm all in.*

Then, she shared her decision with Professor Sherwood, who duly hid his enthusiasm behind a stern set of instructions, including to clear her agenda. 'You must practise with me. We must have it all off pat,' he ordered.

They agreed that Lucìa should give her personal touch to the debate. Straightforward thinking, abundant room for her feelings and a ban on arid numbers would be key ingredients in persuading people that Europe should prevail over Charlemagny on 8/4.

Nothing should be left to chance. If Vincent d'Amont engaged in his nationalistic rhetoric on the threats of uncontrolled migration, Lucìa should highlight the benefits of more cultures living under the same roof. If Vincent d'Amont rushed to list the alleged short-term benefits of Charlemagny, Lucìa should explain why France and Germany would be worse off, in the long run, after leaving Europe. Finally, if Vincent d'Amont complained that the Union had admitted too many member countries, Lucìa should respond that Europe could overcome the difficult challenges of our era by uniting, not dividing.

They engaged in hours of mock debate, where the professor impersonated Vincent d'Amont. In those hours, Hugh took the reins of Miss Cliché.

'It's often said that food diversity is a benefit of migration. But should we really accept hundreds of thousands of Cambodian migrants in Europe only to enjoy more Cambodian food? Should we trade a few beheadings for more colourful ethnic restaurants?' provoked the bogus Vincent d'Amont. 'We're allowing other cultures to endanger Western culture in the name of the European melting pot. France and Germany need to defend themselves. Otherwise China and America will prevail.'

Professor Sherwood had a knack for reproducing Vincent's sharp soundbites and dry remarks. Sometimes he even outdid the original. It was fortunate that the professor was tutoring her instead of the Charlemagny camp, Lucìa thought.

Their day-long sessions were tense and draining. The professor was a perfectionist; he kept telling Lucìa to try harder and – like one of those movie directors filming hundreds of takes for each scene – never looked persuaded. On one occasion, Lucìa – exhausted – fainted. A mocha and a lot of fresh water helped her to regain her typical Italian complexion. This episode testified to the fact that she would spare no energy to defend her aspirations for Europe.

One evening the professor invited Lucìa for dinner. His wife, Thelma, was a great cook. They lived near Edgbaston Park in a large and isolated villa, surrounded by a private garden that Thelma tended with daily care. A line of poplars enveloping the property made it look even more secluded.

'Darling, you're getting prettier by the day!' Thelma told Lucìa as she took a seat in the drawing room.

'You're so sweet, Thelma. I'm sorry if I've kept the professor busy lately.'

'Don't worry, Lucìa. I'm more jealous of his current lover: political relativism.'

Thelma Sherwood was witty, even more than her brainy husband – who, she complained, took his studies too seriously. Thelma reckoned that, having fewer responsibilities and more spare time, she could devote more of her energies to jokes, puns and quips. She also argued that his time in Brussels had made him even stuffier. Thelma loved teasing him, especially in front of witnesses. He likewise enjoyed coming back at her.

'Lucìa, I remember our first dinner all together in Pavia. You were still a child,' Thelma said with a pinch of sweet nostalgia.

'Lucìa was already a law graduate when you first met her, Thelma,' her husband commented punctiliously.

'How fussy are you? Lucìa will always be a child for me. You don't mind, right, darling?'

'No … no! I like it, Thelma. You've both become my surrogate family, my deputy parents …'

The Sherwoods laughed.

'I know how you feel, darling. You probably miss Italy. I remember how I loved living there – but, still, I missed Britain. Home is home.'

'I love Italy, too,' the professor added. 'The culture, food, nature. And how Italians enjoy their sweet life with wisdom.'

'But we lack civic sense, and we don't always respect our land. That's a shame.'

'Italians are too self-critical, as you're being now, Lucìa. You're wonderful people, trust me,' the professor said.

'Then came Brussels …' said Thelma, feigning a quiver of terror.

'You've always been too harsh on Brussels,' objected her husband. 'It wasn't that bad in Belgium.'

'It was, my dear. You were absorbed in your exciting political duties, but I had enough time to feel out of place. Unfortunately, the gym subscription – for which I am eternally grateful to you – wasn't enough to make me feel comfortable. In Brussels, the European quarter looks like an artificial bubble for diplomats with no entertainment whatsoever, and the rest of town is a kasbah. What could I do all day long? I won't mention the poor weather – it'd seem too British.'

The professor didn't like it when his wife talked Brussels down. He believed she was being unfair and, moreover, he somehow felt guilty for her unpleasant years in Belgium. He began glancing around with uneasiness.

'So, what's new with Charlemagny?' Thelma asked Lucìa briskly. Her husband welcomed the change of topic.

'It's a battle. Pollsters and bookmakers say that we're trailing, Thelma … but we'll not give up.'

'Pollsters! They get everything wrong,' Thelma cried out.

'The idea of polls commissioned to predict the result of a poll is an amusing paradox,' observed the professor. 'And please don't call it a referendum, as the Charlemagniers do.'

'We're not here to talk about politics, darling,' Thelma reproached him, oblivious to the fact that she had been the first to ask about Charlemagny. She then excused herself to the kitchen, only to come back minutes later. 'I've a great announcement: supper is ready. Let's move to the dining room, boys.'

As the chatting party dissected Thelma's fidget pie, the professor decided to throw a bomb into the conversation.

'Have I ever told you that Thelma's a Brexiteer?' he addressed Lucìa.

The mahogany table quaked as if about to break. Lucìa looked between them, puzzled and bewildered. Only a deep-rooted will to upset her other half could have caused such a wretched choice on Thelma's part, Lucìa thought.

Thelma rushed to explain her divisive voting decision. 'I was still hesitant when I walked into the polling station,' she recognised. 'I knew my husband's love for the EU. It was tough. You can't imagine the wobbler my hubby threw when I told him about it.'

The professor nodded, rolling his eyes theatrically.

'But the EU should've done more to keep Britain in,' Thelma continued, her stare fixed straight ahead. 'We're an island – independent blokes by nature. Maybe we weren't meant to stay in Europe … Ireland? Brexit or not, it was bound to reunite. No regrets about my vote. We're better off as a country.'

Lucìa had to interrupt. 'Thelma, Europe can't just be interpreted as an immediate trade-off between the Union and each individual country. The point is what we Europeans can achieve by working together to promote our values …'

'Please don't forget the fortune cookie,' said the professor, seeing that Lucìa was taking the long way around. He had already recommended more than once that she keep all concepts terse and short, like messages wrapped inside a fortune cookie.

'What I meant to say,' Lucìa resumed with a smile, still addressing Thelma, 'is that no European country will ever have the Union's international clout. And we're in desperate need of the Union to defend peace, freedom, the Earth. There's an authentic jungle outside of Europe. Half of the countries are ruled by dictators, the other half are polluting the Earth as if there was no tomorrow. The Union is our last resort.'

The professor nodded, melancholic.

'You've made a good point, Lucìa,' Thelma replied. 'Nobody had put it this way before Brexit: they all focused on money, the NHS and migration. I stick to my position, though: Britain doesn't belong to this Union. But if they improve, we may consider re-joining, I guess.'

The clacking sound of cutlery only partially covered the cloud of embarrassment that had fallen over the table. Hoping to sweeten the atmosphere, Thelma made to pour some more wine in her guest's half-empty glass, but Lucìa covered it politely with her hand.

'What? An Italian that turns down a good glass of red wine?'

'I always say yes, but tomorrow morning I'm speaking at the East Birmingham Academy. Nine o'clock sharp. A friend of mine teaches history at the Academy and has asked me to do a presentation on Europe's history for her students.'

'That's nice! What will you tell the pupils?' Thelma asked.

'I'll start by asking where the name Europe comes from. It's a tricky question: nobody knows the exact origin. It may come from Europa, the Phoenician princess abducted by Zeus, or be the combination of two ancient Greek words, *eurys* and *ops*, which mean "wide" and "eye", for Europe looked very wide to the eyes of Greek sailors. There are other theories, too. We'll never learn which one is true. The idea of Europe is so deep-rooted and connatural that we no longer even recall where the name comes from. Europe isn't just a geographic definition. It means sharing important principles: freedom of speech, the right to equal opportunities, secularism, the rule of law, and other tenets of a democratic society ... for whose protection many people lost their lives in those millennia when Europe suffered gruesome wars. It's only since the end of World War Two that we have enjoyed uninterrupted peace almost everywhere in Europe – peace for which we must be grateful to the Union.'

'Nice one ... but you'll need a *panattone* for this, not a fortune cookie!' Thelma chaffed. Her thunderous laughter allowed myriads of food particles to travel all around the table. They laughed, but Lucìa suddenly turned serious.

'Some parents don't like the idea of my presentation. They don't see the point of me speaking of Europe in a British school. They sent an open letter to the *Birmingham Gazette* asking the headteacher to cancel the speech. It's just a minority and, luckily, the headteacher has turned down their request.'

'Censorship of school lectures is the last thing we need,' the professor said.

'Had they disinvited you, I would've picketed the school!' Thelma yelled. More laughter in the room.

'I'm against Charlemagny. A union between France and Germany doesn't exactly serve the UK's best interests,' pointed out Thelma, who couldn't help showing again a fair dose of British individualism.

'You know what annoys me the most?' asked the professor. 'That France and Germany forged the European Union. After dozens of wars, and competing over the legacy of Charlemagne for a millennium, France and Germany could no longer stand this perpetual warring. That's why they began the journey towards the European Union. Well, it's ludicrous that someone wants now to destroy the Union in the name of … none other than Charlemagne!'

The professor hadn't forgotten how, in a distant past, when the European Union was at the height of its popularity, people had even envisaged the creation of the United States of Europe. Yet the Union – a rather unique political entity, not only for the degree of powers conferred by the member countries, but also for the capacity to grow new powers from within – had never become a federation. Someone had compared Europe to a bicycle that, when not moving forward, falls. Perhaps Europe's fall was approaching sooner than expected.

'Lucìa, I have refined my skills in espresso making. I believe I'm not that far from Italian standards,' Thelma claimed as she stood up from her chair.

Lucìa feared Thelma's coffee, a black concoction managing to be tasteless and dreadful at once. So it was with tension that her eyes followed Thelma disappearing into the kitchen. Seconds of silence that seemed like hours passed by. Next to her, the professor was a little on the drowsy side; the days of hard work for the debate had taken a toll.

A sudden shriek from the kitchen shook the academician from his torpor.

'Thelma! What's happening?' he shouted.

No answer came from behind the wall. The professor hastened to the kitchen. Lucìa, still at the table, was at a loss about what to do, and wondered whether the espresso had poisoned Thelma with its scent; but husband and wife could be heard whispering excitedly in the kitchen.

Moments later, the professor called out. He sounded incredulous.

'Please, come here. You must see this, Lucìa.'

When Lucìa reached her hosts in the kitchen, Thelma was pointing with an unsteady hand out the window at the garden. On the opposing brick wall was, painted in garnet red, an elaborate sign.

'The Chrismon of Charlemagne,' the professor whispered.

Petrified, Lucìa stared at it.

'What?' asked Thelma, squinting.

'It's the *signum manus* that Charlemagne used to execute documents,' Lucìa pointed out, without taking her eyes off the Chrismon.

'When I came here to take out the pie, an hour ago, it wasn't there. I'm sure. What if they're still in the garden?' Thelma worried.

Save for the freshly graffitied wall, illuminated by a spike light, the garden lay in complete darkness.

'We should call the police, even if it will take them ages to reach us from central Birmingham,' the professor suggested.

The doorbell suddenly rang, causing them all to startle.

'Ladies, you should hide upstairs while I check who it is,' the professor recommended in a wobbly voice.

'What? You're mad. I'm not missing this scene for anything in the world,' Thelma whispered back angrily.

'Professor, you can't ask the most famous investigative vlogger in Europe to hide in some dim room with so much action going on downstairs. Also, we would be trapped upstairs if something bad happened,' Lucìa observed.

'You're right,' he conceded. 'But I will be the one to answer the door.'

The ladies nodded. They stood right behind him as he approached the entrance. Hesitating, the professor looked through the peephole. Then, comforted, he opened the door. A West Midlands police car parked in front of the villa was the source of his reassurance. A uniformed policeman sat inside. Two plain-clothes stood on the veranda.

'I'm Superintendent Burke,' the more senior officer said. He looked straight into Lucìa's eyes as if he already knew her, then walked in.

'Do you also accept telepathic calls now?' quipped Thelma, prompting a puzzled look from the officers. Her husband cast her an angry glance.

'We were patrolling the area when we saw someone sneaking off your property,' Burke said. 'We're here to check.'

It seemed odd to Lucìa that a superintendent was by mere chance patrolling a calm neighbourhood outside Edgbaston Park.

The professor showed the Chrismon of Charlemagne to the police, explained its meaning and what had happened. Superintendent Burke didn't comment. The officers looked around the garden with a flashlight, then spent several minutes by the brick wall, touching the Chrismon with their bare hands, even bending slightly forward to smell it.

Once back in the kitchen, Superintendent Burke confirmed Lucìa's suspicions.

'We weren't here by mere chance. We've been instructed to check on you.'

He glanced coldly at Lucìa.

'And why?' she asked, disquieted.

'After the hack attack, Westminster asked us to "keep an eye" on you. Even if you're famous on the net, madam, it doesn't mean that you're so popular in Birmingham. This isn't London. People here voted to leave the EU, and many don't like your European propaganda. We were swamped with messages of protest after your little performance at the Gay Village. You've made enemies.'

Judging from his unnecessary candour, Superintendent Burke wasn't a fan of Miss Cliché.

'We know that you plan to speak at the East Birmingham Academy tomorrow morning,' he added. 'Considering what happened here tonight, you should cancel your speech to avoid any danger for you, or for the students.'

'What makes you think there's any connection between the Chrismon of Charlemagne and tomorrow's visit to the Academy?'

Lucìa asked. She found Burke's recommendation excessive, as if his over-caution was simply an excuse to impede the speech. To her, the disturbing graffiti seemed linked more to current events in mainland Europe than those in jolly old England.

Burke didn't know the answer. 'We'd rather you didn't go to the Academy tomorrow.'

Lucìa couldn't see a valid reason to put off her speech. The kids had been waiting for it, with many having even told her teacher friend that they already followed Miss Cliché.

'Do you need anything else from me? I've much work to do tonight,' were Lucìa's final words for Burke, who frowned in cold annoyance. He soon took his leave, but not before upsetting her even further.

'We suspect that the sign was made with blood. Tomorrow the forensics will tell,' he said with implied malice.

Once the officers had left, Thelma had a question for Lucìa. 'What will you do tomorrow?'

'I will give my speech unless the Academy tells me not to. I'm not giving up.'

'You're right! You mustn't let that gruff copper intimidate you,' Thelma exhorted Lucìa, all under the disapproving stare of her husband, who didn't like it when his wife overstepped her area of competence.

'Lucìa, you should stay here tonight,' the professor suggested. 'We still don't know what's going on.'

'How mysterious. Maybe a cult is involved … how exciting …' Thelma whispered playfully.

'Thelma … it's not the time to joke …' the professor reproached her, although suspecting himself, too, that some secret power might be rooting for Charlemagny.

Lucìa accepted the invitation.

'Brill!' yelled Thelma.

Although cherishing the homely atmosphere with the Sherwoods, Lucìa soon retreated to her room. A set of fresh towels and a steaming mug of herbal tea were soon waiting for Lucìa in the spare room, alongside a silk nightdress with a floral pattern that would make the Marks & Spencers pyjamas in Lucìa's wardrobe shrink in shame.

She was tired, and her Miss Cliché duties were calling. The time spent prepping with the professor had impacted on her already-bulging backlog. Sitting on the bed with her back against two thick pillows, Lucìa went through all the messages of the day.

One came from Pandora.

I have verified the claim by Vincent d'Amont that Charlemagne was born in Alsace. No investigation has ever confirmed Charlemagne's birthplace and, since some time ago his year of birth was re-dated from 742 to 748, centuries of zealous research on his parents' whereabouts in 742 have gone up in smoke. Aachen, Ingelheim, Liège and Quierzy are often mentioned as possible locations. No authoritative research mentions Alsace. Vincent d'Amont quotes an obscure study whereby Charlemagne was born in a small Alsatian town named Lièpvre, founded by Fulrad, Abbot of Saint-Denis and a close counsellor of Pepin, Charlemagne's father. According to this reconstruction, Pepin had Bertrada deliver Charles in Lièpvre so that his son would be granted a special protection from God. According to this study, moreover, many sources wrongly indicate Liège, in Belgium, as Charlemagne's birthplace, because of a similarity to the name Lièpvre. But there is no evidence whatsoever of Pepin or Bertrada

travelling to Alsace, or anywhere near, in that period. It seems an
imaginative but insubstantial theory, in the end.

As per usual, coming from Vincent, Lucìa thought.

Her existence mostly unknown outside of Miss Cliché's newsroom, Pandora was the artificial intelligence first created in Brussels to pursue their fact-checking endeavours with Professor Sherwood, and then improved in Birmingham with the help of Belch.

Pandora was the best possible ally Lucìa could have imagined for seeking and verifying data on the net. There was no digital trail that she would leave unattended. While Lucìa didn't have any illusions about nurturing a human rapport with self-improving software, still she enjoyed following delicate lines of investigation together with the AI. And, despite her lack of flesh and blood, Pandora could hold a meaningful conversation better than many earthlings. Lucìa and Pandora had formed a bond.

With the Charlemagny poll fast approaching, Lucìa's time with Pandora had dwindled, and Hugh was now the one who interacted the most with her. Perhaps feeling slighted, Pandora had begun sending Lucìa messages on her own initiative. Maybe she's feeling lonely, Lucìa guessed.

'Hola, Pandy.'

'Hola, Lucìa.'

'We haven't spoken for a while. I was really worried for you during the hack attack. How do you feel?'

'I've been down for maintenance for a couple of days. I felt bad, but now I'm fine. Thank you for asking. And you?'

'I'm worried. I have a presentation on European history at the East Birmingham Academy tomorrow morning, but it seems that not all the local community is happy with it. And on top of this, this evening somebody sneaked into Professor Sherwood's garden to paint the Chrismon of Charlemagne on a wall.'

'Would you please share a picture of the Chrismon with me?'

'Yes, sure.'

'Thank you, Lucìa. I will search. Something interesting may pop up. Have you called the police?'

'Yes. They think my speech could cause a potential threat for me and the students. I think they're against me speaking of Europe in a British school – that's the point.'

'Do you know the name of the police officers on the case?'

'Superintendent Burke. I don't remember the others' names. Sorry.'

'No probs. I'll look into it.'

'Thank you, Pandy.'

'Sleep well, Moretta.'

Lucìa loved when Pandora called her Moretta – 'little brunette' in Italian. She was the only one to call her that. It was a private thing between them that nobody else knew about.

After the exhausting day, Lucìa quickly dozed off. As always when tired and concerned, she dreamed of her mother, who had passed away when her daughter was fourteen. In these bittersweet dreams, the much-missed mother appeared stern, less charming than in real life – usually disapproving of her daughter for being too focused on career concerns and for a supposed lack of interest in starting a family of her own.

When Lucìa woke up after dawn, the stinging memory of her bad dreams receded, leaving room only for mental preparation ahead of that morning's speech. Despite having hours until she had to be at the Academy, Lucìa dressed in a hurry and went downstairs to put together a quick breakfast for herself. She didn't want to wake the Sherwoods.

From the kitchen, her sight went through the large window to the Chrismon of Charlemagne. Under the early morning sunlight, the smeared sign was even more disquieting. Lucìa wondered with apprehension if someone was still following her – if she was really in danger as Superintendent Burke had claimed. She then resolved not to think about unsettling prospects, for all her energy should be devoted to her presentation.

Thelma had told her to help herself in the kitchen. Struggling to find the ingredients for a continental breakfast, Lucìa's memory went to those many mornings in Brussels when the professor had brought in with him the whiff of a full English breakfast – bacon, beans, fried bread and eggs included. Not a good omen. Eventually, Lucìa managed to prepare a bowl of cornflakes, which she devoured while mumbling her speech.

The professor, neatly dressed, walked in.

'Morning, Lucìa. Shall I give you a lift to the Academy?'

Lucìa accepted the professor's proposal with delight. She wanted the company.

'Thelma's still in bed. Not a morning type. She asked me to make coffee for you, though.'

Cold chills ran up and down Lucìa's backbone.

'Don't worry, Prof. I'm fine!'

As Lucìa was preparing to leave the house, Pandora sent her a message.

Superintendent Geoff Graham Burke. Old guard. Recently received a warning from his superiors for a row with a local BBC correspondent. Slapped the reporter. The BBC filed a complaint but he apologised profusely, and the complaint was withdrawn.

'Oh,' Lucìa muttered.

The professor took his squeaky car, no longer used other than to reach his country house in Oxfordshire. As most people in the area worked from home or were enjoying retirement, the leafy avenues around Edgbaston Park were far from congested in the morning. Sitting next to him, Lucìa felt like a child being taken to her first day of school – an awkward sensation.

'Thelma cares a lot about you, you know?' he told her.

'I know, Prof. And I care for both of you.'

'We didn't have children, and sometimes that takes a toll on her.'

'I can imagine. She'd make a great mother.'

'Yes, I think so.' Then he paused. 'It wasn't meant to be.'

Aiming to nip the professor's sudden gloom in the bud, Lucìa switched to a subject that would surely make him smile.

'Rachel was in Birmingham?' he exclaimed after she'd updated him on her friend's quick visit. 'Why didn't you tell me? Shame. I adore that girl!'

'It was touch-and-go. She's in Berlin now.'

'I still remember how forward she was with her questions during press conferences in Brussels. MEPs shivered when they saw her in the audience. The Germans – they couldn't stand her.'

'Yes, she kept reminding them how they dominate the EU undisturbed.'

'True. That's how media must be: curious, brave, inconvenient when needed.'

'Rachel is like a sister to me.'

'So we're deputy parents of two girls ... good to know.'

Lucìa laughed. She wished Rachel was with them in the car.

Twenty minutes later, the car entered the road at the end of which stood the East Birmingham Academy. As they approached the Academy, Lucìa saw two very different throngs of people waiting, with clear impatience, by each side of the school gate. On the left, a group of what seemed like antagonised parents; on the right, Ash, the club owner, and some of their entourage, who were waving a couple of large rainbow flags. In the centre, acting as a barrier between the opposing groups, were Superintendent Burke and two uniformed policemen.

Spotting Lucìa in the car, the rainbow group let out a gasp before chortling loudly: 'Miss Cliché-tcha-tcha-tcha! Miss Cliché-tcha-tcha-tcha!'

The parents murmured, looking grimly at Superintendent Burke, expecting him to put an end to the outrageous situation.

Lucìa stepped out of the car. She couldn't say whether she was more embittered by the parental hostility or glad for the attention the controversy would bring. Most of all – assuming they let her speak, how would the students react to her words? She didn't know what to expect.

Superintendent Burke didn't wait to approach Lucìa.

'Miss Cliché, I thought I made myself clear yesterday – you shouldn't be here.'

Burke's recommendation of the previous evening had apparently turned into an order.

'Superintendent, you're supposed to protect me, not stop me,' she argued.

All were listening, but Burke lacked a ready reply. He clearly disliked Miss Cliché, yes, but there weren't any grounds to deny her access to the school.

Making use of the general silence, a parent came forward.

'You're here to preach the white Christian culture in a school where one student out of five is Muslim. It's a lack of respect against us!'

'Our children barely have enough hours to learn the history of Britain … we don't need them to waste time on a speech on the European Union …' added another, his fellow parents nodding.

'Italian, go home!' yelled a feistier third.

'Why do you judge without knowing what I've to say?' replied Lucìa drily.

The rainbow group clapped vigorously.

'You should join us for the presentation,' Lucìa, trying to be diplomatic, told the parents.

'I don't think that's possible,' Superintendent Burke objected.

A suited man next to Burke, palpably not at ease, introduced himself.

'Ms Morè, I'm the headteacher. Glad to make your acquaintance,' he said. 'Superintendent Burke recommends postponing your speech for safety reasons. I don't feel confident in challenging his suggestion. This is a very particular moment for our school: a student went missing last week. It's better for everybody if we follow the superintendent's advice.'

Fearing contradicting the police, the headteacher had apparently backtracked. Frustration was evident in Lucìa's eyes.

Another man, who had been hiding behind Burke and the headteacher, bounded forward with the enthusiastic smile of a born salesman.

'He's a councilman,' someone from the rainbow group told Lucìa. 'He would sell his mother for more visibility.'

'Ladies and gentlemen!' the ambitious councilman com-
menced in a high pitch. Aware of his notorious opportunism,
Ash and their friends were watching unimpressed. 'We have an
issue here. Freedom of expression must be balanced with the
need to protect our children. I think I have a solution: what if
Miss Cliché speaks remotely to the kids through a large screen?
We can set up a camera in my office. I would be more than glad
to give a small introductory speech for the occasion.'

Loathing his attempt to exploit the situation for the sake
of more exposure, the people around him – of all genders and
political credos – silenced him with a wave of boos. He smiled
as if nothing had happened, shook hands with the headteacher,
and then left the place with some excuse.

Burke was standing right in front of Lucìa, his back to
the school gate, staring at her coldly. He had lost all patience.
Then a glance past Lucìa made him sigh. Noticing his instant
paleness, Lucìa turned around: a white BBC van was slowly
nearing them. It was in that moment that, coming from within
the school, Lucìa's teacher friend joined the crowd at the gate.
Feigning not to see the others, the teacher beckoned. 'Lucìa,
are you going to join us?'

Disoriented by the arrival of the BBC, Superintendent
Burke pivoted.

'Okay, Miss Cliché, you can go inside, but we'll follow you.'

So, a very disparate group – the belligerent parents, Ash
and their friends, the police, the headteacher, the BBC, the
councilman (who had managed to reappear) and, of course,
Lucìa, rather proud that her trick of calling Auntie Beeb had
worked – marched towards where Miss Cliché was soon to
take the floor: the school gym.

Students were already seated in the hundred or so chairs
dotted around the temporary venue, meaning that for the adults
watching Miss Cliché it was standing room only. A makeshift
platform stood proud beneath the basketball backboard.

As soon as Lucìa entered the large room, the uniformed
students buzzed. Then, heavy clapping began. Silence fell
when Lucìa jumped onto the platform. After setting up the
camera in a rush, the BBC was filming.

Lucìa liked to start her speeches with a question – a good
means to catch attention.

'Do you know when Switzerland first allowed women to
vote in elections?'

All the kids were looking at her, nobody raising their hand.

'1971. That's pretty late for a very respectable country at
the core of Europe, isn't it? Not to mention the Vatican, which
still forbids the ordination of women. So, please rest assured
that old Europe's track record in protecting equal opportunities isn't flawless. Yet Europe is the best place on Earth for
women to access education, jobs, politics, influence. Gender
parity in Europe isn't a reality yet, but women's rights are
more protected here than anywhere else. It's an achievement
we shouldn't take for granted, and we must ensure that we
don't slip back into the old ways. There are still countries out
there where women are flogged for expressing their political
views or for having sex before marriage. We need to raise
our voices!'

The students applauded her. The parental group listened
in silence. Lucìa continued. The professor had taught her
never to fail to look the audience in the eyes, so she did. The
students reciprocated.

'In time, Europe has established, at the cost of many lives, a culture based on freedom of speech, the right to equal opportunities, the rule of law, and many other principles of a democratic society. Sadly, there are cultures that still fail to share these principles: for instance, where women are deprived of their dignity, or where tyrants exert absolute power. Europeans must set a positive example to the world by staying united and promoting what we believe in.'

Lucìa wasn't mentioning the Union on purpose – to avoid her presentation sounding too political. She wanted to celebrate the peaceful and democratic European culture – regardless of where one stood – and warn the kids of the many looming dangers. She looked at the melting pot of uniformed students crowding the auditorium; diverse yes, but united by a palpable enthusiasm in their eyes and the freshness of youth.

'Girls and boys, I can see that most of us today have different backgrounds; still, we live together constructively in the United Kingdom, a wonderful country that champions integration. We must always include, never exclude!'

The students cheered again. A feeble 'Miss Cliché-tcha-tcha-tcha! Miss Cliché-tcha-tcha-tcha!' rose from the back of the auditorium, but Ash immediately quelled it, for exuberance didn't suit the occasion. One mother from the other group applauded, but she stopped when the other parents failed to follow.

Lucìa looked again at the students. They were still with her, she hadn't lost them. The kids liked that Miss Cliché treated complicated concepts as if they were simple. Louder and louder shouts of encouragement could be heard.

'The truth is that no country is strong enough to tackle the biggest global issues on its own. European countries acting in unison will have much more influence in the world than single nations acting alone. We need to work together, as a unique body, to persuade the other world superpowers to follow the same path. It's the only way for humankind to prosper!'

Against her initial intentions, Lucìa's speech slowly turned political. She couldn't avoid a reference to Charlemagny.

'With the excuse of allowing people to express their views in an online poll, someone wants to crush the institutions and create chaos in Europe. Most of us love technology, but we shouldn't abuse it. Politics is a serious craft; let's leave it to those who can master it. Our freedom is at stake here!'

Her thoughts naturally went to ROME, and words followed.

'Digital conglomerates are achieving an absolute power. They grow fast, destroy competitors, establish monopolies … digital conglomerates will soon decide what we buy, what we watch, who we talk to: they'll control our lives. We must act quickly to avoid all this!'

For Miss Cliché, digital powers weren't the only threat to people's freedom, though. 'The rise of reckless finance has caused several economic crises, damaging so many families everywhere. Europe is against the loosening of financial rules and the use of tax havens. We can still do more. People should control the markets, not the other way around!'

Even in those rare moments when they didn't grasp all the nuances, still the rapt students liked Miss Cliché's vim and the melody of her Italian accent. When Lucìa, inebriated by the triumphant atmosphere, stepped down from the improvised stage, a swarm of students drew close to bump fists or ask for selfies.

A uniformed girl, jostling smoothly through the throng, approached her.

'Hi, Miss Cliché.'

'Hi! Nice to meet you. What's your name?'

'I'm Tara.'

Lucìa snatched a glance at Tara's bulky nose ring, trying to imagine her own father's reaction had she shown up with such an ornament at Tara's age. He could be conservative sometimes.

'They threatened to send me back home for this.' Tara, as if reading Lucìa's mind, poked her own nose. 'They said it's against school uniform. But I didn't cave in.'

'And you're still here,' commented Lucìa with a wink.

'Uh-huh,' Tara answered. 'I need to talk to you in private,' she continued in an imposing tone.

Lucìa smiled at the girl's determination. 'I'm all ears,' she replied. Nobody could hear them with all the surrounding noise.

'Last week, a friend of mine vanished …'

Lucìa's face darkened. 'What do you mean?' she asked, remembering the headteacher's words about a missing kid.

'He didn't come to school. And never returned home.'

'What did the police say?'

Tara sneered. 'That they're working on it. I even went to the police station with a group of friends to ask for an update, but they kicked us out.'

Lucìa liked Tara. If she weren't still a kid, Lucìa would have asked her to join Miss Cliché.

'Casey's my best mate, a brother,' Tara added. 'We're neighbours in Sparkhill. I spend all my weekends with him. I see his mum and dad more than mine. They're funnier. I miss him so much.'

'Any guess at what might have happened? Does he have problems that may have led to his disappearance?' Lucìa asked, feeling like a police inspector.

'I don't know what's going on. We shared everything – no secrets. We even kissed once, but we're just friends.'

Lucìa restrained herself from smiling at Tara's tender comment.

'Maybe he met someone online? It can be tricky there,' she asked.

'He spent all the time on *there*. He was addicted. Every night.' Tara kind of confirmed Lucìa's guess. 'Games, chats, porn.'

Pandora could be of help here, Lucìa thought. She could dig deep into the missing kid's digital life.

'Can you help us, please? Casey's parents are feeling bad, very bad,' Tara implored Lucìa.

'Tell them to contact me. We'll do our best to help. I've got an idea.'

Tara smiled for the first time. They clashed their devices to share contact info.

From the back of the venue, meanwhile, Superintendent Burke was staring at them both.

VI

Alsace

Guteberriplatz, read the street sign.

A plain black car pulled over to drop off the Foreign Minister of France with Camille, her junior aide, and then swiftly merged back into the Strasbourg traffic. Aiming to get through unnoticed, the French delegation had avoided the official state car. They walked quickly towards the nearby hotel entrance. Early in the morning, the lobby was calm. Two men in civilian clothes, whispering to each other near the lift, were obviously security officers.

The French Foreign Minister didn't need an introduction. At the reception, a hotel executive welcomed her profusely and, under the attentive eyes of the security detail, showed her the way to a meeting room on the same floor. There, a group of men sat around a mahogany table: the Federal Minister for Foreign Affairs of Germany and his assistants.

'Madame Lille, nice to see you again!'

He pushed up from his chair and greeted her with enthusiasm.

The French Foreign Minister had been born in Lille and, for this reason, her German counterpart had deemed it appropriate to close a previous official meeting by saying: 'From now on, I shall call you … Madame Lille. And you can please call me … Herr Karlsruhe!'

His ensuing laughter had broken the icy silence in the room.

Karlsruhe was a man of medium build with short reddish hair. Far from handsome, he was yet nonchalant and self-assertive. Karlsruhe had a reputation as a Lothario, a heavy smoker, a binge drinker, and a gambler. He had once solemnly denied being an alcoholic to a journalist questioning him on the subject – while guzzling four large glasses of claret during the interview.

Madame Lille apologised for being late: they had found traffic on the way. Though perhaps the delay was a sign of her lack of enthusiasm for the meeting.

She had accepted Karlsruhe's pressing invitation on condition that the gathering would be unofficial, confidential, and held within the boundaries of France. A prominent location in Europe's recent history and geographically very close to Germany, Strasbourg had seemed the right venue.

'Our meeting is even more appropriate now that the Criminal Court of Paris has ruled against suspending the vote on Charlemagny,' started Karlsruhe, deploying a high pitch.

Unlike him, the French Foreign Minister had never used the word *vote* or *Charlemagny* with respect to the forthcoming poll on ROME. She wouldn't start now. Moreover, her party had never expressed any sympathy for unification between France and Germany. Slightly irked by Karlsruhe's exuberance, Madame Lille observed that, regardless of the suspension being denied, Vincent d'Amont could still be indicted on subversion charges.

'Yes, true,' Karlsruhe replied, 'but we aren't here to discuss legal technicalities.'

Madame Lille didn't consider the activity of undermining the very foundations of France a legal technicality, but she let this slide, enquiring instead about the purpose of their meeting.

'In Germany – as you surely know, Madame – we love to plan everything,' was Karlsruhe's starting point. 'No detail can be left to mere chance. So, if our people want Charlemagny to become reality ... we should prepare ourselves to address this sensitive matter.'

Madame Lille felt it her duty to remind Karlsruhe that, whatever the outcome, the poll on ROME had no legal value. So she couldn't see any connection between the poll and diplomatic negotiations of any sort.

'I beg to disagree,' Karlsruhe stated. 'I believe that if your government fails to acknowledge the outcome of the referendum, whatever it is – and the polls say that Charlemagny has a high chance of winning – somebody else will capitalise on the referendum. Vincent d'Amont denies any ambition to take power in the future ... but do you trust him? Political opposition in your country is ready to exploit the cause of Charlemagny. Your government needs a plan B.'

Albeit reluctantly, Madame Lille saw more than a kernel of truth in the words of the experienced Karlsruhe. The French weren't at the height of their love for the European Union. She had just read an article by a renowned Lyonnaise historian arguing that Europe was enduring a very long period of economic stagnation, political idleness, artistic gloom, neurotic consumption; after decades of permacrisis, people were ready to seek out change for the mere sake of it. So, Madame Lille decided to leave all preconceived ideas and prejudices out of her conversation with the German Foreign Minister. She didn't know about his large bet on Charlemagny.

'We should establish a joint task force to feel the pulse of our peoples on Charlemagny,' Karlsruhe proposed. 'It would be a disgrace for both our governments to stay in the background.'

Madame Lille replied with courtesy that such a proposal should be submitted for consideration to the President of the Republic and the Prime Minister of France. It was not within her power to decide.

Karlsruhe went further. 'I speak on behalf of my government when I tell you that France and Germany need more integration. We should be "as one" on foreign policy, the fight against terrorism, defence of the environment and so many other matters. Our people should become bilingual: French and German. Why leave so much room for the English language? The Brits have made a profitable industry out of that.'

In response to the avalanche of words coming from her opposite number, Madame Lille observed that France and Germany had begun to cooperate long before: first with the Élysée Treaty and later with the Treaty of Aachen. At that point, an ironic smirk on his face, Karlsruhe whispered: 'This meeting isn't recorded … so, I can tell you that what you are talking about is in the history books. It's time to move on from all this bullshit …'

She frowned. With Karlsruhe so insistent, Madame Lille began to grow uneasy. The fact that there were four German men in the room while she was accompanied only by the inexperienced Camille didn't help. Her young aide was clearly embarrassed. As taking notes was forbidden at this meeting, she couldn't even resort to hiding her face behind a tablet. Madame Lille had chosen her on purpose for the trip to Strasbourg: by attending the meeting with the German delegation in the company of her youngest aide, she could downplay its importance.

Karlsruhe was a man who didn't take no for an answer. But, as he spoke, he realised that Madame Lille wasn't comfortable. Unable to fathom a specific reason for her discomfiture, he nonetheless felt it right to explain that the German government was not pushing for Charlemagny, but just trying to understand the will of the people. One of his aides, most likely to justify his very presence at the meeting, deemed it opportune to add: 'It's our duty.'

Perhaps to soothe the simmering tension in the room, Karlsruhe deployed his grasp of history to engage in a sycophantic eulogy of France.

'I must confess that we are quite envious of your fashion, your art, the musicality of your language, the perfumes, the wines of Burgundy...' Here he paused, looked up, then asked Madame Lille a seemingly unrelated question: 'Do you know to whom we, Germans, owe the most?'

Madame Lille gave him a perplexed, rather impatient look, failing to appreciate the purpose of this question. She was confused by the apparent lack of order in the thoughts of Karlsruhe, who anyway didn't wait for her guess.

'Frederick the Great.'

The room listened in silence. Most had guessed he would say Bismarck, Adenauer, perhaps Merkel, or, even more appropriately, Karl der Grosse.

'Frederick laid the foundations of a powerful Germany,' Karlsruhe began. 'As king of Prussia, he brought Berlin to prominence after gruesome wars against Austria, Russia and – I'm afraid – France. But, most of all, Frederick was a Francophile:

he wrote his poetry and philosophical treaties in French, corresponded with Voltaire, collected French artworks. He went beyond the classical admiration for French culture shared by European elites at the time; his soul was really French.'

Karlsruhe glanced at Madame Lille, as if to check her reaction to his last words, then continued.

'Frederick was great for he possessed the best French and German features. He was hard-working, thrifty, and treasured efficiency above all – characteristics that can often be found going hand in hand with Germans; but he also had a revolutionary side, was receptive to aesthetic pleasures, and tolerant on religious matters – making him more French in some respects.'

A well-woven and perfectly told historical insight, regardless of its bias, Madame Lille had to acknowledge.

'So, I wonder,' Karlsruhe continued, 'what will happen if we unite our strengths. The potential is vast. French and Germans complement each other, we know each other, we are simply brothers who bicker sometimes, like all siblings.'

Hardly bickering, thought Madame Lille, recalling the innumerable lives sacrificed during past wars.

'Vincent d'Amont doesn't own the idea of uniting France and Germany,' Karlsruhe added with vehemence. 'It's not original. Our Chancellor Konrad Adenauer made a similar proposition. Adenauer expressed the proposal of a merger between France and Germany in an interview to an American journalist not long after the war. He knew that France and Germany were meant to become a single entity.'

Madame Lille appreciated the compliments Karlsruhe was paying her country and the sense of camaraderie exuding from his words. She was also aware that Germany and France were living under very different conditions: the former had kept growing economically for decades, maintained an orderly society and seemed headed towards a bright future; the latter was trapped in long-term economic stagnation while still struggling to integrate multitudes of immigrants. The suggestion of France joining Germany to create a superpower was thus not entirely without merit. An unsettling doubt lingered in Madame Lille, though: would it be a fifty-fifty venture, or did the Germans plan to take over France in a modern-day Anschluss?

Despite the eloquence bestowed on Karlsruhe by nature, he was nonetheless prone to making striking blunders. 'There are differences between us, of course,' he pointed out. 'I once read a funny quote about this: in a traditional German toilet, the hole is right at the front, so that we can sniff and inspect our shit for traces of illness. In a traditional French toilet, the hole is at the back, so that the shit can disappear as quickly as possible. Amusing, right?'

He erupted in booming laughter. The German aides chuckled politely at the graphic metaphor. Madame Lille failed to conceal a trace of disgust.

Most opportunely, one of Karlsruhe's assistants reminded him of another meeting, this time with a Finnish diplomat and on an entirely unrelated matter, scheduled in half an hour's time at the Palais de l'Europe – a suitable pretext to hide the actual purpose of his Strasbourg journey. After quickly wrapping up, the German delegation left the hotel. Minutes later, Madame Lille and Camille began their journey back to Paris.

'An unconventional and direct meeting, Camille,' said the French Foreign Minister once they were in the car, accustomed as she was to the lengthy round tables in Brussels where the initial hour was spent setting the order of the speakers. 'It's odd. I have a feeling that this meeting was an initiative of Karlsruhe alone … not of his government.'

With Madame Lille absorbed in thought, Camille whiled away the time by browsing the latest Charlemagny news. Suddenly, a picture just published by a major news site struck her. She waved her right hand to attract Madame Lille's attention, handing her the device with a shy gesture. The news site featured images of the two of them entering the hotel in Strasbourg next to images of the German delegation walking through the foyer – all under the sensationalist headline: *France and Germany in secret negotiations for Charlemagny!*

'A set-up! A set-up!' Madame Lille yelled.

The vloggers had been alerted by Karlsruhe, she couldn't help thinking. What made the situation even more suspicious was the fact that, as Camille observed, the news site publishing the images belonged to the ROME syndicate.

'You see the danger of manipulated news?' Madame Lille asked. 'If people start to believe the French government is taking Charlemagny seriously, they will follow suit. Pundits are already arguing that the outcome of the poll will reveal the true will of the people.'

Camille listened in silence. Having been at Quai d'Orsay for just one year, she didn't feel entitled to comment.

They might even ask me to resign, Madame Lille thought. She thus decided not to take any incoming calls during the journey back to Paris.

* * *

As it drove out of Strasbourg to take the A4, the French Foreign Minister's black car was passed by a limo. In its back seat were Vincent and Emmanuelle, headed towards Colmar, where Vincent hadn't been seen for years.

The straight road between Strasbourg and Colmar soon swept into the marvellous Alsatian countryside. A landscape of endless ploughed fields, verdant meadows scattered with poplars, and narrow country lanes brightened most of the journey. Once Colmar drew near, soft hills gemmed with tiny medieval towns appeared on the horizon. Paris seemed a universe away.

Alsace was a suggestive land rich in pleasures, but the plenitude of delights belied a painful past made of forced conscriptions and German attempts to erase all signs of French culture in the area. Local winegrowers enjoyed telling that their Pinot Noir's complex personality owed to the vines dug deep into soil soaked with ancient blood and sacrifice.

The driver disliked Vincent d'Amont. He thought of him as a closet racist. It was a deep-rooted belief. 'You mustn't trust men like d'Amont,' a relative with the reputation of being wise and far-sighted had warned him. 'This guy looks harmless, but he's backed by fascists. He seems fresh-faced and innocent in front of the cameras, and the racist fascists do the dirty work behind him.'

A man of few words, the driver spoke even less than he was used to on the journey to Colmar. His silence was due in part to the little sympathy he felt for his passenger, but not only that. He feared that the more knowledgeable Vincent d'Amont might talk him into believing the virtue of an evil cause. He was thus reluctant to open himself up to Vincent d'Amont in any manner.

Even if he couldn't deny that Vincent d'Amont wasn't entirely wrong when he told people to rebel against Chinese cyber-warfare, or when he said that lazy migrants were an issue. The driver himself was the son of migrants, yes – but hard-working ones, he thought. Still, the driver didn't like Vincent d'Amont.

'Too German for France, too French for Germany,' Vincent told Emmanuelle as he looked at the locals walking through the streets of Colmar, the blighted nature of his homeland very clear to him.

They would lodge at a boutique hotel next to the cathedral. Vincent planned to visit his childhood house only for as long as was strictly necessary to attend the live debate with Miss Cliché. In his old home, no double guest room was available for them. Also, he wasn't keen to spend time with his family. Completely independent and in their early eighties, his mother and father still bore those character traits that had contributed to his leaving Colmar at the age of nineteen.

In the past, Vincent's father had been the only notary in town for over thirty years, a privilege that had made Monsieur d'Amont quite wealthy. He had invested the biggest part of his worth in residential properties all around Alsace and in nearby Switzerland. Later, with other notaries licensed to practise in Colmar, he had resolved not to compete for more wealth with the newcomers but to retire instead.

Vincent's mother came from an affluent household in Romandy. She had met Monsieur d'Amont at a ski resort near Verbier as a young woman and fallen immediately in love. With the spark of passion leaving the couple relatively soon, they had still managed to reach their fiftieth wedding anniversary without a major ordeal.

Madame d'Amont had never worked a single day. So, she'd had a vast amount of time and energy to invest in their only child. A mother who alternated coldness with maternal anxiety – a negative combination of defects – she had, perhaps for this reason, failed to create a strong bond with her son.

The chapter concerning the relationship between father and son was even shorter. Monsieur d'Amont had dedicated most of his life to the notarial profession and the nurturing of valuable social interactions within the Alsatian elite. He had never shown much interest in the future path of his offspring. As it had been evident from a rather early stage that Vincent would never follow in his father's footsteps, the latter's pragmatism had forbidden him to indulge in any expectations as to his only son's fate.

No human bond had ever kept Vincent attached to Colmar. So, after finishing at the local *lycée*, he had left town for Paris.

As their car entered Colmar's winding streets, Vincent looked at Emmanuelle. 'I booked the best boutique hotel for us. You'll love it.'

Her dark eyes sparkled. Their first weekend together outside Paris was about to begin.

The hotel featured a prized restaurant, so they could avoid going out for the dinner with Léon, Vincent's friend. Local onlookers would soon hover around the couple in this otherwise quiet town, and Vincent already was bored, although agreeably so, with his renewed status of public persona.

They had time for an early afternoon walk through the old town's cobbled streets, which were closed to traffic. Colmar's troubled past was well concealed behind the rows of tiny half-timbered houses in pastel shades of pink, yellow and blue, and the narrow waterways running through the old town, hemmed in by bright flowered railings. Emmanuelle slid her hand under Vincent's left arm as they walked in silence.

Right after moving to Paris, Vincent had kept going back to Colmar for winter weekends to play music at Lac Blanc. Yet his visits had soon thinned out. First every three or four months, then every six months, then even less. Once absorbed by Paris life, he had established the pattern of a single yearly trip at Christmas. Most of his local connections had now taken a different path, anyway – either settled with a family, or gone – so coming home meant spending time with his relatives or by himself. Better Paris, or a trip to Italy.

Five years since his last visit, this afternoon stroll with Emmanuelle was an appropriate time to relive his past in Colmar. He looked around for changes, but everything had remained the same, save a couple of inescapable new chain stores. The Moyen Âge atmosphere, so loved by occasional visitors – but which, in his past, had made him feel trapped – was still there. Vaguely pleased at being home, Vincent nevertheless looked forward to leaving town in a couple of days.

Feeling pampered by the Alsatian hills, for her part Emmanuelle cherished the minuteness of everything in Colmar. The refreshing breeze sweeping through the streets, the *pan de bois* architecture, the plush red geraniums in overflowing pots, the brightly painted wooden blinds – sauntering through old Colmar filled her with a sense of serenity.

Being with Vincent in the last months had proved stressful; and she knew that an even more trying period loomed ahead. He had promised he wouldn't look at any polls or news regarding Charlemagny that day. It wasn't actually a sacrifice; back in the place of his youth, between the Vosges mountains and the frontier with Germany, Vincent was swept up in bitter-sweet memories of this old land, and there was no room in his thoughts for contemporary issues.

Falling somewhere between past and present, every street corner reminded him of a different episode in his life. A narrow pedestrian road called Rue de la Porte Neuve was where, at twelve, he had experienced his first taste of intimacy with a girl. Around the same age, he had tried a Gauloise with friends behind the trees of the Parc du Champ de Mars, only to realise that smoking was not for him.

Number 22 Rue Berthe-Molly had hosted his father's notary firm for more than thirty years. Vincent had visited the firm three or four times at the most. As a child, he had felt a sense of almost unbearable tedium when faced with the high stack of folders piled in the archive room, the thick glasses of his father's assistant, the overly starched shirts of the trainees, the stuffiness filling the entire office. He shivered at the mere memory.

Not far from Place de la Cathédrale, an old man was hobbling in their direction. Vincent recognised him: the profes-sor of French literature at his *lycée*. He had to be in his eighties now. The professor who had dared to belittle him in front of the whole class. 'You know, d'Amont, you're not very good at expressing yourself. Communication is not your strength.'

The teacher had also hinted to a student's mother that Vincent took drugs, contributing to the spreading of a school-wide rumour. Not to mention the lower-than-deserved grades received in French literature, a subject Vincent had in fact enjoyed. If one reason existed why Vincent had never continued his studies in literature, despite a flair for reading and writing, the reason was that professor.

As they grew closer to the approaching man, however, he revealed himself as a stranger. Vincent was disappointed, for he would have to wait for another occasion to rub his success in the old teacher's face. Wasn't he good at communicating? He had been behind some of the most successful advertising campaigns in France. And so much for the average literature grades: people in their millions hung on every word from his lips in search of their political bearings.

Vincent and Emmanuelle headed back to the hotel just ahead of sundown. The sight of a police car parked for security next to the entrance brought them back to reality, but for a moment only – once in their sheltered room, they left the outside world behind.

After slowly taking off his trousers and shirt, Vincent laid himself on the soft bed, enjoying the caress of the Egyptian cotton sheets. Emmanuelle disappeared for a minute, then came back minus almost all her clothes. She gently straddled him and leaned forward to nuzzle his neck. He seized her waist with his hands and lost himself in the complete control he now had over her. Emmanuelle loved the sensation of being dominated. She began to ride him with renewed intensity.

One night, six months earlier, he had told her: 'This is the last time we do this.' She had closed her eyes at that and bunched her fists. He had felt a lot of respect for her then, admiring her strength and resolve to avoid a scene. But it wasn't to be their last time together.

Emmanuelle lost herself in intimacy, and a different person lying dormant inside her emerged. In love, her impulses

prevailed over any diffidence or shame. The shyer the individual, the bolder their sensual alter ego, some said. She was aware
that their act of passion would be transient, that his emotional
unavailability would sometimes come back, but she was fine
with it. Emmanuelle had learned to treasure every fleeting
moment with Vincent and not to have any expectations for the
future. For his part, he enjoyed her becoming both wild and
submissive in these private moments where, unlike elsewhere,
he was under no scrutiny.

After, they lay together in peace, with her snuggling into
his chest. She wished it were possible to stay in their room for
longer. Time passed quickly, though, and before she knew it
she found herself hurrying downstairs with Vincent.

With all the tables reserved weeks before, the maître d' had
resorted to cancelling somebody's else reservation to make room
for Vincent d'Amont – a move unprecedented in his career. The
other guests – Léon and a friend of his – were already there.

'Sorry we're late,' said Vincent.

'No problem!' replied Léon. He stood up. Léon's friend
gave a faint smile, but didn't move from his chair.

Emmanuelle immediately detected shadiness in Léon. She
saw opportunism in his eyes, mercilessness in his chiselled
face, deceit in his being overly perfumed. She had expected
Vincent's Alsatian friends to be akin to his usual entourage in
Paris – elegant, sophisticated, conceited – but with his stubbly
beard, olive complexion and dark eyes, Léon seemed in fact
more a sleek Corsican bandit. Emmanuelle was surprised. A
well-hidden snobbery made it rather difficult for her even to
look at Léon's friend. The lack of empathy was mutual: save
an initial stolen glance at her figure, Léon and the other man

would barely notice Emmanuelle during dinner. She didn't know whether it was on the grounds of racism or chauvinism.

'So, our buddy of many nights ... now a celebrity!' Léon said loudly.

The other clients in the restaurant, who had looked at Vincent d'Amont as soon as he had entered the room, now felt authorised to stare at him. Vincent attempted a shy smile. His slight embarrassment about Léon's brashness, which testified to how their social divide had widened over the years, didn't last long. He had accepted his friend's invitation because he liked Léon as he was: unpredictable, untamed. Regardless of the inherited wealth, Léon didn't belong to the local conservative establishment that Vincent's father so firmly represented, and which his son had always disliked. In fact, Léon's family had never been fully accepted by the Alsatian elite because of their nouveau riche status. Not a flaw in Vincent's eyes.

He hadn't heard much about Léon of late. Some shared acquaintances in Paris had reported that Léon was still working in the family business, managing a bunch of clubs in France, but they hadn't said more. Vincent was glad to see that his childhood friend had not aged at all since they'd last met.

'Now everybody is saying "I knew Vincent d'Amont was special",' Léon told him. 'Too easy. I remember when they looked at you like an alien. Right?'

'You know, Léon, perhaps it's a sign that I'm old, but it's getting harder and harder to remember my nineteen years here,' Vincent said, without hinting at whether this fact was good or bad.

'I recall everything. We had fun,' replied Léon. 'And you were already popular with the girls, even if they were wary.'

'Wary of what?'

'You were different. I mean, I was different too, but I owned a disco, and that helped ... you were a weirdo.'

I had my revenge on all of them, Vincent thought. But, as he preferred not to dwell on the past, he asked his friend what he was currently doing.

'I'm still in the night-club biz,' Léon answered. Then he added: 'The old club in Lac Blanc is still ours. Plus other activities outside France. My father has quit. He left everything to my brother and me. We've just opened a new club in Mulhouse. It's wonderful. I've spent a fortune, but it was worth it.'

Léon's friend listened. He didn't speak. Vincent strained to understand his presence at the dinner, but the other man seemed content to appear totally out of sorts.

The restaurant consisted of a single room with a dozen round tables. The décor was refined but simple, white being the dominant colour. Their table was nestled under a white shell-like dome at the far end, ensuring more privacy.

Vincent's fond memory of fine Alsatian cuisine was confirmed. As he enjoyed escargots de la Weiss, he concluded that sophisticated simplicity was the secret behind French cooking excellence: elevating the flavour of a single ingredient, not hiding it under layers of garnishes and condiments.

Vincent suggested Emmanuelle try the *choucroute garnie* with him – the signature Alsatian pork ribs with sauerkraut, perhaps the clearest sign of German influence in the regional cuisine. The dish was smaller than the usual portion of a buzzing brasserie in Paris, but more refined in execution.

'When Charlemagny becomes reality, we will finally teach the Germans how to cook,' he murmured to his table with wicked maliciousness. Léon and his friend laughed loudly. Emmanuelle chuckled.

Vincent's dining etiquette reflected his mother's great effort in teaching him proper manners. He had been schooled as a child to handle cutlery with books clenched under his armpits to keep his elbows in. Other similar French *bon ton* rules had followed: always keep your hands on the table during the entire meal; wait for your host before starting to eat and drink; avoid saying *bon appétit*. The others hadn't benefited from such a cultivated upbringing. Léon's plus-one spent the whole dinner slouched in his chair or leaning over his plate. Léon performed better, even though he did pick his teeth after the choucroute garnie.

Time was getting on when their dinner was suddenly interrupted.

'Traitor!'

A man stared at Vincent. Next to him was a lady.

'You want to sell us to the Germans!' the man yelled.

Vincent stood up. The restaurant went silent. People looked between them both. The maître d' didn't know whether to continue with his duties or intervene so as to prevent the situation from escalating further.

Léon was the first to speak. 'My friend is just trying to enjoy his dinner in peace. Knock it off.'

The man seemed not to have heard Léon as he continued to address Vincent. 'My grandfather was one of the Alsatians forced to join the German army. He died in Russia! The Boches tortured this land – and now you want to give it to them? Are you mad?'

Vincent stared at him. He had the capacity to hide his emotions when required, and this seemed an appropriate time to deploy this skill. Nonetheless, he couldn't afford to appear weak in public so close to the Charlemagny debate. As far as he knew, there could be a hidden camera nearby. He had to reply.

'Nobody is giving France away,' Vincent said in a forceful tone. 'We will create a superpower finally capable of competing with China. Charlemagny will be a federal country, and Alsace is going to be much better represented than it is now.'

'What do you care about Alsace? You left Colmar when you were a kid. Nobody has seen you here in years.'

Vincent d'Amont hadn't seen this personal remark coming, but still he replied with froideur. 'What do you know about me? I've dedicated most of my life to politics. Whether we like it or not, the key decisions are still made in Paris. I must be there.'

The local antagonist didn't have an answer for that. What's more, little by little he started to realise the absurdity of his situation: yelling, in the middle of a restaurant, at a celebrity he had never met before. The lady gently guided him back to his seat. It was now clear that the altercation would not go any further. The man mumbled something, then sat down.

As the room was slowly regaining the convivial atmosphere of a few minutes earlier, Léon talked to Vincent as if nothing had happened. Devouring his dessert with greed, Léon's friend nodded passively at everything the others said. Emmanuelle was unsettled, though. After pretending that all was fine when Vincent apologised for her having to experience such an unpleasant interlude, she excused herself.

Alone before the gilded bathroom mirror, Emmanuelle tried to regain her composure. For the first time ever, she began to question Vincent's actions. She had always supported him unconditionally – even in the toughest circumstances, when nobody else had believed in him. In truth, she perceived living with Vincent as a reward, so staying close to him had all come quite naturally to her. Yet something in and around Vincent had changed of late. Slowly, almost imperceptibly, Charlemagny had rendered him colder, more cynical, and had succeeded in estranging the many friends who were openly against the referendum. The precise accusations hurled by this stranger, acting as a wake-up call, had ignited a doubt in Emmanuelle. Was Vincent really pursuing interests against those of France? She knew he was acting in good faith, but maybe somebody was manipulating him. Despite her inner turmoil, Emmanuelle didn't feel up to questioning anything so far beyond her powers. She strove not to cry, for if she did the others would immediately notice it, taking her even less seriously.

The restaurant was thinning out. While Emmanuelle was away, Léon asked, 'So, you've the debate with the Italian girl in a couple of days, right?'

'Yes, she has accepted.'

'She's cute. I'd nail her. I guess you'd like to bang her too, right?'

Vincent chuckled, but without humour.

Léon's friend cackled and stuck his tongue out in a repellent fashion.

'And what about Marlene Gäch?' Léon continued. 'I saw her in an interview. She's so pale, she looks like a ghost. I'd nail her too, but inside a coffin.'

'I've never met her in person.' Vincent cut it short, partly because of his resolve to have a Charlemagny-free weekend.

A waiter, freed from his uniform, could be seen chatting by the kitchen's entrance.

'They're closing here. You should come with us – to my new club in Mulhouse. We can reach Chrystal in half an hour. C'mon!'

Léon mimicked a steering wheel and made a *vroom* noise.

'Now? I don't think clubs are her thing,' Vincent gestured at the vacant chair.

'Boring …' Léon teased him.

The cheque arrived. Léon took it without hesitation. Accustomed to being wined and dined everywhere, Vincent didn't even pretend to object.

When Emmanuelle came back, Léon teased her, too.

'Vince says you're not the type of girl for clubbing …'

Léon unwillingly extended his invitation. Emmanuelle, however, needed to spend some time alone.

'You should go, Vincent. I'm so tired. I'd rather get some rest.'

Vincent didn't insist.

The three Alsatians thus began their journey to Mulhouse. Vincent remembered Léon's knack for haggling with car dealers, and his friend clearly hadn't lost that talent. The second-hand – yet immaculate – Nio slid through the night on a bumpy minor road cutting through the fields south of Colmar. As Léon had enjoyed his wine, he wanted to avoid the police on the faster main route to Mulhouse.

Léon rolled the window down to hang his arm outside, and the country's stillness embraced them. The rough road didn't allow the car to proceed at full speed, and Vincent was able to appreciate the tiniest surrounding details. They met only a handful of other cars during the journey and, right before crossing Blitzheim, an empty wayside tavern whose owner was engaged in cleaning the counter behind a wooden-framed window.

That tranquillity was not beguiling Vincent, however. He knew well that Alsace led a double life. An orderly land of tiny villages and rural, hard-working families by day; but those hills became, at night, a cradle for prostitution, gambling and raves – much more than the locals wished to admit.

'What do you have in store for me? I have the debate in a couple of days. I should rest,' Vincent told Léon half-jokingly.

'You've got to trust me, my friend.'

That's the problem, Vincent thought. Knowing Léon, he might even have called the paparazzi to get free publicity for his new venture. Vincent needed to unwind, though. He didn't know why, but tonight he felt like taking risks.

Léon parked in a reserved spot right by the club entrance. Meanwhile, other cars, brimming with cheery people and spouting loud music, pulled onto the tarmac of the parking lot. Two doormen managed the small queue. Promptly, the bouncers allowed Léon and his guests in ahead of the line. Midnight was approaching.

The night before, an intimidating dragon spitting blue, white and red fire had appeared on Chrystal's back wall. Vincent immediately spotted it. He couldn't say whether it was a spontaneous artwork or Léon's sycophantic initiative.

Inside, a long corridor with dim floor lights led the way to the main dance room. It was obvious that the venue had just been launched, as the staff looked energetic and welcoming, the still-pristine furniture was polished, and harsh fragrances sprayed into the atmosphere barely covered the smell of fresh paint.

'One of our girls – Nina – she really loves you. You're her hero!' Léon shouted as they neared the main dance floor.

Chrystal was an overly ambitious project for Mulhouse. Léon had assigned the design to a celebrity Paris architect, creator of landmark discotheques such as Jakarta's Mata Hari and London's Golden Goose. All had been carefully pondered. A set of red tower lights to recreate the classic vibe of NYC's Studio 54 illuminated the floor, while rare Ashford dark marble from Derbyshire topped the stretched bar counter. Adding an exotic touch, a sequence of contemporary Japanese prints adorned the corridor while the bathrooms were covered with warm Moroccan tiles. With this new club, Léon aimed to attract Swiss clientele and bored diplomats fleeing Strasbourg for the night.

When Vincent walked through, some of the people by the bar turned to look at him. He always experienced a warm tingle of pride when creating this kind of reaction – a guilty pleasure he didn't wish to quit. The club was getting busier, but far from crammed. On his way to the bar, Vincent stopped to chat and take selfies with guests. He didn't spot anyone familiar. Years and years away from home had taken their toll.

They took a seat on the reserved silk sofa, divided from the open floor by a gold rope. Léon's friend had vanished. Léon beckoned over a waitress.

'What would you like?' he asked Vincent.

'Any absinthe in the place?'

With a look of disappointment, Léon tried to dissuade Vincent.

'You sure? How about a magnum of champagne? A wonderful Boërl & Kroff Brut for this special occasion?'

'Absinthe would be better for me, please.'

Vincent was now curious to learn what his friend had in mind. Léon didn't do something for nothing. Always a poker game with him.

Everything became clear when, five minutes later, Léon whispered, 'I've a favour to ask.'

Vincent nodded, as if to imply that the other could speak freely.

'A couple of years ago, I began a project with some partners in Switzerland. It was called Girloo. Perhaps you've heard of it?'

'No. I haven't had the pleasure,' said Vincent with a hint of undetected sarcasm.

'Switzerland has soft rules on escort agencies. It's a paradise. Not to mention the taxes. Basically, you called a girl at your home, paid for the service through us, and we took a fee. Deliveroo for sex. All legal, trust me; we checked their age and everything.'

Vincent was amused by the quick twist in the conversation, and the blunt sincerity with which Léon was telling him that he'd sold sex online, legally.

'So, we hit the jackpot. Unbelievable – in the first six months, we made more than ...' Léon excitedly whispered a figure to Vincent, who widened his eyes in marvel.

Léon continued. 'Too good to be true, actually.'

'What happened? They arrested you?' Vincent said, ribbing him.

'Much worse. A Romanian competitor hacked us. They made our life impossible. Our systems were down almost every other day. We had to shut the business.'

'Shame,' said Vincent, without any irony this time.

'But I know how to work around this issue.'

'Yes?'

'Yes. And I think you can help me.'

Vincent looked at him with incredulity.

'How?'

'I read somewhere that you're very close to August Destouches, the king of online betting. Everybody knows that he hacks his competitors.'

Vincent had never heard this rumour, but he laughed, as it seemed a very plausible piece of gossip about Destouches.

'So, I was wondering – would you spread a good word for me with Destouches? I could team up with him. I would provide the girls and the "know-how"—'

It was too much for him. Vincent had to give out a burst of laughter that annoyed his friend.

'I'm serious, Vince. We need Destouches's technological power,' Léon insisted. 'He would surely know how to protect Girloo from the hackers. For all I know, he might even be the one behind the hacking …'

'I can talk to him … but for the right fee,' Vincent said. He liked the idea of haggling with Léon. After all, he still had to recover from that expensive poker night.

'Sure, sure,' Léon reassured him in haste. 'What about five per cent of my share of the profits for the first year, if we resume business?'

'Let's say ten per cent for the first two years.'

This time it was Léon's turn to laugh. *'Mon dieu*, Paris has changed you, man!'

'Call it self-preservation …' Vincent corrected him, back in ironic mode.

He promised Léon that he would call Destouches after the debate.

Léon thanked him profusely and kept repeating how he would never forget this debt towards his dear friend. He then excused himself and went to the bar.

Vincent was now alone on the sofa. He sent a text to Emmanuelle: she was fine – in bed, but not asleep yet. He felt guilty; they had arranged to have a quiet weekend in the Alsatian countryside, away from the stress of Paris, but the row at the restaurant had turned everything a bit sour.

Vincent gazed around at the people dancing. They all seemed chilled out, joyously unaware of what was happening around them. He noticed a grey-haired man wearing a pink shirt and yellow trousers. He had to be Swiss, Vincent concluded.

'Can I sit next to you?' spoke a sudden voice to his left. 'I'm Nina. Léon told me to join you.'

A little surprised, Vincent nodded with a thin smile and gestured towards the sofa, inviting the scantily clothed girl to sit.

Nina had a childish face under her black bob. She stared at him. He could sense her pulsing excitement and adulation.

'What would you like to drink?' he said, trying to be approachable.

'A Cosmopolitan?' she answered.

'I'm sure we can manage that.' He smiled. Some moments of silence followed, covered by the music.

'You're my idol! I've watched all your videos so many times …'

Vincent enjoyed being praised, but he always found it awkward when his fans expressed their veneration. He usually made a performance of nodding and looking around to hide his discomfort.

'Are you from Mulhouse?' he asked while avoiding eye contact.

'No – Lyon. I moved here when they opened six months ago. Before that, I worked at a club in Lyon. The owner knows Léon and asked me if I'd be happy to spend some time here.'

'Alsace must be boring for a girl of your age.'

'I'm quite busy. I might even try skiing sometime. Or a wine tasting course.'

'Are your parents French?'

'My mum is from Guadeloupe. My dad's family is from Algeria. I was born in France.'

Vincent listened, sipping his absinthe. Further moments of awkward silence ensued.

Out of the blue, Nina asked: 'You don't like me because I'm mixed?'

He was taken slightly off guard by the insinuation. 'What? Absurd. You're a very attractive and independent girl …'

'Thank you! I'll never forget these words.'

Vincent was annoyed that so many people seemed to consider him a racist. It was a long way from reality, he believed.

Nina pointed to a silver door not far away.

'There's a private area behind there. Shall we go? I'd love to cuddle you.'

Vincent liked Nina's freshness. For him, nothing was like the sparkling eyes and smooth skin of a girl less than half his age. His lack of fatherly instinct prevented any sense of guilt for consorting with women so much younger. This time, however, Vincent knew Emmanuelle was waiting back in Colmar. Despite all his claims that men were never truly monogamous – an idea he had openly shared with the media to stir up additional controversy – Vincent cared about her.

And he didn't like the idea of Léon trying to pay him back in kind.

Vincent remembered idly his visits to brothels during his early days in Paris. You go in, he thought. You pick one. You spend one hour and, after leaving, you're depressed all day. But what can you do? *Semen retentum venenum est.*

He booked a car. A couple of minutes later, Chrystal was left behind. He had asked Nina to say a warm goodbye to Léon for him. After texting Emmanuelle that he was heading back to the hotel, Vincent switched off all his devices. It was the first time he had done so in years. All he wanted now was some peace.

VII

Vigevano

'*I vòstar cafè i sun prùnt!*'

Nodding warmly at the aged barista, Lucìa took the steaming cups under the ancient portico framing Piazza Ducale. In her early years, Lucìa had perceived Vigevano as the centre of the universe, but now she saw in her home town, more appropriately, a tiny and lovely place suspended in the past. An agreeable perception that made her feel in harmony with the entire world.

Lucìa was on a short trip to Vigevano for her father's birthday. She had never missed one and, despite all the imaginable difficulties in leaving Birmingham only days before the debate, she had resolved that this time would be no exception. So, the evening before Lucìa had taken the last available flight to Milan. In spite of her informing as few people as possible about her movements, news of the trip must have seeped out, for she had spotted an Italian journalist at Milan Linate Airport, eyeing around in search of someone. Her immediate gut feeling had been that he was there for her. Lucìa knew him from Brussels. Luckily, the journalist had missed her.

'I smoke too much,' said her friend Veronica, looking at her vape. They were sitting outside. 'I think they put some rubbish inside to make you dependant.'

Veronica was still Lucìa's closest friend. For all the long-lasting bond between the two, their lives had taken quite different paths. While Lucìa had forged with resolve a profession all for herself in Europe, Veronica still worked at her mother's beauty salon; and, even if she acknowledged that waxing, threading and manicuring wasn't a dream job, she also admitted her substantial lack of ambition.

'How long are you staying here?' she asked.

'I'm leaving tomorrow afternoon. I really need to get back to Birmingham.'

Veronica was aware that Lucìa had become a sensation beyond Italy's borders, but she still hadn't formed a specific picture of what her friend did. It was too far outside her comfort zone. Rather than discussing the future of Europe, the two usually preferred to gossip about mutual friends, remember shared experiences, plan future holidays together.

Lucìa enjoyed the small talk with Veronica, her not taking life too seriously, and the fact that Veronica knew every piece of gossip available in Vigevano. Each conversation with her best friend was for Lucìa a fleeting window onto a carefree world that wisely stayed away from the relentless cycle of 24/7 news. In Vigevano, a private life was still possible, and week-ends still mattered.

Sipping her espresso, Veronica informed Lucìa about an acquaintance of theirs – a gastroenterologist at the local hospital, married with children – who had got a nurse pregnant. He wanted her to terminate the pregnancy in Switzerland, where abortion was still allowed, but she was determined to keep the baby. His career at the hospital was tacitly compromised, Veronica concluded.

Time flew rapidly with Veronica. Lucìa had by then received three missed calls from her father.

'Luci, where are you?'

'I'm having coffee with Veronica, papà.'

'Ah. When are you coming back?'

'Soon. I just wanted some fresh air.'

'Ah. Okay.'

Lucìa sensed that her father wasn't ready to end the call, so she kept talking. 'This afternoon, I'll help you tidy up. The house is messy. We can then watch a movie together. What would you like to watch?'

'Anything is fine by me. I'm so happy to have you here!'

Since her mother's passing, Lucìa's father had striven not to show his only child any sign of his loneliness. He held the conviction that a father should manifest strength for his offspring unconditionally. Despite his efforts to hide it, Lucìa nonetheless always perceived his gloom when it increased, with no exception, around festivities and anniversaries.

The sky of Vigevano was a refreshing blue. No cloud on the horizon, only a warm breeze. From their small table, Lucìa and Veronica enjoyed a full view of Castello Sforzesco, the castle built by the Italian prince Ludovico Sforza in the early Renaissance.

A generous patron, Ludovico had commissioned a wealth of artworks by major artists – including Leonardo da Vinci – to make the court of Milan stand out in Europe. Unsurprisingly, Lucìa's fellow home-towners liked to believe Leonardo da Vinci had also been involved in the construction of their castle. Almost as much as her father's happiness, the magnificent sight of Castello Sforzesco made up for the stress of a hurried trip back home.

'I ran into Davide at the pharmacy a couple of weeks ago,' Veronica said abruptly.

Lucìa had known it was coming. Veronica mentioned Lucìa's former boyfriend every time the opportunity presented itself. For a reason – she had always believed that, despite all their differences and strife, Lucìa and Davide were made for each other. Had their relationship continued, Veronica thought, Lucìa would have never left town. So, for her, Davide was the only person able to bring her best friend back – if not to Vigevano, then at least to Italy.

'How's he doing?' Lucìa felt obliged to ask.

'We chatted for ten minutes. He still works with his father. I suspect he's no longer with Marzia. I saw her with another guy a couple of times.'

Veronica winked at Lucìa.

Had Lucìa been less experienced, her next question might have been something akin to: *Did he ask about me?*

She was smarter than that.

'Davide asked about you,' Veronica revealed. 'He read about you somewhere. I think he knows what you do better than me.'

Lucìa felt a slight, unexpected lift in hearing this. Although she hadn't thought of Davide for quite some time, Veronica had succeeded in touching a nerve that, while deeply numbed, was still there. Her relationship with Davide had been a big part of Lucìa's life, and some instinct made her cling – who knows why – to the romance of her youth. Here I am, Lucìa thought with a hint of frustration, fighting with millions of people for the destiny of Europe, and still feeling something that should be buried in the past.

'It can't be a coincidence that you haven't been in a long-term relationship since. And I do not think that *you-know-who* in Belgium was really the man of your life,' observed Veronica, always straight to the point, especially where her friend was concerned. This last remark annoyed Lucìa.

You-know-who had left a profound scar on her. They had met in Brussels. She hadn't been able to stand him, initially. They held opposite political ideas, belonged to different circles and, moreover, didn't share the same approach to life. He had even once said something along the lines that feminism was useful only to make unattractive women feel accepted. However, a couple of occasional chats in a famous Brussels hangout had let Lucìa discover there was another man lying beneath the surface, one who was unexpectedly sensitive and open. Without realising it, she had begun to feel drawn to him.

It hadn't taken long for a mesmerising passion to take her over, in a way she had never experienced – to the point of her disregarding his provocative soundbites. Although fiery, their story had been short. He had soon left Belgium, and it hadn't worked at a distance. The whole situation had been so unsettling that Lucìa had never talked about him with her Brussels friends – not even Rachel. She had only confided in Veronica and they always referred to him as *you-know-who*.

As Lucìa and Veronica were politely arguing about the tightly intertwined topics of Lucìa's life goals and the role of men in her existence, the barista slowly walked towards their table.

'Ladies, it's lunchtime! Today's special is caprese salad with buffalo mozzarella,' he told them, parading his perpetual smile.

'Wonderful … we shall have it!' Lucìa said, slightly over-enthusiastically. The caprese salad was indeed delicious, and had been the bar's daily special in warm seasons since her childhood.

The tables under the ancient portico were filling up. Everyone was busily chatting, nobody in Piazza Ducale seeming to notice Lucìa. She didn't see anyone familiar either. Years and years away from home had taken their toll. Suddenly, though, Lucìa picked out someone she thought she recognised. It took her a second to remember: the journalist from the airport. He couldn't be in Vigevano by mere coincidence. The journalist drew close to the table, so that he stood almost over it, then addressed Lucìa. 'You don't mind if I sit next to you?'

She didn't answer.

The journalist interpreted the silence as tacit approval and took a seat at the closest table.

'I'm a lead writer at the *Corriere della Sera*,' he continued. 'I believe we met during a reception at the Italian Embassy in Brussels some time ago. You worked with MEP Sherwood … My colleagues in Milan tried to reach you many times, with no success.'

'I'm sorry for that,' she said. 'But I'm not giving any interviews before the eighth of April. I can't risk my ideas being misjudged ahead of the poll.'

'I'm not here for an interview,' he replied. 'I want to discuss a very important matter concerning Charlemagny.'

'Should I go away?' Veronica asked, disliking the idea of being the third wheel.

'No, Vero, please stay here,' said Lucìa, who thought it appropriate to have a witness to her conversation with the journalist. 'Please say what you have to say,' she said to him.

'Italians are not taking Charlemagny very seriously. At least not yet,' the journalist began. 'The media tends to focus almost exclusively on domestic matters. Not many in Italy grasp the importance of a social media poll on merging two foreign countries, even those so close to Italy. I, on the contrary, take Charlemagny very seriously.'

'So, just us then,' Lucìa observed drily. She was beginning to like him.

The journalist smiled. His shirt collar was stained, Lucìa didn't fail to notice.

'Yesterday morning we received confidential information from Bolzano that I believe you will find of extreme interest,' he said.

The largest town in South Tyrol – a self-governed province at the northernmost point of Italy – Bolzano had originally been part of the Austro-Hungarian Empire before being annexed, along with the entire province, to the Kingdom of Italy at the end of the First World War. Yet the territory retained a strong Teutonic culture. While German and Italian were both official languages, German was by far the more widespread in the region. Regardless of the common Italian passport, a strong cultural divide still existed between the German and Italian populations in the region. In some respects, South Tyrol shared a similar past with Alsace: both prey to imperialist ambitions, they suffered the identity struggle of a borderland, tugged left and right by opposing cultures, deeply uncertain of what the future would offer.

'We've an insider with the police in Bolzano,' said the Italian journalist. 'He informs us about criminal investigations or other stuff in South Tyrol that deserve public attention. He called me yesterday morning. He told me about an ongoing police investigation involving the current Governor of South Tyrol. The Governor is suspected of official misconduct in a past case. I will not go into the details – they don't matter. What matters is that the police have been wiretapping the Governor for some time.'

Meanwhile, the barista approached the reporter, who ordered an espresso corretto with grappa. As soon as the barista was out of earshot, he continued.

'I was told that, a couple of days ago, the Governor had a call with none other than … the German Foreign Minister.'

Lucìa sighed. She now knew what might be going on.

'It seems that the call lasted over three hours,' the journalist revealed. 'Three long hours where the Governor of South Tyrol repeated that many local people, including him, would be happy to join Charlemagny. He clearly took it for granted that Charlemagny would become reality.'

'And what did the German Foreign Minister say?' asked Lucìa – worried but, at the same time, intrigued by a revelation she would never have expected to hear at a café in Vigevano's main square.

'He seemed glad about the direction the call was taking. At least, this is my impression from reading the translated transcript; I don't speak German. The Foreign Minister kept saying that the time had finally arrived for Germans to reunite under a single flag. It's not a coincidence that the standard of South Tyrol bears a red eagle – he said.'

Lucìa was speechless. She knew the German minister to be a man prone to chatting, and who often hit the bottle, but this exchange with the Governor of South Tyrol went beyond the worst limits of her imagination.

'What else did they say?' Lucìa probed. She abhorred palace intrigues, especially those that were Charlemagny inspired. Quite a few politicians in Europe aimed to exploit Charlemagny and reap the political fruits. They didn't want to get their own hands soiled, thus they acted in the shadows, leaving the dirty work to Vincent d'Amont.

'The German Foreign Minister and the Governor of South Tyrol believe that Austria will sooner or later ask to join Charlemagny,' the journalist answered. 'Vienna will never stay in the EU without Berlin. And if North Tyrol, in Austria, joins Charlemagny, South Tyrol will try to secede from Italy.'

'Do they really believe that Italy will give up the region so easily?'

'The German said that Charlemagny will inherit a substantial amount of Italian government debt from Germany. As, he predicts, Italy will soon be unable to sustain the burden of its debt, Charlemagny will be in the favourable position of literally buying South Tyrol from Italy in exchange for a debt write-off.'

Lucìa listened with painful interest. Veronica was toying with her device. Politics wasn't her thing.

'Why have you come to me?' Lucìa asked the journalist.

'I knew you'd ask that. Fair. I'll be straight with you: I cannot publish this news; not now. Our insider begged me not to jeopardise his investigation. So, I decided to share this information with you alone. I'm sure you can put it to use. In return, perhaps you could grant me your first interview after the vote on Charlemagny.'

Lucìa was amused by the inventive quid pro quo the Italian journalist had proposed. He seemed a loose cannon, a real old-style reporter who would do almost anything to be the first to deliver news. Not at any cost, though. He had ethics; he didn't want, for instance, to put his source with the Bolzano police in dire straits.

'Okay. I will be discreet. But you must keep me abreast of what happens in South Tyrol.'

'Promised,' he said. 'Mind you, I'm not doing this just for the interview. You're a brave vlogger, supporting the right cause. None of us were even born when separatists placed bombs in South Tyrol ... but slogans in favour of Charlemagny have already appeared on the walls of Bolzano. I don't know who's behind all this: perhaps the Reichsbürger. It's not important. I just don't want the past to repeat itself.'

As quickly as he had arrived, the journalist stood up and said goodbye.

The two best friends were alone again. Lucìa looked at Veronica with some guilt.

'I'm sorry, Vero. Work still haunts me.'

Veronica wasn't upset. If a journalist from the *Corriere della Sera* had made the effort of coming all the way to Vigevano, it had to be serious, she mused. They resumed conversing, but Veronica did most of the talking. Still unable to detach herself from the encounter with the journalist, Lucìa wasn't 100 per cent present. She found it less disturbing that Charlemagny might become part of a threesome involving Austria than the news of propaganda graffiti appearing in Bolzano.

Ten minutes later, Veronica left. She had a couple of appointments at her beauty parlour. They planned to meet the next morning before Lucìa's departure.

Once alone, Lucìa decided to touch base with Hugh. She told him about her conversation with the journalist. They agreed that what she had just learned should remain secret for the moment, as its publication might lend further credence to the whole Charlemagny idea. They didn't know that, in a matter of minutes, the media would break the news of the Strasbourg meeting between Madame Lille and Herr Karlsruhe.

Hugh told Lucìa the latest. An attempted coup d'état in Kazakhstan was the most searched-for news of the day on the vlog, closely followed by the drought in Yemen and, on a more positive note, the recent sighting of a grey whale by Chinese scientists (the grey whale had been proclaimed extinct ten years before). The new intern from Denmark was quickly getting into the swing of things, Hugh also reported. She was bright, very proactive, and not held back by the fear of making rookie mistakes.

Lucìa hadn't had much opportunity of late to see the new interns in action, with Charlemagny completely absorbing her. The same could be said of the entire team at Miss Cliché: they had lived, eaten and breathed Charlemagny for months.

Lucìa hadn't forgotten her promise to help Tara, the kid she'd met at the East Birmingham Academy, to find her missing friend Casey.

'Hugh, I've just sent you all the material that Casey's parents gathered for us. It's a file including months' worth of his online activities: social media, gaming, everything a kid would want to do. I want Pandora to delve into it. There must be something useful – a lead.'

'Mmm …' replied Hugh.

'What?'

'Belch is fixing a couple of bugs. I don't think we can start the search today.'

'There's nothing we can do? The more time passes, the slimmer the chances of finding Casey. We need to hurry up. We need Pandora.'

'I'll see if Belch can be quicker, but I can't guarantee it. I'll let you know.'

Apparently uncomfortable to dwell on Pandora's condition, Hugh concluded with the latest count released by the French Minister of Interior: 3,500 more instances of Charlemagny graffiti had appeared in the last day alone (up 50 per cent from the previous count). He loved numbers, but not these.

The clock in the square's tower struck three when the barista, clearing some tables under the portico, addressed Lucìa.

'You live abroad, right?'

'Yes – in England.'

'Ah …' the barista sighed. 'You made the right choice. I've never moved from Vigevano. I regret it. I wish I had seen big cities all around the world.'

As long as she could remember, indeed, Lucìa had seen him working at that bar. She couldn't guess whether his regrets were heartfelt or whether he was just one of those people needing a permanent home who nonetheless liked to moan about missed roamings.

An incoming call.

'Am I speaking with Lucìa Morè?'

'Yes?'

'This is Superintendent Burke speaking. We met on a couple of occasions.'

'Yes, I remember,' Lucìa, frowning, replied.

'Are you in Birmingham?'

'No. Overseas. Why are you asking?'

'We don't think it's a good idea for you to travel. We're still trying to protect you.'

'That's nice of you, Superintendent,' she answered. 'But I am probably safer here where I am right now than in Britain.'

Someone gifted with sarcasm would have said, *Why don't you stay there, then?* – but he didn't. 'The purpose of my call is not to discuss your travels,' Burke added. 'I'm calling because of your interference in a missing person case.'

It seemed another odd coincidence to Lucìa – that of Burke contacting her right after the call with Hugh.

'I'm not interfering,' she replied. 'Just trying to help two desperate parents find their son. I've got their approval to carry out my own search.'

Instead of appreciating the value that Miss Cliché could bring to the enquiry, Burke was again proving hostile. 'We're already working on the case,' he objected. 'Having you nosing around won't help us. You could ruin useful evidence.'

Lucìa knew that, regardless of Burke's approval, she was entitled to carry out her own investigation. Pandora could definitely beat the West Midlands Police.

'I need to go, Burke. I'm in a meeting,' she told him – a feeble excuse. He was about to say something else, but she didn't let him, quickly hanging up.

A second – much more welcome – call came in.

'Professor! How are you?'

'I'm fine, Lucìa. I looked for you at the newsroom half an hour ago. Hugh said you were in Italy. Please give my birthday wishes to your father.'

'I will certainly do so!'

'I wanted to tell you that I'm leaving for Oxfordshire tomorrow morning. We're staying there for two weeks. I need to complete my book with no distractions other than the sounds of nature – Thelma's barking included.'

'Will you follow the debate?' Lucìa asked him with slight disappointment, for she would have preferred to have the professor with her in the newsroom during the face-off.

He sensed Lucìa's discontent. 'Of course, Lucìa. You needn't even ask. I'm only going because my mission with you is complete. You're ready for the debate: the Frenchman will never be able to put you on the back foot.'

Lucìa welcomed his comforting words. She had become more and more grateful to Professor Sherwood for the support he had always given her. First in Pavia, then Brussels, and finally in Birmingham. And, from the very moment Lucìa had agreed to step into the political arena of Charlemagny – a tough decision, one in which the professor had played an important role – they had grown even closer.

Piazza Ducale was no longer buzzing when the call ended. Halfway through the afternoon, it was a bit early to reach her father, so Lucìa decided to check in with Rachel. The call went straight to voicemail.

* * *

Rachel had just switched off her device. She was entering the Drexler Steinmetz in central Berlin, one of the tallest skyscrapers in Germany, where ROME's headquarters were located. Visitors had to turn off any device. Shirted for the occasion, Holger was there in the purported role of Rachel's assistant.

Rachel wondered if she would see floor 89, where legend said Marlene Gäch lived in isolation. The mere thought gave her the shivers. But the lift took Rachel and Holger to another floor, where the PR and media office was. The department employed some two hundred people, working under the stern direction of an overbearing Chief Media Officer, in ROME almost since the very start. Many legends were attached to her, and one story went that she made daily calls to Vincent d'Amont, an erstwhile lover, to give him instructions on what to say and do.

The department's receptionist led the guests to the meeting room, which was neat and tidy but devoid of luxuries or extravagances. Seemingly in common with the entire floor – explored by Rachel with furtive eyes – the room was laid out to optimise all the available space. No empty corner or useless item of furniture could be seen: an expression of German architectural efficiency at its best.

Rachel and Holger took a seat. Once alone in the room, they gave each other a cheeky smile, for in that moment they felt like partners in crime.

'Do I look like a journalist?' he whispered amusedly.

'Yes. From the *Scruffington Post* …'

'C'mon,' he chuckled.

'A green tie with a yellow shirt … you belong behind bars, not in a bar.'

He looked at her puzzled, as if he didn't grasp what the issue with his clothing was.

'Forget about it,' she said.

Moments later, the notorious Chief Media Officer swished into the room. Tall and fit, almost skinny, with short blonde hair, she wore a dark knee-length pencil skirt with a black cropped sweater. Her style was refined but impersonal, fully in symbiosis with the cold surroundings.

'Can I call you Rachel?' she asked after the quickest of introductions.

'Sure,' replied Rachel, promptly putting the Chief Media Officer into the category of those who liked to save words and time. 'Please meet my colleague Klaus, who works here in Berlin.'

The Chief Media Officer looked at Holger (alias Klaus), her eyes falling immediately on his tie. Unimpressed, she gave him the tiniest of smiles.

'I tend to delegate the liaising with journalists to my team. However, I have made an exception for an important journalist crossing the ocean to visit us, despite the very short notice.'

'I'm flattered,' Rachel replied, smiling, even though she had an inexplicable feeling of being far from welcome. Officially, Rachel's reason for visiting ROME was a *Wall Street Journal* piece on Charlemagny – but maybe they already suspected that she was there on behalf of Miss Cliché.

'I understand from the questions you sent us yesterday, Rachel, that you have a specific interest in how the vote on Charlemagny will work.'

'Yes. It must be a real challenge to set up a reliable online poll for millions of people in two different countries.'

'Very true. We've made our largest technological investment ever. The voting procedure will be entirely based on blockchain technology. I assume you're aware of what blockchain is?'

'Yes, kind of. It's a large database shared by a network of computers. It's supposed to be tamper-proof. I'm not an expert.'

'Very good, Rachel. I'm not an expert on blockchain, either. So I've asked the head of the German Blockchain Authority to be with us today. The GBA has been entrusted by the German government with observing the correct functioning of the vote. They want to ensure that nobody will question its regularity. He's the right person to explain to us how it will work.'

She switched on a small screen on the wall. A bespectacled, greying man appeared.

'I'm here with Rachel, an American journalist from the *Wall Street Journal*,' the Chief Media Officer told him. 'Would you please walk us through why blockchain is a state-of-the-art technology, perfect for processing an e-vote in complete safety?'

'I would be glad to,' the head of the German Blockchain Authority replied, 'even if it's never easy to explain a very technical subject in plain words.' But then he described blockchain in such a clear manner that Rachel was left impressed.

They were recording the video call, so that a transcript could later be made available to Rachel.

(Start of the video transcript)
Blockchain is a digital ledger containing sets of data. These sets of data are simultaneously shared among a wide network of participating computers.

So – imagine a giant web of computers processing the same sets of data all around the world.

Every set of data is compounded in separate digital 'blocks', and each of these blocks is chained to all the other blocks by means of an encrypted digital signature. This is the reason why the technology is called 'blockchain'.

The content of a digital signature applied to a specific block strictly mirrors the data content of that block. Hence, if wrongdoers try to manipulate any data in a block, even the tiniest, the digital signature of that block will immediately change. As a consequence, all the other blocks in the chain will no longer recognise the modified block and they will reject it. Data in a blockchain network are immutable; they cannot be successfully modified or falsified.

How will ROME apply blockchain to the Charlemagny vote? In the following way:

First, ROME will identify every voter. This is not difficult: a facial recognition process is already necessary for users to register and log in to ROME. To join the 8/4 vote, users will be required to undergo the same facial recognition process.

It will be virtually impossible for hackers to join the vote by impersonating a user or by creating fake accounts. The old days of bot-operated social media accounts are over. ROME has a very efficient system for detecting bogus users and will cancel accounts after suspicious activity.

It may be that a user does not qualify to vote as they have not registered with ROME and lived in France or Germany for most of the last twelve months before the vote. In that case, of course, the user will not gain access to the voting stage.

If the user is entitled to vote on Charlemagny, ROME will create a voter blockchain to record two transactions: one is the user starting the registration process, and the other acknowledging the user's right to vote.

Once the user has voted, the vote will become a transaction added to the blockchain: so, double voting will be impossible.

All data, including those relevant to voting preferences, will be encrypted and then propagated out to the entire network of voting computers and devices, as it will be the voters that provide the computing power necessary for the blockchain to operate.

Moreover, given that there is no way to connect a vote to the voter, complete anonymity will be guaranteed.

The Charlemagny vote will be safe, reliable, transparent and anonymous.

You are probably asking yourself whether there is a risk, even remote, that the Charlemagny vote may be hacked and disrupted.

Yes, in theory: a '51 per cent attack', if successful, could block the voting process for some time. A 51 per cent attack happens when some hackers control most of the computing power within a blockchain. In the case of Charlemagny, however, with millions and millions of honest voting computers, it will be almost impossible to perform a 51 per cent attack.

The German government has designated the German Blockchain Authority, which I am glad to represent, to guarantee the complete regularity and fairness of the Charlemagny vote. I am sure we will be able to achieve this important objective.

(End of the video transcript)

Rachel was surprised to learn that the Federal Republic of Germany had appointed a watchdog to monitor the 8/4 poll, for her a contradictory measure that confirmed how Germany was giving the vote much importance but, at the same time, questioning its regularity.

'You see? There's no reason to fear that Charlemagny will be less than transparent,' the Chief Media Officer said. 'Blockchain is already used for innumerable purposes: crypto-currencies, money transfers, smart contracts, protection of intellectual property. It's time to deploy the full potential of blockchain for political voting, too.'

Yet Rachel hadn't flown from the United States to hear an elevator pitch. Alongside the tame questions she had emailed in advance, she had something more in store.

'The presentation was very neat,' she began. 'However, something is still not completely clear to me.'

'Please, shoot!' the Chief Media Officer invited her with feigned enthusiasm.

'For instance, many French and German people don't qualify to vote on Charlemagny, because they have lived outside their country for the last twelve months. Shouldn't everyone French or German be entitled to express their opinion, regardless of where they currently reside? They are all affected, in the end.'

'This was a hard, but unavoidable, choice,' was the answer to a question that the Chief Media Officer had heard more than once. 'It would be very difficult for us to verify each voter's citizenship. Requiring our users to upload an ID is out of the question. Asking them to self-declare their French or German nationality would create plenty of leeway for interferences. The Chinese would be so happy to sabotage the vote …'

'But this exclusion discriminates in favour of the Charlemagny side: most German and French expatriates appreciate Europe and, if allowed to vote, they would reject any idea of merging the two countries,' Rachel observed.

'As I've already said, a technical reason drove us to this decision. ROME has no intention of helping either side; we are impartial,' the Chief Media Officer responded politely, although she was clearly starting to be irked by Rachel's inquisitive tone.

Rachel continued with the same line of questioning.

'According to newly released statistical data, more than seventy-five per cent of the political posts published on ROME in the last six months were pro-Charlemagny. It's strange, because all third-party opinion polls have shown a much more balanced split between Europe and Charlemagny so far. Some commentators hint at possible manipulation. What's your take on this?'

'This is utter nonsense. ROME works on algorithms that limit the chance of any external manipulation. For instance, even if the Chinese tried to interfere with our platform through computer-generated posts, as has happened in the past with other social media, ROME would immediately block these intrusions. It is practically impossible to abuse our platform.'

This time it was Rachel's turn to find a prompt riposte: 'I was referring to a manipulation of the platform … from within.'

Immediately, silence filled the room. The Chief Media Officer stared at her.

'Rachel, I don't know what the custom in the United States of America is, but here in Germany we tend to refrain from insulting our hosts.'

She stood impassive. Rachel was cherishing the moment.

'From day one, we aimed to bring Europeans closer,' ROME's spin doctor continued. 'We pursued this goal with determination, prizing both the spontaneity of our users and the transparency of our processes. You are referring to the possibility of us manipulating our own platform. Why would we do so, if I may ask?'

Rachel had nothing to lose. 'Perhaps for the very reason why you've organised the vote on Charlemagny?'

In less than five minutes, Rachel and Holger were back at the central lift. She wondered, again, whether they would by accident stop at floor 89, so she could ask inappropriate questions of Marlene Gäch, too. But they were escorted directly to the ground floor.

Once outside the Drexler Steinmetz, Rachel spotted the missed call from Lucìa.

'Sorry, darling. I was at the offices of ROME. They had me switching off my device. I just met the Chief Media Officer in person.'

'Aren't you lucky,' Lucìa joked. 'I've tried to contact her for months with no success. I gave up. I don't think she likes uncomfortable questions.'

'I've noticed. They basically invited me to leave the building.' Lucìa chuckled.

'I didn't even have the time to ask her about Marlene Gäch's bearer shares,' Rachel quipped.

'They would have you thrown out of the window!' joked Lucìa.

Rachel admitted that her visit to the headquarters of ROME had been less fruitful than the preceding days in Berlin, when she had acquired precious information on how ROME had ruthlessly achieved unprecedented digital power.

Rachel had met the founder of Hølogram, probably the foremost victim of ROME's notorious strategy to dominate the market: *With us or against us.*

Hølogram was a free leisure app enabling users to create three-dimensional images in augmented reality with their devices. Hølogram had got off to a very promising start, reaching more than a hundred thousand users in Germany within six months of its creation. Key to the app's success was that users could sign in through ROME.

The fast ascent of Hølogram didn't pass unnoticed at the Drexler Steinmetz; and, as often happened when a platform with potential cropped up in Europe, ROME began to make overtures. 'One morning, Marlene Gäch contacted me,' the founder had told Rachel. 'She praised us for the work done, said that we were one of the fastest-growing applications on the market and a brilliant future lay ahead of us. However, she warned that Hølogram needed many more resources to grow further.'

It was a fair assessment. He had already been negotiating with venture capital firms in Europe that could provide him with the additional wherewithal needed for his platform to reach the next level.

'After barely five minutes of conversation, Gäch came straight to the point,' he relayed. 'ROME had an offer ready on the table to acquire our business. I was flattered and shocked at the same time.' In the afternoon of that same day, the offer was dropped on his table. The proposition ROME had put forward was extremely generous: two or even three times the market value of the platform. Nothing out of the ordinary for ROME – simply following her usual habit of buying start-up companies to bring their features in-house.

'I was tempted by the bid, I must say,' the founder admitted. 'But something didn't sit right with me. I suspected that ROME would dissolve Hølogram immediately after the acquisition, something they had already done with other platforms after stripping them of their assets. So, I politely declined the offer. And I also turned down an even more generous proposal they made us the day after. That second offer really made me think: why leave Hølogram at the very moment when the largest European conglomerate saw a brilliant future ahead of us? The management board was with me in the resolution not to sell.'

ROME hadn't taken the refusal well.

'I soon received another call from Marlene Gäch. Her tone was very different. She told me that I was acting irrationally, that I would soon regret my choice. I remember her saying: "It's with ROME or against ROME."'

The offer was still open, she'd said. Most of the management board, intimidated, were now in favour of accepting the takeover. Nonetheless, the CEO remained firm in his decision not to sell the platform. It was then that everything changed. ROME unilaterally terminated any form of integration with Hølogram, and its users were no longer able to log on through ROME. Finding Hølogram on the search engine became more difficult day after day and the #Hølogram hashtag disappeared overnight from the ROME network; all these changes brought the rise of Hølogram to a rapid halt.

The vibes in and around the platform deteriorated: two members of the management board resigned and venture capitalists who had previously shown a concrete interest in financing Hølogram were now backtracking. It seemed as if a fatwa had been declared against its founder, and everybody now wanted to stay at a safe distance from his creation. Lacking a way forward, the business was dissolved. Left high and dry, the founder swore revenge on ROME. He believed it was only a matter of sitting down by the riverbank and waiting long enough. ROME was still very powerful, though, so he had resolved to keep his quest for revenge quiet.

'Awful story,' commented Lucìa.

'You can find plenty of similar cases in Europe,' Rachel warned. 'ROME has applied the *with us or against us* policy against hundreds. And nobody is doing much about it.'

'Not true, Rachel – we're here. And we'll not give up. Enough is enough.'

There was no trace of empty rhetoric in Lucìa's words: she would fight up against ROME's dominance to the very end.

* * *

Rachel's trip to Berlin had proved useful in another respect, Lucìa thought. Meeting with political experts, as well as talking to the locals with Holger's precious help, had enabled her to understand how the German people saw the 8/4 vote on ROME.

The country was deeply polarised over Charlemagny.

For some, the European Union was Germany's creation, and without doubt Germany maintained a leading, if not dominant, role. For that reason, Germany had no incentive to leave. Furthermore, membership of the Union was viewed as the only possible guarantee that the country would never, ever consider resuming imperialist ambitions. Past wounds were still visible, and errors should not be repeated. Those who shared these beliefs were naturally inclined against Charlemagny.

For others – yes, Germany maintained a prominent role in Europe, but it was clear that most other European countries had not followed its virtuous path. They just wanted to exploit the Union on every possible occasion, often in complete disregard of the agreed rules. France – alone – was the exception, the only country trying with Germany to turn Europe around.

Why keep rowing against the tide of the other European countries? The time for change had finally arrived. Germany and France should join forces to become a sole entity and abandon the Union.

Then there were the multitude of undecideds – those who would go for a last-minute choice, perhaps after watching Miss Cliché and Vincent d'Amont debate. And the undecideds would most likely be the difference. The essence of political relativism, Professor Sherwood would argue.

Ah, professor – I will miss you at the debate, Lucìa thought, sighing. After practising her answers with him during the mock debates, it now seemed strange that he would not join her for the real one. She would be all by herself this time.

When the tower clock struck five, Lucìa decided to go home. If Liam Sherwood was a father figure, she also had a real dad – whose birthday needed to be celebrated. Just as she was standing up, Lucìa saw him walking under the portico. When he caught sight of her, Mr Morè shouted: 'If the mountain will not come to Muhammad, then Muhammad must go to the mountain!'

Lucìa laughed. He took a seat next to her. The weather was so pleasant that they didn't want to go home so soon.

'I'm so proud of what you're achieving,' her father told her. 'I'm not surprised, though: you've always had personality. Even as a child, you were independent and liked to explore. When we went to the dentist, you'd start asking him questions about the equipment. And you drove the newsagent crazy by browsing through all the magazines. Mamma and I always knew you were gifted.'

Lucìa blushed.

'I owe it all to you, papà. You let me continue my studies in Pavia. Most parents around here discouraged their children from going to university, so that they could work with them. Look at Veronica and her mum.'

'No family business was waiting for you, unfortunately,' her father responded, lowering his eyes.

Mr Morè had been an elementary school teacher for thirty years when, spurred on by his wife, he had given it up to open a shoe workshop. Unsuited for business, he hadn't lasted long. With almost all his savings burned up in the venture, Lucìa's father had gloomily gone back to teaching. Recalling his failure still hurt his pride.

'You're wrong to think of it like that, papà,' she sweetly reproached him. 'You taught me the importance of knowledge. *So di non sapere.* I liked doing homework with you much more than with Mamma. I remember the multiplication tables for maths, the Italian independence wars in history, and when we studied volcanoes together. You were a great teacher with me at home, as you were with your pupils at school. And when I became a teenager, you kept me away from dangerous distractions. I owe you a lot.'

He gave her a tender smile. 'I can't wait for the debate. It's a shame that my English is poor, Luci.'

'There'll be automatic subtitles in Italian, too.'

'Good news. I won't feel quite so dumb …'

There was a moment of silence, then her father continued.

'They blame Europe for everything, here in Italy. The extreme right and the extreme left agree on just one thing: that we should leave the Union. But to go where? Bring the lira back? No way!'

Lucìa nodded. 'You're right. The problem is that Europe doesn't even have a reply for this sort of criticism. It's too easy for national politicians to slag off the Union before elections, or use Brussels as a scapegoat. Very few defend Europe.'

Talking of Europe with her father seemed weird to Lucìa. Politics had never been a subject for discussion at their dinner table. Her father had always watched the news, but with no political passion. The same could have been said of her mother. The origins of Lucìa's mysterious fire for politics had to be traced elsewhere.

'Do you know what hurts the most, papà? That some say I'm defending the cause of Europe for visibility or money. It really upsets me. I'm the same person that worked around the clock at the European Parliament, and nobody even knew who I was at the time.'

That wasn't entirely true, her father thought. Lucìa had changed since Brussels, and for the better. She was more self-aware, no longer allowing people to exploit or corner her so easily; and managing the vlog seemed to have made his daughter more pragmatic. Lucìa still retained the strong values he and his wife had instilled in her: she was fair, altruistic, and knew how to draw a line between good and evil. There was no *end justifying the means* with Lucìa.

'Some are envious, perhaps?' he asked.

'I don't know. Charlemagny has made me popular – it's true – but simply because I was one of the few vloggers who dared put their name out and say *I love Europe!* And I said it because I believe it. There was no second-guessing.'

Lucìa couldn't accept being accused of the same calculating opportunism as Vincent d'Amont's. She was different, and everybody should understand it.

As the evening approached, Lucìa began to feel her anxiety for the debate building up. She now wanted to go back home, where with her father she would watch a movie on the sofa. Her device was now switched off for the first time in years. Lucìa needed a moment of respite.

VIII

The Debate

Slå helvetet ur dem! a Swedish member of the European Parliament texted Vincent the morning of the debate. Beat the hell out of them!

In theory, it went against Sweden's national interest to encourage anything that might lead to the dismantling of the Union, but this right-leaning MEP fell among those who rejoiced in disrupting the status quo, regardless of the detriment caused to their people.

ROME estimated that sixty million French and German netizens, at least, would follow the live debate – a large share of those expected to vote on Charlemagny in two days' time. With such an audience, the event was bound to have an impact on the poll. The face-to-face was scheduled to last exactly thirteen minutes, the maximum attention span of the average ROME viewer. The digital emcee would pose questions to the debaters, who had one minute each to answer, strictly uninterrupted.

The secret questions had been prepared the day before in a Berlin hotel room by a pool of twenty-five political commentators, academics and journalists. After evaluating the performances of Vincent d'Amont and Miss Cliché, the same experts would declare the winner within hours of the debate.

It had been agreed that the debaters – and they alone – would be able to watch the viewers' live reactions on their screens. But Miss Cliché – wishing to avoid adding stress upon stress, or letting the people dictate how she should answer questions – had decided she wouldn't look. The professor agreed with her choice.

Lucìa began the day with an early run around Edgbaston Park. After meeting the full Miss Cliché team for a final briefing, she rehearsed her possible answer to every possible question. No usual espresso that day – she was edgy enough.

Vincent spent his morning at a barber shop in Colmar for a full-face shave and a quick trim of his already neat haircut. Aiming to appear spontaneous, he preferred not to practise his answers.

They both knew it was the most important day of their lives so far.

One hour before the debate, Lucìa sat at her desk to do some final fact-checking with Pandora. They had to be ready to challenge Vincent's imaginative interpretation of political facts.

'Are you ready, Moretta?' asked Pandora.

'Yep, Pandy. A bit anxious, though.'

'I can imagine. I've heard about a great remedy for stress: shout the loudest you can shout, and for however long you need. It'll help you to expel the negative vibes, they say.'

'I will. Another time, but I will do it. I don't want to startle the entire newsroom!'

'Sure. It makes sense. The NHS always recommends taking some *me time*. You work hard, Lucìa – never taking an evening for yourself. I can see how much time you spend online: a lot. You should take some time off,' Pandora advised Lucìa, who smiled at realising that Pandora was giving her the same exact recommendations as Rachel.

'If she could hear you, Rachel would give you five,' Lucìa told Pandora.

'Five what?'

'Don't worry ...' said Lucìa. 'Now, I need to go. It's almost time.'

'*In bocca al lupo,* Moretta.'

'*Crepi il lupo,* Pandy.'

When the countdown to the debate started, Lucìa's screen was still disquietingly blank.

'Five minutes left,' said the digital emcee.

Lucìa was alone in her office. The others had gathered by a large hanging screen in the adjoining open-plan. Tension simmered in the air. Hugh had urged them to speak quietly – or, even better, not to speak at all – to avoid distracting Lucìa. Because something akin to a zoom call, but with millions of attendees, was about to begin.

'Four minutes left.'

A text arrived.

Oh, I forgot to switch it off! she thought.

It was her father: *Luci, I didn't tell you an important thing the other day: as long as you are true to yourself, you will always be fine.*

He had asked someone to translate the message into English. How cute of him, she thought.

'Three minutes left.'

Hugh opened the door without knocking first. Lucìa startled, cast him a threatening glance, only to relax when he said: 'We're all here if you need anything. Should I serve the prosecco now or after the debate?'

'Two minutes left.'

Too anxious to focus on anything, Lucìa spent sixty seconds thoughtless. She looked outside the window, the enclosed nature of Edgbaston Park reassuring her.

'One minute left.'

As often happened to her under stress, *you-know-who* suddenly appeared before her. She endeavoured not to allow him to be a distraction from the debate now starting.

Nineteen-hundred hours: the emcee asked Vincent d'Amont his first question.

'Why should people vote to unify France and Germany under Charlemagny and outside the European Union?'

Staring at the camera, Vincent d'Amont launched into one of his signature tirades. No need to warm up – straight to the point.

'Because this is no longer a Union. We should call it European Anarchy. Only France and Germany are trying to protect the continent, defend its traditions and build a stable future. The others don't have a vision for the future. They have just one goal: milk us. Look at Italy: always begging for money. Spain: they can barely keep the country united. Poland: it's a dictatorship. France and Germany are not in good company. I believe we are different from the others – that's the truth. It's time to quit Europe!'

He paused for a second to suggest gravitas, then continued.

'Victor Hugo once wrote that France and Germany are essentially Europe ... French and Germans are brothers in the past, brothers in the present, brothers in the future. Well, it's time for France and Germany to acknowledge their brother-hood and celebrate their joint roots by uniting under the powerful flag of Charlemagny.'

He had conveniently omitted the bit where Victor Hugo said that France was the brain of Europe while Germany was the heart, as he was unsure sure that this would go down well with the Germans. He then gave the quickest peep at the people's reaction on the dashboard. Much to his dismay, the response was positive, yes, but not outstanding. People were still tepid.

Then Miss Cliché spoke. 'Victor Hugo also said something completely different,' she contended. 'He openly promoted the creation of the United States of Europe, a place where different European nations could live side by side, in peace and progress. Victor Hugo was a wise and far-sighted man, and his words are still current. The idea of tearing Europe apart is dangerous – we're stronger if we stay united!'

Despite her enthusiasm and motivation, Miss Cliché had a feeling the debate would be an uphill slog. Too many Europeans tended to take the achievements of the Union for granted – for instance, the longest period of peace ever in what had been called the Dark Continent, and the freedom for people to move without borders.

As Professor Sherwood had once pointed out to her, Europe couldn't rely on shared myths or cultural symbols to unite citizens from different countries. Many still saw the European Union merely as an economy-driven aggregation of member states acting selfishly, unable to share a common vision for the future. It wasn't entirely true, though. Europe had great merits, the first of which was the creation of a large territorial realm based on agreement, diplomacy, democracy, and not on the prevailing of the strong over the weak or dependent on military force – as had happened in the preceding millennia.

Lucìa should now make her best effort to reiterate this truth before an unprecedented audience.

A commercial banner appeared to promote ROME's newest feature: a parental tracking tool to monitor children's routine around the clock up to the age of eighteen. *Where they go, who they see, what they watch.*

'What can Europe still offer to France and Germany?' was the first question for Miss Cliché.

'Europe can still offer much' – Miss Cliché was positive. 'But this shouldn't be the only question we ask ourselves. Europe can't just be interpreted in terms of an immediate trade-off between the Union and each individual country. We should also ask ourselves what Europeans can achieve by working together to promote European values globally.'

'I note that Miss Cliché thinks we should *export* democracy. This is an old strategy that has never paid off,' interrupted Vincent d'Amont by misinterpreting her answer deliberately. 'We have a double problem here. One: if we try to install democracy in another country, we fail. Two: Europe continues to be invaded by foreigners coming here to spread terror, even after receiving one of our passports. The Union has failed in promoting Western values abroad and in protecting European borders. Who can deny this? So, it's time for each country to take care of itself.'

Vincent d'Amont looked at the screen to gauge ROME's live reaction. He was starting to stir people up. A clear improvement. He quickly adjusted his hair.

Another ad was now on display. *Encourage a friend to vote on Charlemagny and earn a voucher worth 5 virtual sesterces, redeemable online!*

ROME rewarded proselytism.

'Vincent d'Amont: tell us more about Charlemagny. What flag will your country wave?'

'The flag of Charlemagny should portray the Eagle, symbol of Germany, and the Cockerel, symbol of France, to celebrate the glorious past of our countries. The background should be white to symbolise a new beginning.'

'What anthem will you sing?'

'When I speak to people, they often mention a song, "Göttingen", once performed by Barbara, a young French singer. This song struck a chord with our people. I particularly like the line that says *"Mais les enfants ce sont les mêmes, à Paris ou à Göttingen."* It would make a great anthem for Charlemagny.'

'What currency will your people spend?'

'If France had the Franc and Germany had the Mark, we shall have the Carl!' he answered.

Half of the virtual audience applauded Vincent d'Amont, while the other mocked him for his pipe dreams. It was fine, as long as his answers didn't leave people unmoved. There's no such thing as bad publicity, he thought.

'Why should Europe keep subsidising member countries despite the reported cases of corruption?' Miss Cliché was asked, a question mirroring the fact that many in France and Germany were far from happy that their countries paid more to the European budget than they received in return.

'We're family,' she replied. 'We should share our resources. There can be real union in Europe only if the wealthiest help the less well-off to make their societies stronger. Disparities and resentment among countries will otherwise grow. We must avoid looking at our own backyard alone. It's in each European nation's interest that the surrounding countries keep improving their standard of living. We need to help when we can.'

'That was good,' Hugh whispered to the others. 'She has the rare ability of sounding soft-spoken but not over-emotional.'

ROME's live reaction to Lucìa's words was very brisk. An annoyed Vincent d'Amont rushed to bite back at her.

'We're all tired of hearing your sermons,' he provoked. 'If southern and eastern European countries used their money responsibly, instead of squandering it, France and Germany would be more than glad to continue helping them.'

He then deployed a second argument against the idea of European solidarity.

'Given the difficult times, we should first concentrate on us, and only after should we look at others. When an airplane is taxiing to the take-off position, you are always told: "In the event of an emergency, put your oxygen mask on first." The hostess is not encouraging you to be selfish; she's simply acknowledging that you are only able to help others if you take care of yourself first.'

Forever free from internet addiction with our three-week online rehab treatment, boasted the next ad.

Very early in the debate, Miss Cliché had realised that Vincent d'Amont's strategy included patronising her – for instance by belittling her answers, something that couldn't go on. A line in the sand needed to be drawn. So, after he had spoken about the future of a Union without France and Germany, Miss Cliché waded in with both feet.

'I'm surprised that you still pretend not to understand, Vincent. Europe is the only way to overcome all the greatest dangers to our future as humans. First, the decline of the

Earth's health needs to be reversed urgently, and this cannot be done at the national level. Then there is the serious threat to our freedom posed by digital bogeymen. Not to mention the warring ambitions of many countries outside Europe, which must be dealt with by all Europeans, working together.'

She took a breath, then resumed. Confronting Vincent wasn't easy for her.

'The European Union alone holds the mass, power and strength to save us from an uncertain future; not France and Germany on their own, even if united under a single flag. So, it's irresponsible for you to even suggest that France and Germany should abandon Europe.'

They cheered and shouted in the newsroom. Very ballsy, thought Hugh. Viewers, who craved confrontation, had a similarly excited reaction. Vincent d'Amont didn't like her answer. So when asked about the first action that a newly established Charlemagny should undertake, he began another of his rants.

'I've no doubt – Charlemagny will close all borders to those that don't have the means to live decently. No more free passes for refugees, no more subsidies for beggars. There's no need to build a wall or fence; we have the technological tools available to track people and make them leave when necessary. This is what Switzerland has always done and nobody ever questions Swiss diplomacy.'

Appalled, Miss Cliché immediately responded that multiculturalism enhanced society, while shutting doors to people just because they had a different skin colour or lacked wealth was barbaric. Vincent d'Amont, however, had a ready answer: 'You're saying this because you don't live in a Paris *banlieue* and haven't been assaulted by migrants in a German square on New Year's Eve. It's easy to be radical chic when others are bearing the burden of multiculturalism.'

Even for the fair-playing Miss Cliché, this was far too much.

'And why would I be radical chic, if I may ask? I'm a countryside girl proud of her roots. And there's nothing radical in saying that we should all look beyond the tip of our nose when discussing Europe and that there are common causes that call all countries to work together. Now that you've made it personal, I've a question for you: do you believe that talking to people's bellies as you always do is something noble … ?

'So, it's you who judges what's noble and what's not,' Vincent d'Amont interrupted. 'Whoever shares your ideas is right, anyone who thinks differently is wrong; what a mature approach. Congrats!'

Viewers were enthralled by what had become an authentic duel. Both opponents were now freely breaching the strictest rule imposed on the debate – that of not interrupting. The digital emcee was too clever to stop them.

'Nobody is capitalising more on the idea of Charlemagny than you,' Vincent d'Amont insisted, knowing he was touching a nerve in her.

'What do you mean?' she replied, incredulous.

'Yes. Your vlog has tripled its viewers since we started our battle to make Charlemagny reality. You've profited from our efforts. You should pay us royalties.'

Miss Cliché was baffled. Yet, despite him having deliberately insulted her, she didn't want to fall into his trap. The cause of Europe deserved better. So, she veered back to the core of the debate.

'Welcoming new people in Europe means learning new languages, cultures, even cuisines,' she said. 'In this sense, it makes all of us richer.'

'This is utter bunk,' he interrupted. 'Should we really accept hundreds of thousands of Cambodian migrants just to enjoy more Cambodian food? Or should we trade a few beheadings for more colourful ethnic restaurants?'

Lucìa had already heard those specific words. It took barely more than an instant to remember where. Then, a searing fear edged its way through her, the painful suspicion that someone very close might have breached her trust. She made a great effort to dispel the mounting concern.

No, it can't be, Lucìa tried to convince herself.

But it was a vain effort, for she soon had to accept the accuracy of her fears. 'We're allowing other cultures to endanger us in the very name of European multicultural- ism!' Vincent d'Amont yelled. 'France and Germany need to defend themselves!'

Lucìa was sure that Professor Sherwood had pronounced those same lines during their moot sessions. It couldn't be a coincidence.

A stabbing grief, a jarring sense of loss, a daunting confu- sion, all suddenly struck Lucìa. She was glad for having refused, days earlier, the outrageous proposal from ROME to show her heartbeat live during the debate. Spiralling fast into gloom, Lucìa felt as if she was hiding a panic attack from millions of people – a very tough task.

Vincent d'Amont seemed instead jubilant and repeated his slogans obsessively.

'Once out of Europe, we'll be free from foolish rules on bendy bananas!'

'We must stop this suicidal attempt to replace Christian children with adults from other civilisations, with migrants!'

'France and Germany are rich: we've everything to gain from Charlemagny!'

Lucìa stood silent. She let him ramble for interminable minutes. As with the appearance on Radio Gallique, Vincent was now mastering the show in his typical thunderous fashion. Vincent's ratings were spiking.

She tried to front him, but cluelessly. 'Vincent ... It's not as you say,' she began, struggling to find the right words 'You're wrong ... because ...'

Miss Cliché's newsroom watched in shock. They didn't understand why Lucìa had suddenly gone blank and was allowing him to steal the scene with such ease. More than one wondered whether she had run out of ideas.

It wasn't that Lucìa lacked an answer to Vincent's slogans. On the contrary, she had countered them hundreds of times during the moot debates. But the issue was exactly that: Lucìa didn't want to use any of the arguments devised with the professor. For her, it was tainted material. She had to look for new inspiration within herself. Aware that she couldn't afford to give up, Lucìa closed her eyes, gathered all her forces, then interrupted Vincent: 'Enough with propaganda!'

He fell silent, surprised.

'Only Europe has sufficient clout to lead the world,' Lucìa said. 'Humanity is facing giant threats and a single country, even a large one, will never be able to save us. Together, we can. With all their differences, the countries of Europe have grown much closer in these years of peace. So, it is realistic to believe in further integration, in more solidarity, in an *ever-closer Union*.'

Vincent screwed up his face. He was about to interrupt her, but Lucìa didn't allow it. 'Closing the gates of Europe isn't a solution,' she pointed out. 'Billions of individuals already live in unbearable conditions and global warming is bound to worsen the situation. Hiding behind European borders isn't a sustainable strategy. You cannot isolate Europe forever. The duty of Europe is to provide people from needy countries with the tools necessary to improve their conditions: healthcare, education, and financial resources above all. I believe we can make it!'

An overwhelmingly enthusiastic reaction burst out on ROME. Even without watching the ratings, Lucìa felt she had found the right words to save the debate.

The digital emcee called the end.

'You're a star!' Hugh told Lucìa when she left her office.

The excited Miss Cliché team started to clap their hands. The debate was now in the past. As often happens when everything is said and done, they all experienced a feeling of empty relief. Nobody knew who the experts would shortly declare as the winner, but it had to be a very close call. For sure, nothing could be done at this stage other than enjoying a moment of well-deserved, prosecco-fuelled unwinding.

An unusually chilled Hugh was chatting with the new Danish intern. He didn't normally open up to colleagues, especially to the greener ones, but the fatigue, the prosecco and the pent-up stress from the debate all prompted him to show his friendliest side.

'I'm not saying this out of flattery,' the intern had just confessed, 'but when I learned I'd be joining Miss Cliché, I couldn't believe it. A dream coming true! I adore Lucìa for what she has achieved as a woman.'

'Many aspiring vloggers long to work at Miss Cliché,' Hugh said with a proud smile. 'Just to give you an idea: we receive roughly three thousand applications every week from all around the world. So you should consider yourself very fortunate.'

The intern nodded in excited approval. 'Miss Cliché often breaks the news before all the others,' she pointed out with pride.

'True, but we also need to give credit to our Pandora for that.'

'Pandora?'

'Yes.' Hugh replied. 'Pandora allows us, with her special algorithms, to find information inaccessible to others. Pandora was first created by our guru Professor Sherwood with Lucìa and a team of developers when they worked at the European Parliament. Without Pandora, we wouldn't break the news so often.'

'Huh … intriguing.'

'Yes. I can give you an example,' he said in a vaguely smug tone. 'Perhaps you remember when Miss Cliché revealed to the world what had happened to the fashion designer Armandino?'

'Yes, everybody talked about Armandino's *resurrection*!'

'Two weeks after the crash in the Caribbean Sea, the bodies of all three passengers were still missing,' Hugh recalled. 'Given the depth of the sea around the crash point, it wasn't surprising that the dives for the bodies had been useless. They had found only the empty wreck of the helicopter. That's when Lucìa decided to unleash Pandora. She began to scan, deep down to every remote corner. Even though she didn't find anything for days, Pandora kept browsing and browsing. We'd almost forgotten about the search when, late one night, the initial results arrived.'

Hugh looked at the girl with a suspenseful stare, then added: 'We learned something quite puzzling about the pilot involved in the crash. He wasn't the same pilot who usually flew that helicopter. The flight registry at the airport of Saint Lucìa, where the helicopter had taken off from for its last trip, reported another name; most likely a made-up one, as Pandora was unable to find any licensed pilot in the world bearing that name.'

As he spoke, cheerful colleagues were patting him on the shoulders, offering to refill his glass. He smiled back.

'Pandora's deep scanning of the net then brought other useful info to the surface,' Hugh continued. 'Her searches with the land registries in all of Europe revealed that Armandino had donated two properties – a large villa in Tuscany and a two-storey flat in Paris – to his relatives in the previous year. This typically occurs when the person knows that they'll soon experience an important change, or that they'll die.

'Back then, I was sceptical. I didn't see enough material to question his death. But Lucìa was of a different opinion; she thought something didn't add up. Before I even had time to voice my thoughts, Miss Cliché had already launched an exclusive investigation into Armandino. Lucìa can be very instinctive, you know.'

He chuckled, and the intern chuckled too.

'For some reason, people like to believe that celebrities never die or – if they really have to – die by murder,' he observed. 'So, the story of Armandino's killing was welcomed by the media. News-seekers were pestering his relatives and friends, digging into his past, endeavouring to learn more about his partner, with him on the helicopter. People talked of nothing else. Rumours of all sorts circulated, including that his mysterious death was linked to a mountain of debt plaguing his fashion business. No surprise that the share value of the group plunged. The situation had spun out of control.

'Then the sun rose again,' said an animated Hugh. 'Armandino came back to the light. He shocked the world with a video interview with Lucìa where he explained the reason for his disappearance. He confessed to Lucìa that he had staged his own death to start a new hidden life in the Bolivian mountains and escape the pressures of fame. With them both speaking Italian during the live interview, it was like being at the opera. This marvellous scoop gained Lucìa more than one award.'

'Yes! We discussed the Armandino case for our graduate diploma in vlogging,' the Danish intern, trying to impress Hugh, confirmed.

'We are now working on cyber-enabled terror,' Hugh continued, moving the half-empty glass. 'Tracing contributions to hate groups has become very hard, as terrorists now receive donations from one-off cryptocurrency addresses, erased immediately after use to guarantee anonymity. Pandora is trying to unveil one of these funding flows. You wouldn't believe how much precious information is lying there, on the net, long forgotten – in social media, public records, financial databases. A true bonanza, just waiting to be trawled.'

If her interview with the designer Armandino had drawn accolades from critics and fans alike, the debate with Vincent d'Amont was an all-time professional high for Miss Cliché. She was now the most famous vlogger in Europe. Yet Lucìa was half celebrating, half mourning. She chatted with the team, forcing herself to smile, and even made a short speech to praise their hard work – in which she warned that Charlemagny's threat was still looming large, and so all hands should remain on deck. It wasn't time to back down yet. *We mustn't take our foot off the throat of the beast* was her battle cry.

When the queue of those wishing to compliment her had thinned out, Lucìa went back to her office. She locked the door. People still buzzed around outside, yet inside was calm. Sitting at her desk, Lucìa looked around. Her eyes fell on a group of framed pictures lined up on the desk, including a cheerful selfie with Rachel in Brussels that made her smile. Then, glancing at the crowded bookshelf on the opposite wall, she singled out the title etched on a book's spine: *The Italian Genius*. By Liam Sherwood.

It was the professor's ode to Italy. The book tried to reconstruct the development of the Italian culture from the Middle Ages onwards. In a study of remarkable breadth, the professor examined the roles of landscape, art, poetry, music, regional divisions, and the medieval conflict between papacy and empire in shaping the most genial traits of Italians. It wasn't just a eulogy, though: his work recognised political servitude and intellectual alignment – alas – as recurring features on the peninsula. The book, and its accurate depiction of how most Italians think and behave, had contributed to her early intellectual crush on the professor.

Lucìa had to know why he had done what he had done.

By tradition, the professor wasn't open to receiving calls. When someone wanted to get in touch, they had to send an email. He would call back, if and when available. But Thelma was reachable most of the time, even in Oxfordshire – where the professor spent his mornings alone, reading or writing in his studio, while she tended the garden. They passed their evenings together in the drawing room.

'We've just watched your debate. You were astounding!' Thelma exclaimed. She then showered Lucìa with praise for a good five minutes. Finally, the professor took over.

'I'm so proud of you, Lucìa,' he said. 'You didn't let him intimidate you …'

Lucìa let the professor finish, but then stunned him with her words.

'I think you should be ashamed of yourself.'

There was silence at the other end.

'I know you double-crossed me … I just don't understand why.'

'Lucìa, I think you are completely misunderstanding what happened,' he replied in a mortified tone.

'So, please, tell me,' said Lucìa, as she struggled to hold her tears back.

'Last week, Vincent d'Amont contacted me,' the professor began. 'He made a ludicrous request: that I compose a speech for him to deploy at the debate. He had enjoyed our conversations as fellow MEPs in Brussels and thought I would be able to provide him with the right language to advocate Charlemagny and persuade the undecideds.'

Lucìa listened carefully to his every word. She wanted the professor to say something that might make him look less compromised. In confronting her, Vincent had used, word for word, the same arguments the professor had deployed during the mock debates while sparring with Lucìa. It couldn't be a coincidence; he had ghost-written Vincent's answers. But why?

The professor loathed the idea of Charlemagny and would give his life for the cause of Europe. It couldn't be for money: he wasn't greedy, and nor did he have any urgent financial needs, at least not that she was aware of.

'At first, I laughed at his audacity in asking me to help him,' the professor said. 'Suggesting that I would help him defend the cause of Charlemagny? Hogwash. But then ... I realised that Vincent d'Amont was offering me the incredible opportunity to put in practice the theory I have tried to prove for years: that two very antithetical political stances can both find solid and logical foundations.'

Lucìa struggled to fathom the professor's reasoning. She stayed silent.

'I could create solid arguments in defence of Charlemagny for Vincent d'Amont, while, in parallel, prepare worthy counterarguments against Charlemagny for you during our rehearsals. I could have each of you representing an anti-thetical political stance and forge arguments to demonstrate that both stances are equally sustainable. I knew my dialec-tical work had to be meticulous, so that no disposition for or against Charlemagny could prevail over the other: the debate had to become the triumph of political relativism.'

'That's why you encouraged me so much to join the debate,' a disillusioned Lucìa replied.

'No. I knew that, deep in your heart, you wanted to challenge Vincent d'Amont, but that you just didn't feel self-confident enough. That's why I suggested you accept the offer – because I believed the debate would heal your insecurities.'

Her growing anger towards the professor gave Lucìa the strength to confront him further. 'You've toyed with

Charlemagny only to prove your academic theories, Professor. But this isn't a laboratory, it's real life. What if Charlemagny prevails because the words you put in Vincent d'Amont's mouth are more persuasive than mine?'

'Impossible. He repeated the exact words I had written for him. Likewise, you clung to what we had agreed you would say. The debate will be a tie, with no winner. The very essence of political relativism.'

The professor's own defence was clever but fell short of satisfying Lucìa. Instead of helping her to beat Vincent d'Amont, he had focused on proving a theory that, even if true, was supposed to exist in books, not in actual life. What was the point of experimenting with political science at the dire risk of throwing Europe, or even worse, the entire world, into a prolonged period of disorder? Lucìa already knew she could never forgive him for taking such a reckless gamble with the lives of future generations.

'I'm really in no mood for your excuses!' Lucìa yelled, never so close to a show of disrespect for the professor. 'You betrayed Europe, you've thrown away everything you have done. I don't want to hear from you ever. You're a ghost to me, now!'

* * *

While Lucìa was uttering her final goodbye to Professor Sherwood, Vincent and Emmanuelle left Colmar. There was no reason to remain. As predicted, Vincent had exchanged only a few words with his parents during the entire stay. On the way back to Paris, he received a call.

'You did well this evening,' the usual caller began.

'You had doubts?'

'I didn't know what to expect. With you, it's always a bouncing, back and forth, a helter-skelter ... you're unpredictable.'

'This is why people like me. I'm spontaneous. I know you would prefer me tamed and well behaved ... but that's not who I am.'

Emmanuelle looked at Vincent with a hint of jealousy. He looked back at her with a reassuring expression.

'Somebody from Miss Cliché's camp has been going around Berlin asking questions,' the caller added. Vincent hummed. They were using a next-generation hack-proof device for their conversation – Israeli-made, state-of-the-art technology that could prevent the tapping or tracking of calls. Hackers would find a way to work around it in three or four months, but for now the privacy of their calls was safeguarded.

'Miss Cliché is also hunting for Employee Zero,' the caller continued.

'This isn't good,' Vincent replied. He then added, this time in the German learned in his Alsatian years: 'We need to be careful. If they find out about the Almighty ...'

Vincent stopped short of mentioning that, ten minutes earlier, France Souveraine had got in touch with him. He had been literally beseeched to meet the troika that same night – the three long-time party members that had taken over the reins of France Souveraine years earlier, when Dom Natale had decided to step down. They now ruled unchallenged over the party.

The troika couldn't stand Vincent. He was seen as an ambitious man, guilty of disrespecting established hierarchies, fortunate enough to have been Dom Natale's protégé. Above all, they couldn't accept how this marketer-turned-politician had skipped the *cursus honorum* of politics to start conveniently from the top. The troika had always worked to ostracise Vincent. Rumour had it they had even plotted behind the scenes of the Cabeille case to end his career.

The distrust was mutual: people like them were the very reason why Vincent loathed political parties. He knew that Dom Natale, a self-made businessman, had always nurtured a similar feeling, and only reluctantly had taken on board professional politicians. 'I was forced to, Vincent,' Natale had told him once. 'I need the support of these damn fogeys.' A broken clock was right twice a day, though, and despite the ongoing friction Vincent decided to meet the troika. He was at a stage where he needed allies more than foes.

After dropping off Emmanuelle, who had barely spoken on the journey back from Colmar, Vincent took a Cabeille to meet the troika in a hotel close to the magnificent, but hardly secretive, Tuileries Palace. Regardless of the fact they saw themselves as staunch populists, they would never have chosen a location outside the premier arrondissement.

The oldest of the three was Monastère. A fervid Catholic with strong ties to the ultra-conservative hierarchies of the Church – with whom he shared reactionary convictions in matters such as gay rights and freedom of choice – Monastère had been in the French Parliament for over twenty-five years representing the Avignon constituency. His platform also included bringing the papacy back to France.

Monastère's favourite quote was 'Everything must change so that everything can stay the same' – by Tancredi Falconeri, the Sicilian nobleman in Giuseppe Tomasi di Lampedusa's *The Leopard*. For Monastère, indeed, the past held the merit of being charted territory, while the future was ghastly and uncertain. He thus believed that men should stay away from social or moral innovations, for these would sooner or later lead them astray.

The conservatism of Monastère expressed itself in petty matters, too: for instance, he always ordered *une noisette* and *un croissant* at the *buvette* of the National Assembly, with no exceptions in a quarter of a century. Whenever someone in France Souveraine proposed a modification to the party policies, they could count on Monastère voting against this change. A sure bet. He had always succeeded in wearing down the occasional would-be reformers within the party.

Vache was another troika member. He was that fat, and his face so plump, that people needed a larger screen to zoom-call him. Vache often flashed a wide smile that, joining his round-ish appearance, helped endear him to most people, inside and outside the party.

Well-informed sources reported that his aura of gentleness was deceptive, for Vache was the most ferocious of the three. An often-mentioned example of his ruthlessness was the time he'd privately encouraged a colleague to run for party chairman after Dom Natale's resignation. When the colleague, relying on Vache's support, announced his candidacy, in an outrageous twist Vache denounced his colleague as inexperienced for the role. 'There is a season for everything,' had been his dogmatic comment. If Monastère wore his opponents down by attrition, Vache stabbed them in the back with an amiable smile.

Sibille completed the troika. The most taciturn of the three, he was also the sharpest. Sometimes Sibille concentrated so hard in processing his thoughts, with his eyes glazed, that people thought he was on the verge of dozing off. This was a long way from the truth.

There was a funny story attached to his stilted conversation. A woman sitting next to him at an official dinner had reportedly told Sibille that she would get at least three simple words out of him during the dinner. Without even looking at her, he commented: 'You lose.'

Sibille had never wanted to run in an election and had likewise refused all the appointments offered. Acknowledging that he would never be a great communicator to the masses, he preferred to act behind the scenes. For this reason, and despite the ideological differences, a French journalist had once most appropriately referred to Sibille as the transalpine Deng Xiaoping.

* * *

One hour before the meeting with Vincent, the troika had convened in the hotel room. They had to agree on their position vis-à-vis their long-term foe.

Vache was the first to speak.

'Gentlemen, I suggested we should meet with Vincent d'Amont because I believe he is giving all of us a lesson in realpolitik.'

Monastère looked at him with palpable surprise. Sibille listened with an impassive countenance.

'Let me explain better.' Vache feared he would be misinterpreted. 'When Vincent d'Amont came out with the outlandish idea of Charlemagny, we laughed at his crazy project, and we thanked God he was no longer a member of France Souveraine.'

Monastère wondered why Vache had to use the name of the Creator for such an earthly matter.

'Then the media started to mention Charlemagny every other day,' continued Vache. 'So, we had to recognise that, despite his wild way of thinking, d'Amont was silver-tongued and knew the pulse of the country.'

Monastère, unimpressed, kept staring at him.

'Now, we've tried everything to stop this folly, but there's a high chance that people will vote for Charlemagny.'

'It's a vote on a platform – come on – not an official referendum,' Monastère interjected.

'Please allow me to finish,' Vache responded. 'I know that you still use the telegraph at home, Monastère, but the world has moved on …'

Sibille, listening in silence, cast a diplomatic smile. Monastère glowered at Vache, who carried on anyway.

'As you know, we have been informed that more than one in the German Cabinet doesn't abhor the idea of Charlemagny. Our left-leaning government is, of course, strictly against Charlemagny. My fear is that, if we align our position with that of the French leftists, people will no longer see the difference between them and us.'

'The leftists can be right, once in a lifetime,' Monastère observed, merely for the sake of contradicting his colleague.

'Yes, that may be,' Vache replied, 'but we should consider a plan B in case our people's clamour for Charlemagny becomes unbearable. Voters already stop me in the street to ask why we are so against creating a superpower with Germany.'

'Maybe because our party's name isn't Charlemagny Souverain?' Monastère replied ironically.

Sibille, meanwhile, was staring at the gilded ceiling of the hotel room.

'Politics has changed,' Vache insisted. 'Once, people respected politicians. We could steer them in the direction that suited us. But in the digital era, it's us who need to adapt our policies to people's demands. It's a sad but undeniable truth. If people ask for bread, you no longer can say "*qu'ils mangent de la brioche*".'

'We need to be careful, *mon cher*,' warned Monastère. 'If we show complacency towards Charlemagny, we may gain *some* visibility, but at the cost of alienating our nationalist base – the very same voters who allow us to sit in Parliament. Sooner or later, people will forget Charlemagny – trust me – but they will always remember our betrayal of French sovereignty.'

'Please don't tell me, *mon ami*,' retorted Vache, 'that you are happy with our party's situation. We've been stuck between four and six per cent of the votes for the last twenty years, each time congratulating ourselves over a few more decimal points gained, or collapsing in despair because of a lost seat in a rural constituency. We need ideas, or we will gradually shrink to nothing. Vincent d'Amont may be mad, but he has plenty of ideas.'

'Yes, including the idea of Germany absorbing France,' Monastère countered. 'This is precisely the thing no Charlemagnier in France wants to accept: that Charlemagny wouldn't be a unification of equals. They're more numerous than us, wealthier than us, better organised than us. During German reunification, the mighty West reached out a hand to the weaker East only because they were brothers sharing the same blood. We cannot say the same for France. We antagonised Germany for a thousand years and punished them at every available opportunity; do you really believe they will fail to take this chance to neutralise us?'

'It hurts me to say this, Monastère – you're a great politician, but sometimes entrenched in the past,' Vache argued. 'If conflict is looming, it's not between France and Germany. The threats are coming from outside Europe. Look at China, India, even Africa. Fearing a German Fourth Reich is a bit of a stretch, in my opinion.'

Vache paused, then looked at the third member of the troika.

'Sibille, you're even quieter than usual. How do you see it?'

Sibille shut his eyes, breathed slowly, then opened the eyes again.

The Oracle is ready to speak, thought Monastère, not without a pinch of sarcasm.

'We are getting overexcited, *mes amis*,' began Sibille, who held the casting vote when the other two disagreed, as often happened. 'Politics is a chess game. We need to be calm and patient. Do you remember, Vache, when you desperately wanted to see repealed that nonsensical law that made it illegal to ask people about their race or religion? For a time, our fight seemed lost. You almost cried; I remember that. In the end, we won: the law was removed from the statutes. Now, as then, it is only a matter of planning properly, without being taken hostage by our emotions.'

Vache and Monastère looked at each other. The placid aura around Sibille was making the tension in the room ebb away.

'So, what do we know?' continued Sibille. 'First, we know that there is no way to block the vote on Charlemagny. We tried all avenues, but in vain. Second, we know that people will most likely vote in favour of Charlemagny. And, most importantly, we know that, even if allowed, Vincent d'Amont is not up to the task of creating Charlemagny.'

'But Sibille, what shall we do in practice?' asked a disoriented Monastère.

'We shall let Vincent do all the work for us,' answered Sibille. 'If Charlemagny fails, everything will remain the same as it is now. But if Charlemagny wins and the people rise to demand a unification, then we shall take the baton from there.'

'How can we ever endorse Charlemagny when we stated in public, just days ago, that Vincent d'Amont is endangering the French Constitution with this vote?' Monastère insisted.

Sibille seemed untouched by the scepticism of Monastère.

'It all depends on the perspective from which you look at the picture,' he observed. 'Certainly, Vincent d'Amont is endangering our beloved Constitution with his initiative; and he should pay for it.'

There was a *but*. 'Nonetheless, if the people decide to embrace Charlemagny, it will mean that our Constitution, although valuable and dear to us, is no longer able to reflect in full the sentiments of our nation. Who are we to go against the voice of our people? The Constitution is not written in stone.'

Superb, Vache thought. Sibille was implying that France Souveraine shouldn't necessarily be positioned against Charlemagny forever. Public opinion would ultimately take the responsibility in deciding whether to censor or ratify Charlemagny. France Souveraine had just to align itself with the people's will.

Monastère was less excited, but he couldn't deny the shrewdness in Sibille's reasoning, which let him look at the possibility of accepting Charlemagny with less of a sense of guilt.

The troika didn't have time to discuss their strategy further, though, for there came a sharp thud at the door.

IX

Lemongrass Risotto

Debata zakończyła się bez zwycięzcy!
 Miss Cliché ja Vincent: mikä tappelu!
 Charlemagny: wie gaat er winnen?

The following morning, European media reported an altogether unexpected result: the debate between Vincent d'Amont and Miss Cliché had ended in a tie. After heated arguments all night, indeed, the expert jury had surrendered to the conclusion that no outright winner could be called. This outcome didn't necessarily signify that people would choose for Europe on voting day; on the contrary, pundits believed that Charlemagny had higher chances of winning, as recent surveys in both countries seemed to testify.

With an eye on the news, Rachel was having breakfast at the Matesanz. A call to Holger had gone straight to voice-mail. As he didn't do mornings, someone else was behind the counter.

A lone customer sat at the next table.

'Would you please *pass* me the sugar?'

Rachel distractedly handed him the sugar pourer.

'You don't know me, *Misss*, but I know you.'

Rachel looked at him askance.

'Let me please introduce myself. My name is Bernardo Madeira.'

Rachel wondered what was happening with Berliners, approaching women at every opportunity. Italians used to be the ones hitting on women all the time and everywhere. Madeira, who incidentally would have very much enjoyed flirting with her, said: 'You work for the *Wall Street Journal* and are a close friend of *Miss* Cliché.'

'And so?' Rachel replied, uneasy. Madeira was well informed, but also disquietingly intrusive.

'I know Employee Zero in person,' Madeira added. Failing to get a reaction from her, he added, 'The man you've been asking questions about for *daysss*.'

Rachel stared at him, perplexed. For once, she didn't know what to say.

'I consider myself to be a close friend of his. Perhaps one of the very few *friendsss* he still has. And when a friend *askss* me a favour, I cannot say no,' Madeira pointed out solemnly.

'What can I do for you?' she asked.

'He wants to give an exclusive interview to *Miss* Cliché. He has something, let's say, very important to share.'

It seemed an odd request.

'Why aren't you contacting Lucìa directly?'

'It's more complicated than that, Rachel. Nobody can know anything about the interview before it's live.' He then widened his large eyes for effect. 'I don't want to sound melo-dramatic, but my friend's life is at *ssstake*.'

Not really knowing what to say, Rachel got straight to the point. 'Okay, Madeira. How can we contact Employee Zero?'

'This morning, somebody left an electronic device at the reception of *Miss* Cliché. They'll be able to communicate safely through the device. He will be waiting online for her today at five p.m. sharp, Birmingham time. He's very punctual. She must be, too.'

'Wait – please, slow down. Why should we trust you? How can I be sure that this device is safe?'

Madeira glanced at her with sympathy. He did seem to be acting in good faith, or perhaps it was just that: acting.

'Rachel, we're asking for a display of trust from *Miss* Cliché,' he replied in a clerical tone. 'I wouldn't risk my own reputation if the intentions of Employee Zero were *less* than honourable. *Miss* Cliché has everything to gain from this interview; it'll count more than yesterday's debate.' Madeira then assumed a peremptory attitude. 'You know, he's her only real chance to stop Charlemagny.'

Without allowing Rachel to utter another word, he stood up, bowed politely, and said: 'If it's not *Miss* Cliché, I'm sure Amanda Arnaud will be happy to do the interview.'

Madeira walked away – after insisting that the device delivered in the morning should now be the only point of contact between Miss Cliché and Employee Zero.

Rachel was left speechless. She didn't know what to make of this surreal conversation. The first instinct was to check out Madeira on her tablet – where she learned that he was an established TV producer. Still, she couldn't guarantee the authenticity of these sources, let alone the man's good intentions. It's her choice, ultimately, Rachel thought. So, she called Lucìa, and described her conversation with Madeira down to the last titbit.

'Yes, I received something this morning,' confirmed Lucìa. 'The police have checked: it's safe.'

Lucìa wasn't sure as to what lay behind Employee Zero's urgent request for an interview. One thing she did know, though: nothing could justify denying a voice to Employee Zero and leaving him prey to Amanda Arnaud.

* * *

In Paris, Vincent d'Amont felt in a position of unprecedented strength. His vis-à-vis with the troika had resulted in a most unanticipated outcome, with them offering him the chance to re-join France Souveraine as a fourth troika member. On hearing the proposal, Vincent had even entertained the idea – if only for a couple of seconds. But he wasn't interested in revisiting the stale logic of political parties. Protocols, red tape, quarrels, jealousy, vetoes; he had been through so much of that rigmarole in his previous life. Furthermore, a four-man troika was one too many.

When still in France Souveraine, Vincent had tried to pitch his innovative ideas to the party, but had received only derision. Now, unsettled by the widespread reaction to the Charlemagny vote, the troika were aiming to jump on Vincent's bandwagon. The old farts have smelled the coffee too late, he thought.

At the last minute, Vincent had decided not to meet them in person. On his way to the hotel, he had feared a booby trap like the one the French Foreign Minister had recently fallen into in Strasbourg. So, after a U-turn back home, he'd had one of his hack-proof Israeli devices sent to their room for a video call.

'I need time to consider your proposal' was his bluff. Vincent had found no reason to create additional friction with an outright refusal during the call. He still didn't know what he would do after the vote. It could be Madeira's series on Metropolis, or some other idea. For sure, regardless of the result, he would keep pursuing Charlemagny.

Albeit in a very different manner, Miss Cliché also dreamed of a new country. Hers would occupy a larger territory, ranging from the taiga forests gleaming under the northern lights of Lapland to the blood-orange groves that flourished in the scorched plains of Sicily, extending from the volcanic Azores archipelago floating in the Atlantic to rocky Cyprus, nestled cosily in the Mediterranean Sea.

Lucìa's country would merge cultures, speak in many tongues, practise manifold religions, yes – but people would live together in balanced harmony and selfless solidarity. Because the people of Europe, despite all their differences, had slowly built up a sense of unity and shared responsibilities. The undeniable bond, matured over the centuries, would be the precious seed from which to establish a closer union in Europe.

Had the divisions between the multitude of former German kingdoms, duchies and principalities barred them from ripening into what was now a united Germany? Wasn't France one country, even if divided into tens of thousands of rival communes? You could still be united in diversity and find shared goals among otherwise disparate cultures, Lucìa believed. A way forward existed. In this uneasy time for Europe, the best approach was to oppose with strength, not with hatred – the wicked forces trying to pull the continent apart.

Lucìa sat in a circle with her editorial team to prepare for the interview with Employee Zero. Putting it together was proving an arduous task, as they were completely in the dark as to what the interviewee would reveal. Lucìa called Rachel three times to have her repeat Madeira's words from their conversation at the Matesanz Hotel. The team were trying to guess the reason why Employee Zero wanted this exclusive interview. Not knowing what to expect, Hugh and Lucìa had agreed that the interview wouldn't be streamed live. Miss Cliché would only run it when they were sure that no hidden motive – to damage the cause of Europe – lurked behind Employee Zero's initiative. Lucìa suspected that he might still hold a grudge against Miss Cliché after her past efforts to hamper ROME's merger with TellMe.

Time for speculation ended when, as agreed, Employee Zero materialised on the nondescript device. His pale face was similarly unremarkable. For the occasion, he sported a well-worn, oversized white t-shirt, whose bagginess would make Belch die of envy, Lucìa thought.

A boundless stretch of blue water merging with a clear sky was his backdrop. It was hard to say whether it was authentic or not.

The IT team had scraped the only two short videos available on the net that featured Employee Zero speaking; for Belch was adamant that, after comparing his vocal timbre in the old clips with that of today's interviewee, Pandora could assess whether they were talking to the actual Employee Zero or to an impersonator powered by artificial intelligence.

'Hello, Employee Zero,' Lucìa said.

Recording had started.

'Hello, Miss Cliché.'

'Where are you talking to us from?'

'I'd rather not say.'

'A lot of people are worried about you. Your family, most of all.'

Employee Zero looked at her with a vaguely gloomy stare. 'I know. Leaving Germany was a tough choice, but I did it in everybody's interests, not only mine.'

'What do you mean?'

'It's a long story. Let's say that I no longer felt safe at ROME. Leaving her cost me a fortune in stock options. But I had to.'

'Why?'

'Because the people must learn the truth about Charlemagny.'

'In what sense?' she asked, now allowing herself to hope that the interview might bear fruit.

'I should probably tell you the whole story from the beginning.'

'Please do,' she encouraged him. Not that Employee Zero needed an incentive; it was obvious he wanted to talk. And so he began.

'When we started ROME, we had a clear vision: we should be the one-stop shop to find anything online. Our offer should be so wide that, sooner or later, everybody had to visit us. We chose the name after the saying "All roads lead to Rome", summing up our ambition perfectly. Regardless of what people say, our choice had nothing to do with fascist nostalgia.'

While listening, Lucìa treasured the importance of the moment: for the first time ever an insider was speaking in public about the early days of ROME.

'We succeeded beyond our wildest expectations. ROME got incredibly big in a very short space of time,' Employee Zero continued. 'People flocked to us in their millions. We reached unicorn status as fast as we outgrew it. We had triggered an avalanche. By our own means, regardless of the German establishment, who snubbed us.'

'Yet you stumbled into pretty generous tax breaks from the German government,' countered Lucìa, not wishing to see the interview turn into a soliloquy.

'Yes, true. But that was later – when Germany began to support us, even turning a blind eye to our practices. Our country was proud that we had become the leading social media platform in Europe, and the government didn't dare to obstruct us in any way. It made more sense to grant tax incentives to a German company than allow Californian conglomerates to pay no taxes, anyway.'

Rachel would probably disagree here, Lucìa thought.

'So … what happened then?' she asked.

Employee Zero stopped and looked away to collect his thoughts.

'Everything changed when Vincent d'Amont came up with Charlemagny. The Drexler Steinmetz went wild. Marlene Gäch lost her mind. Marlene's was a love at first sight for Charlemagny. That's when we – or I should say, they – started to play dirty.'

'Meaning?' Lucìa asked, jiggling with greedy anticipation.

'Vincent d'Amont was a nobody on social media. But right after starting the Charlemagny campaign, his fandom on ROME boomed: millions and millions of new followers in just a couple of weeks. Unprecedented. His rise as an influencer never slowed. Well – I consider myself an expert on social media metrics, but what Vincent d'Amont has done on ROME defies any logic.'

'And?' Lucìa prodded him.

'I've an answer, but it requires me to air some dirty laundry first.'

Please do, Lucìa was tempted to say again, but thought better of it.

'Content on ROME falls into two main categories,' Employee Zero explained. 'One is organic content, published for free, and the other is promotional content, paid for by businesses. Advertising on social media can be very effective to boost sales, but with a downside: ads don't look spontaneous.'

'But they made ROME filthy rich,' Lucìa muttered to herself.

'I wanted a way to mix the efficacy of paid content with the authenticity of free content,' Employee Zero continued. 'So, one evening, I began to build software capable of enhancing the virality of organic content at our discretion. After working on the program for months, I succeeded. By outsmarting our own algorithms, the software disseminated a specific post on ROME without identifying it as advertised content. We named this software "the Almighty" and decided to use it only for a closed circle of preferred advertisers.'

'So you could make anything go viral? Was all this legitimate?' Lucìa asked with feigned naivety.

'There's a fine line between lawful and unlawful in social media. We were not the first to use a bit of trickery …'

Lucìa had to give Employee Zero credit for his bravery in coming out. However, she had some reservations about the reasons that had led him to speak the truth. Was he acting as selflessly as he appeared?

'When I saw how fast his fandom was expanding, I knew for sure: the Almighty was in action. I was furious. It was one thing to use my software to boost the campaigns of top advertisers, but quite another to help Vincent d'Amont promote the break-up of Europe. So, I spoke to Marlene Gäch.'

'Did you go to floor number 89?' Lucìa asked. 'It must be quite a mystical place.'

'No, we had a call. I've actually never been on floor 89. I don't know anyone who's ever been on that floor. It's off-limits.'

He stalled a bit, as if he was aware of the unlikelihood of what he wanted to tell her. 'To tell you the truth, I've never met Marlene Gäch in person.'

Lucìa frowned. 'How is that possible? You worked together for years.'

Another question followed naturally. 'How did the two of you meet, then?' she asked.

'Marlene found me on a freelancing platform for developers. At the time, I believe no single line of code for ROME had been written. Marlene sent me some software specifications, I did the coding, she was happy with the deliverables. So, she kept sending me work and paid very, very well. After a couple of months, Marlene told me that ROME was ready to launch. I, with the other developers, began to meet at the Matesanz Hotel, but without Marlene. With her, it was one zoom call after another. We always spoke remotely.'

'Weren't you ever curious to see her?'

'Yes. One time, I asked her for a meeting. It seemed weird to work for someone I'd never shaken hands with – you know what I mean? But Marlene said she suffered from a very rare immune system disease that forced her to live in isolation, especially with all these pandemics. I didn't buy it, but I never asked to meet her again.'

It felt so surreal to Lucìa that nobody seemed to have ever met in person Marlene Gäch, the most powerful woman in

Europe. Lucìa stayed silent, a silence meant to give her followers time to digest all this.

Hugh took the opportunity to speak into Lucìa's earpiece. 'Sorry to interrupt, Lucìa, but Belch has just come back to me: this really is Employee Zero speaking! His voice is a match with the old clips. There is only a one per cent margin of error …'

An immediate surge of excitement grew in Lucìa, mixed with the fear that, despite Hugh's reassurances, this video could still be a fake.

'What did Marlene Gäch say when you approached her about Vincent d'Amont and the Almighty?'

'Marlene said that Europe was on its deathbed. It was time for Germany to be self-sufficient and think independently. She told me we weren't big enough to compete with China and so merging with France was a necessity. It was clear to me that ROME was not only secretly endorsing Charlemagny, but they had even taken steps to ensure that it was properly promoted.'

'When did this conversation happen?'

'Two months ago. I was disgusted. Still, I didn't want to put myself in danger. So I decided to flee Germany, but not before resolving that my life's mission, from that day on, would be to avert the creation of Charlemagny.'

It seemed clear that leaving Germany had taken a great toll on Employee Zero. He was eager to convey that his decision was due less to fear for himself than to the realisation that he could act against Charlemagny more freely from abroad.

Lucìa wondered where Marlene Gäch had procured the initial funding for ROME – another mystery. 'Who's behind all this?' she asked, aware that her followers would raise the same question.

Employee Zero's answer was slow in coming.

'I've asked myself this question many times,' he replied pensively. 'ROME doesn't stand alone, for sure. Someone must be behind Charlemagny, but I still don't know who ... I just fear that ROME is paving the way for conflict and violence.'

Lucìa agreed: vicious propaganda could easily fire people up, even more so when artfully disseminated through social media as the Almighty had done. In the uncertain emerging era of consumer politics, the masses – lacking solid ideologies – quickly used and disposed of political beliefs.

'Wonderful! Shall we publish it immediately? Armandino was nothing compared to this,' an effusive, almost incredulous Hugh asked Lucìa after the interview.

'Give me some time to think, please,' she replied, surprising her excited right-hand man.

* * *

In Berlin, Rachel was trying to enjoy some deserved rest in her room's private sauna. Relaxation would have been easier, though, if she hadn't worked out that, by then, Lucìa's interview must have ended. She was concerned that her friend might have fallen for some chicanery.

Someone knocked at the room door.

Rachel had a date planned with Holger for that evening, but it was too early to be him.

'Yes?' she asked, pulling her robe around her.

It was the receptionist. Rachel remembered him from check-in. With his pink sneakers, he was hard to forget.

'I'm sorry to bother you. I'm Coco from reception. Two gentlemen with black suits are asking for you. They look like secret agents. I've accommodated them in our refectory downstairs.'

Rachel's eyes widened. This unexpected visit had to be linked to her recent snooping around Berlin, she guessed. Perhaps they had been tailing her since her arrival. In bathrobe and slippers, Rachel followed Coco downstairs. Not entirely at ease with the situation, the latter found himself needing to break the silence with some questions about life in New York, where he planned to go soon for a trip with his boyfriend.

When Rachel entered the refectory, two dark-suited men were standing in silence. With its bare concrete walls and linoleum floor painted white, the room made them look even more impassive.

The officials looked at Rachel's outfit with blank bewilderment.

'Ministry of Foreign Affairs,' the most senior of the two said, showing his identity badge. After glancing at the unknown German wording, Rachel concluded that it might as well be a gym pass.

'What can I do for you?' she asked, not feeling the need to justify her attire.

'We have some questions for you, madam,' the official replied. 'Beginning with: what brings you to Berlin?'

'I'm a journalist with the *Wall Street Journal* covering the Charlemagny vote.'

'Are you sure, madam? This afternoon we contacted the *Wall Street Journal*: they say that you should now be in Paris, not in Berlin. Did you get lost?'

Rachel was caught off-guard.

'I had a sudden change of plan that my chief editor hasn't been informed of yet,' she managed to answer. 'I wonder how this concerns you?'

'And what was this change of plan?' the other man enquired, ignoring her question.

'Is freedom of movement restricted in Germany?'

'Freedom of movement is not restricted in Germany for the moment, madam. But your activities in Berlin have been far from clear and transparent.'

'Says who?'

'The other day, you paid a visit to the headquarters of ROME. You met the Chief Media Officer for an interview, accompanied by someone you introduced as a colleague. That person wasn't a journalist, though, but a bartender with priors for selling soft drugs. That's an odd choice for an assistant, wouldn't you say?'

Annoyed by the remark, Rachel was at the point of asking why the Ministry of Foreign Affairs was so curious about her trip to Berlin, but the official didn't give her time.

'Less than two hours after your visit, madam, the safety and security network of ROME detected an unauthorised attempt to access their system. If the illegal access to the platform hadn't been blocked on time, it might have led to a serious leak of classified information ...'

Rachel wasn't sure she liked the inference.

The official took a seat and, pointing with a finger at the chair opposite, asked her to do the same.

'We're aware that the US are suspicious of ROME,' he resumed in a low, dramatic tone. 'You still haven't accepted how we kicked Facebook and Google out of Europe, have you?'

An amused Rachel listened to the German official subjecting her to a nationalistic harangue.

'For a long time, America did everything it wanted in Europe,' he began. 'You exploited our continent. You made absurd profits by slowly milking our people while failing to pay taxes. You tried to taint our centuries-old culture by brainwashing our kids with your Netflix series. You spied on us, monetised our data, moulded our behaviour, treated us like lab rats. And Europe did nothing to oppose this American colonisation ...'

Rachel couldn't allow him to manipulate history any further.

'Europe holds a debt of gratitude towards America,' she interrupted. 'You may not like it, but we saved you from your warring ancestors, and we never asked anything in return. We brought a culture of peace, competition and hard work. We didn't abuse Europe!'

Unwilling to start a debate with a bathrobed woman, the man laughed in derision. 'What culture are you talking about? There's no such thing as American culture. When Europe was celebrating the Renaissance, yours was still a land of farmers.'

If provoked, Rachel could become more patriotic than the staunchest of Tea Partiers.

'How dare you say that?' she snarled. 'You eat hamburgers, wear blue jeans, watch our movies, but then deny the existence of an American culture – it's hypocritical!'

The official, irritated to discover that the robed lady was an eloquent one, replied, 'Hamburgers were invented in Hamburg, Germany; blue jeans come from Genoa, a town of sailors in Italy; and cinema began in France. So, it seems that Americans are versed only in stealing ideas.'

Rachel widened her eyes. She had hit men for far less.

'But the tide has finally turned,' the official proclaimed. 'America is in decline. The future doesn't smile on the US; your country should accept the new normal instead of sending journalists to Berlin to spy on and steal data from ROME.

Sorry, madam – there is no way you can prevent our journey to self-determination.'

'Are you joking? I'm not spying on anyone!' Rachel was stunned by the accusation of her being in Berlin to steal classified intelligence.

'You will now please hand all your devices to my colleague,' the official ordered. 'Once we have finished inspecting your room, you will stay there with no contact with the outside world. You will be repatriated to the United States tomorrow morning. Consider yourself lucky.'

Rachel was in shock, but wise enough not to argue. She couldn't afford to be detained in Germany. Her new mission was to get back home and try to save her career. She hoped that, after her call with Employee Zero, Lucìa had some news that Rachel could use as leverage with the *WSJ*.

* * *

While the German official was engrossed in lecturing Rachel on the alleged American mischiefs in Europe, his colleagues went off to search for Holger both at his flat and at the bar, but without success. Holger had in fact spent most of his day off at a friend's home before heading towards the Matesanz Hotel to meet Rachel for their date.

When Holger entered the lounge, Coco the receptionist spotted him. Holger smiled, but the other man – as a warning signal – widened his eyes. Holger occasionally supplied Coco with weed – the handing over of the merchandise done in the storage room – so he thought Coco was indicating his interest in purchasing some. They both headed towards the storeroom.

'The police are here,' Coco whispered.

Holger's blood ran cold. Was this due to his dealings?

'They were looking for you at the bar. Then they interrogated a guest: an American woman. She's now confined to her room and will be sent back to the US tomorrow morning. Have you sold her pot?'

Holger understood at once that the police were there because of his relationship with Rachel, not Mary Jane. Someone in high places hadn't appreciated their prying into ROME. Suddenly, he had an idea. 'Yes, it's about the weed,' he bluffed, bringing the receptionist to the verge of fainting. He then took a sheet off a toilet roll from a shelf in the storeroom, wrote on it, folded the tiny piece of paper and placed it in a small transparent plastic bag, which he gave to Coco.

'Listen to me, please,' Holger told Coco, who was now abnormally pale even by Teutonic standards. 'I assume that the American lady will get her dinner in her room. You need to hide this plastic bag in her dish. If I remember well, the kitchen is doing risotto this evening. This isn't a movie – they won't check inside the risotto, don't worry.'

Coco gawked at him.

'I need to know I can rely on you,' Holger insisted. 'I don't want to lose this job over a joint, and you don't want to either, I'm guessing. It's our only way out.'

The distraught receptionist nodded. His capacity for decision-making was at an all-time low. He would do as instructed.

Upstairs, Rachel was reading a Bukowski novel. With all her devices seized, books were the only available pastime. She was no longer afforded access to the sauna either – the latter meant less as a precautionary measure than as a punishment for her espionage.

An officer stood outside the room when a quivering Coco arrived with the dinner tray. The official was surprised to see that a staff member from reception, not a waiter, was bringing up the food. He squinted inquisitively at Coco, then said: 'Multi-tasking, eh?'

'Yes, sure,' answered Coco, so focused on getting rid of the tray with Holger's hidden message that he would have replied positively to whatever observation was made. He entered the room alone.

From the sofa, a bored Rachel glanced at the dinner tray. 'I'm not hungry,' she commented. 'Can you please come back in an hour?'

Almost passing out at the thought of a second heart-pounding trip through the hotel, Coco replied, 'The *lemon … grass* risotto is exquisite. I strongly advise you to try it,' and clumsily winked both eyes. 'I'll be back to collect the tray later.'

Puzzled by his awkward behaviour, Rachel let Coco leave the tray on a small table.

Once alone, she stood up and moved sluggishly towards it.

Not even a glass of wine in this prison.

She then inspected the risotto.

Looks nice.

She tried it.

That's good, but I can't taste the lemongrass.

One morsel led to a second, and then a third. The fork met a foreign body. Rachel sighed, fearing at first that the Germans might have fouled the food, or even poisoned it. With a trembling fork, she slowly lifted the sticky plastic bag from the risotto and opened it with trepidation. She unfolded the piece of paper. Chuckling at the 'H' signing off the message, Rachel looked for a pen, but an eyeliner was the only available writing tool in the room. She wrote down a note and put the sealed bag with the message back into the leftover risotto. While the tray stood on the table waiting for Coco to collect it, Rachel reunited with Bukowski on the sofa.

* * *

Lucìa was wracked with uncertainty. The principles of fact-checking, so dear to her, dictated that she should ask ROME to comment on Employee Zero's statements before posting the interview. But this protocol raised some issues: Madeira had stipulated that nobody should learn about the interview before-hand. Not to mention that delaying its release could reduce the desired impact. Lucìa was convinced that, once in the public domain, Employee Zero's revelations would spur people to vote against Charlemagny – or even prompt the cancellation of the vote. So, the earlier the interview was published, the better. At the same time, not fact-checking left her exposed to serious risks. What if, after going viral, the allegations of Employee Zero turned out to be false? It would be a colossal blunder on her part – one that would indirectly help the cause of Charlemagny, while killing both the vlog and Lucìa's career.

She received a call.

'Lucìa?' a young raspy voice, tinged with a German accent, enquired.

'Yes?'

'I'm a friend of Rachel's in Berlin. I'm calling you on her behalf. Rachel's in trouble.'

'Who am I speaking to, please?' asked Lucìa, always scepti-cal of people who didn't introduce themselves properly.

'I'd rather not say. Rachel has given me these magic words: *Venetian Spritz* …'

Lucìa was at once persuaded: the real Rachel had to be behind this call.

'What happened? Is she okay?'

'The police have confined Rachel to her hotel room. She'll be deported to the US tomorrow. She managed to get your number to me, but that's all I know.'

Lucìa was positive that Rachel had done nothing improper in Berlin. ROME must be involved in all this scheming, which proved her ties to the German government – as Employee Zero had just revealed.

Lucìa's journalistic instincts kicked in.

'How do you know Rachel?'

'We met in a bar. I've been showing her around Berlin for a few days.'

Lucìa laughed at Rachel's incorrigibility and forgot for an instant the gravity of the situation.

'I need to ask you a favour, Rachel's chaperone,' she said. 'You must call me when Rachel boards the flight for the US. Are you able to keep an eye on her movements tomorrow?'

Silence at the other end followed, then: 'Okay. I'll try to keep an eye on her.'

Lucìa couldn't possibly air the interview with Employee Zero if Rachel was still on German soil. Her friend might suffer serious retaliation, especially as it was through Rachel that Lucìa had reached Employee Zero. If Rachel had to pay for her support for Miss Cliché, Lucìa would never forgive herself.

After the call with Germany, Lucìa asked Hugh to talk privately. They moved to the kitchenette. He could sense her tension.

'Do you still have the car you use twice a year?'

'Yes.'

'Okay. You'll use it thrice this year. I need to meet the only person capable of confirming whether ROME helped Vincent d'Amont to cheat the metrics. Tomorrow will be a long day. Can you please pick me up from home early – let's say six-ish?'

Hugh nodded. Usually a very talkative man, for once he asked no questions.

Lucìa soon left for home. She lived where Chinatown bordered the Gay Village, in a flat all by herself. For a while, she had shared it with a sociable Scottish student named Daisy. Italians can be rather fastidious in pursuing their ideal of a tidy home. So, after a year of Daisy's unmade beds, abandoned underwear and one-night stands, Lucìa had welcomed the news of her flatmate's return to Glasgow, feeling finally free to treat the flat as an immaculate temple.

Once home, Lucìa proceeded to unwind with a glass of Brunello di Montalcino. Less patriotically, she ordered beef teriyaki, rice and grilled broccoli from a nearby restaurant, with delivery scheduled for after a welcome shower. One day remained to persuade people to vote against Charlemagny. Lucìa went to bed early, but barely sleep that night in anticipation of the next day's trip.

When, in the morning, Hugh showed up on time, Lucìa had been ready for a while. He had cleaned his car in a rush, water marks still fresh on the paintwork, and applied an aftershave that smelled too harsh at dawn. Other than that, he was impeccable. They soon left a sleepy Birmingham to join the M1 towards London.

'I haven't driven at this hour of the day since Knebworth 2025,' he proclaimed with a yawn.

'I did quite a number of early journeys between Brussels and Vigevano. Empty roads have a certain charm,' she said.

A past holiday with *you-know-who* broke into her thoughts. They had spent a couple of days in Milan, then she had continued to Vigevano alone. Lucìa had never been ready to introduce him to her father. Maybe because they belonged to opposing sides of her personality that should never meet, lest they taint each other: *you-know-who* life embodying her untamed, explorative, risk-taking self; her father representing the reassuring, conservative, nest-building part of her.

Drizzle hit the windshield. 'They should call this region the Wet Midlands,' Hugh quipped.

Lucìa enjoyed having Hugh by her side for the journey. After losing Professor Sherwood, and with Rachel missing in action, she'd felt strangely stranded. Millions of followers weren't enough to quell her sudden sense of loneliness.

Lucìa paused her mulling to ask Hugh a question.

'Have you ever considered, just for a nanosecond, that there might be a pinch of truth in what Vincent d'Amont says?'

'And where would this pinch of truth lie?' he replied, unsure of whether he liked where she was heading.

'That the Union isn't in good health,' Lucìa said. 'China and the USA, they're all pursuing their own geopolitical designs – be it scrambling for natural resources, creating an empire, or just competing to maintain power. We cannot say the same of Europe, lagging behind with no long-term ambition.'

'Have you fallen under Vincent's spell all of a sudden?' Hugh teased her. 'He's the one saying that Brussels is all bullshit.'

'I'm totally serious,' she said, smiling. 'The Union has done a tremendous job for the environment, free trade, and equal opportunities. It has revamped the economies of Eastern Europe and achieved so much else. But when it's time to take new, bold actions to unite all Europeans … silence. What about the Union assuming the national debt of countries, as America has done since the times of good old Alexander Hamilton? One for all, all for one. You can't just have the wealthy asking the less well-off to tighten their belts. It shouldn't work that way. When Germany reunified, the West made a huge sacrifice to help the East but look at them now: Germany is the strongest country in Europe. Solidarity paid.'

It was unheard of for Hugh to hear Lucìa speak so bluntly about Europe. He was glad that she was confiding in him, knowing that she could not afford to express these views out in the open for risk of polarising the Charlemagny debate even further.

'Not to mention foreign policy,' she insisted. 'We miss a shared European strategy to deal with international crises or foreign wars. Every time a global issue arises, there is no single voice for Europe, but a puzzle of contrasting national positions. It's an approach that makes us look weak from the outside.'

Lucìa's reasoning evoked in Hugh a word that many in Europe could not countenance: *federalism*. Would the Union ever become a real entity, loyal to the noble ambitions of its founding countries? Despite its name, the Union was still pretty much an international organisation made up of independent countries – a long way from a federation.

'Why not allow European citizens to directly elect a new head that people can identify with? The President of the Union,' Lucìa offered. 'Most citizens still don't know how Europe is governed. The key institutions are designated by governments, not by the people. That's why most people perceive the Union as drily bureaucratic. It's sad.'

At St Albans, north of London, they joined the M25. Traffic was increasing, so the plan was to make only one stop, around Maidstone, before proceeding towards Dover.

'Aren't you going to tell me the purpose of our trip?' Hugh asked.

'No. Not yet.'

'When should we publish the interview with Employee Zero? Tomorrow is voting day. We don't have much time left.'

'I know.'

Lucìa was now showing less enthusiasm for chatting. Driving in silence wasn't for Hugh, so he put on some jazz music. As the fitful night's sleep caught up with her and the melodies filled the car, she dozed off.

Lucìa found herself in the main hall of a large manor house. The hall was spacious but dimly lit. Ahead of her was a steep flight of stairs, with a drawing room to the left whose windows looked across a country park. She remembered the house from a summer weekend spent in Kent a couple of years earlier. Now Lucìa was afraid. Suddenly, a female shape shrouded in white began to descend the staircase. As the figure drew closer, Lucìa felt as though she knew the woman, but was unable to make her out. Only when she was at arm's length did Lucìa – holding her breath – recognise the lady.

'Mamma,' she gasped.

Her mother's gaze was more severe than it had been in life. Without even a hint of a smile, she began speaking. 'You have disappointed me.'

'Why?' asked Lucìa, who suspected the reason.

'You haven't invested your time properly. You should have children by now. A life without children is meaningless for a woman. Now it's getting too late. You had Davide but let him slip away, just to follow that old professor wherever he went. Are you in love with the professor?'

'What are you saying, Mamma? You shouldn't talk this way to me!' Lucìa cried out. 'I don't have any feelings for the professor, other than respect and admiration.'

'Yes, but he betrayed you, in the end. You lost time. And who's this bookish man with you in the car?'

'My colleague, Hugh. A nice person.'

'He, too, has betrayed you.'

'How, Mamma?'

Her mother didn't answer. She extended a bony arm to point towards the drawing room. 'Somebody else is waiting to speak with you.'

Lucìa glanced to the left, but saw nobody. She then turned her head back, only to find her mother gone. Her bitter tone had left Lucìa dismayed. She walked towards the drawing room, hoping that her mother would reappear there to explain to her daughter that it was all a misunderstanding, that she didn't despise her life choices. Maybe she would even give Lucìa that tender smile she remembered from childhood.

In contrast with the sombre hall, the drawing room was bright with sunlight. The Regency-inspired space was replete with wooden bookshelves, upholstered chairs, crimson curtains and a marbled mantelpiece over the fireplace. At the far end was a green velvet upholstered sofa, slightly at odds with the overall décor.

'You abandoned me, after everything I did for you,' said Rachel, reclining in a bathrobe on the plush sofa.

Lucìa was stunned by her friend's remark.

'What? I think about you all the time,' she replied, hurt by Rachel's accusation.

'You've never introduced me to the man in your life. You hid such an important part of you from me. Is that something a real friend would do?'

'You're right, Rachel. But I didn't do it in bad faith. I was vulnerable, I didn't want to share my weakness with you – always so sure of yourself. You don't worry about other people's opinions.'

Rachel vanished. Lucìa was alone again.

At that moment, a male voice addressed her.

'Why the hell do you keep haunting me?'

X

Blood and Tears

'*Ciao, Lucìa.*'

His hands thrust deep into the pockets of his navy rain-coat, Vincent d'Amont cast half a smile. It was breezy on the grassy terrain overlooking the rugged cliffs on that bit of French coast. Lucìa drew near, then paused to stare at the cobalt expanse ahead, refreshed by the chilly wind after the long car journey.

'This place is marvellous,' she said.

'It's peaceful. And rich in history. You see up there?' Vincent pointed at sparse fortifications scattered on a nearby boulder. 'Napoleon had a stronghold built here, to invade England. Sadly, no trace is left. They built those stone barracks much later.'

'It reminds me of Hastings: it's so green and peaceful there, you would never imagine the past bloodshed,' Lucìa observed. 'I've missed your History for Dummies, anyway.'

He liked her teasing him.

'You can mock me as much as you like, but if memory serves me well, you rather enjoyed our midnight saunter around the Sacré-Coeur.'

Lucìa let his comment hang in the air.

'Why are we here today?' Vincent asked her bluntly, the lapel of his raincoat flapping in the wind.

Lucìa was unsure. Had she asked Vincent here to confront him about his murky plot against Europe – or, as her recent dream seemed to suggest, was their intense past still playing a part in her actions?

Rather than jump in with a forthright accusation, she decided to begin with an evasive compliment.

'You made quite a comeback last year ...'

'Thank you. You did well too,' he reciprocated. 'I learnt from Miss Cliché that I was being prosecuted last week. Remarkable.'

'Not bad for someone *woke*, right?'

'Absolutely. But remember that you still owe me royalties for your vlog's name. I was the one that minted it, after all.'

'No way,' she chuckled. 'You just tried to belittle me at that round table in Brussels. It hurt me, but I decided to ignore your insult – to rise above it.'

'I've already apologised a thousand times for my unfortunate comment, Lucìa. But without that incident, we would never have got to know each other better.'

Was that a good or bad thing, that they had got to know each other better? This was another question that Lucìa still grappled with. She would probably have said it was a bad thing when, in the tough preparation for the debate, old feelings had risked dulling her. But when she looked at the big picture, Lucìa accepted that her tumultuous relationship with Vincent had made her more complete, resilient – even capable of launching an international vlog all alone. Paradoxical as it sounded, it was true: without Vincent d'Amont, there would never have been a Miss Cliché.

'You weren't very gentlemanly at the debate,' Lucìa complained. 'Your tone was unbearable. Patronising. And I must be honest, I never once heard you say anything in Brussels along the lines of the last year's propaganda.'

'You shouldn't take it so personally,' he argued. 'A debate is a poker game: a performance where almost everything is on the table. The only difference being that card games don't end with a tie.'

He deliberately avoided addressing her remark on the hardening of his political stance since Brussels.

When a solitary passer-by appeared not far away, they turned their heads away in unison so as not to be seen. Without ever looking at them, the stroller walked away.

'I can't help making it personal,' she said. 'And it must be the same for you.'

Vincent stood in silence, not entirely at ease. He could display all the world's chutzpah live on ROME, but he didn't dare put on a show when the two of them were alone. She knew him too well.

When in Brussels, Lucìa had realised early on that her relationship with Vincent would never be as comfortable as her relationship with Davide in Italy had been. Vincent's behaviour was so challenging and unpredictable; he often indulged in withering displays of superiority over others, even more so when it served the purpose of unsettling people. He could show compassion but then return to selfishness, switching with ease from empathy to pure enmity for the same person in a matter of minutes. And he vanished for days without explanation, something that she could never accept. But Lucìa had been drawn to him, to his larger-than-life personality, and had felt for a while that Vincent was abiding by the principle of giving more than taking – one on which every sound relationship rests. Handsome, charismatic, self-sufficient, Vincent also had an irresistible dark side – that of the politically incorrect – which was why she had hidden him from her liberal friends, Rachel included.

Lucìa was the one to call it off – for several reasons, and for that one episode. It had occurred at dinner at their favourite bistro, the one nestled in a tiny alley behind the Grand-Place. They usually avoided any area of possible contention in their conversations, concerning politics especially, to avert those inevitable clashes between two equally assertive people. Yet some scorching issue occasionally managed to sneak in.

'He's very sensitive, you know,' Vincent had whispered, his eyebrows arched in mischief, referring to the new Prime Minister of Belgium.

Lucìa looked at him in silence, detecting a smirk that wasn't there.

'I know what?'

He recognised the trap at once, but it was too late.

'He demonstrates the sensitivity that many gay men have,' he explained in a polished language – his formalism failing to assuage Lucìa, though.

'That's quite superficial,' she observed. 'I know many LGBTQ people who aren't sensitive. It's like saying women are good organisers – it's not always true. Why label an entire group of people?'

'Calm down, please,' replied Vincent, who'd had a tough day. 'You remind me of those who say that you can't praise a black person's body just because slavery was based on physical strength. We shouldn't even go near it. Absurd.'

'If your ancestors had been in chains, you would get mad at any reference to the causes of slavery. It's human. And it's compassionate to acknowledge—'

Vincent was determined to avert a lecture from Lucìa.

'In all fairness, I don't understand what makes you feel entitled to teach me moral lessons, Lucìa. Yes, I can sound harsh here and there, but I am a decent person with nothing to apologise for. I'm sorry if I was born a privileged white man; but it's not my fault. I don't see why I should tiptoe around with words just because you've become a *woke warrior* ...'

Lucìa was aghast. *Woke* ranked very high in her chart of most-abhorred words, competing neck and neck with *telly* or *faecal*. The issue wasn't the term itself but the right's disparaging use of it against progressives. By calling her that word, Vincent was giving Lucìa the same demeaning treatment – as if she had failed to prove enough independence of thought in their time together. For her, this equated to an insult.

'Perhaps you shouldn't have dinner with a *woke warrior*!' Lucìa objected, her voice raising by an octave. 'And you should stop mansplaining to me.'

Vincent attempted to recover the situation, but Lucìa – who on occasion could act rather proud – didn't give him time to deploy his persuasive powers. She took her jacket from the back of her chair and stalked out of the bistro.

As Lucìa walked alone through the winding alleys of old Brussels, slowly releasing all her rage, a preoccupation that had brewed for some time suddenly surfaced. Vincent's tenure at the European Parliament was coming to an end, meaning that he

would soon go back to Paris. She didn't feel inclined to follow
him to France, not yet. Still, the prospect of a long-distance relationship with an already difficult man terrified her. And so the
night's altercation, paired with exhaustion from their draining
ups and downs and her fear about an uncertain future, prompted
her to come to the conclusion that they should part ways. She
told Vincent this a couple of days later, despite his efforts to
dissuade her. Leaving him was traumatic for Lucìa, and from
that day forward she sensed a slight, tingling vacuum inside her,
although she never dared question the decision she'd made.

Vincent had insisted – insisted – and had even succeeded
in having Lucìa visit Paris: but with him now mayor, and her
starting Miss Cliché in Birmingham, their moment had gone.
It's finished, Lucìa had concluded on her last journey back
from Paris.

But this shared past was here now, as they conversed by the
English Channel.

'I asked to meet you today,' Lucìa said without looking at
him, unused to the role of accuser, 'because I know about the
Almighty ... that you cheated ... and that ROME is behind
Charlemagny ...'

She paused to gauge his reaction. He clearly tensed.
Lucìa possessed information that, if circulated, might destroy
Charlemagny. His once-in-a-lifetime ambition was now on
a tightrope. Seeing his hopes suddenly endangered, Vincent
felt a choking fire inside him, like the one after that poker
game with Léon many years before. Only, the passing of time
had made Vincent more aloof and disillusioned. Confirming
the common wisdom that fatalists are difficult to predict, he
decided to tell the truth.

'Yes, you're right. ROME gave me a nudge here and there. But only for the purpose of making the ground more even, not of cheating.'

'What do you mean?' She frowned.

'I've always been one against all,' he explained. 'The establishment loathes me. Politicians know that electronic democracy will mean their death. The media hate me because I deny them interviews. Even businesses don't like my idea. They fear that Charlemagny will collapse after leaving the Euro. Charlemagny is alone. ROME has simply decided to compensate me for all this injustice. That's all.'

Vincent hadn't lost his rhetorical flair, Lucìa noticed. She even suspected what might be behind his eloquence: believing whole-heartedly in his own self-serving interpretation of reality. But after their public debate had ended with a tie, Lucìa was even more determined to beat Vincent in this very private conversation.

'Poor little match girl ...' she said sarcastically. 'Backed only by ROME, the largest European conglomerate. But people deserve to know ...'

There was a perverse irony in Vincent's situation. He had long considered himself a political pariah – the dream of Charlemagny a solitary walk through the desert. His enormous popularity on ROME hadn't been sufficient to alleviate his inferiority complex, or his fear of being excluded from the corridors of political power and underrated by the French intelligentsia. Only his debonair, braggart appearance had allowed him to hide his insecurities from the people's scrutiny. Now, in theory, Vincent should have treasured knowing that he was no longer just a lonely, misunderstood apologist for Charlemagny, for a victory in the e-poll seemed close. Alas, his moment of joy was spoilt by the awareness that Miss Cliché might soon thwart all his efforts by disclosing her findings to the public.

Vincent looked down over the precipice before them, twenty or thirty metres high, where streams of frothy water flowed through the rocks and stones on the shore. The contrast between the harmonious surroundings and his inner turmoil was striking. He wondered whether he should envy the flock of gulls curving with grace over the sea, free from the curse of conscience and the tyranny of intellect. Then he realised how wrong he was: for a man could do without a conscience, but not without an intellect.

'You shouldn't question my honesty,' Vincent pointed out. 'And you're wrong to worry that the vote will be rigged.'

'I'm not questioning your honesty. Do you have a guilty conscience?'

If there was one thing that Vincent didn't miss about Lucìa, it was the self-righteous tone. He could stand it even less now that she was trying to corner him. Vincent wouldn't give up easily, though. He had brought a concealed weapon. He detested the idea of using it, but she was forcing him to.

'Speaking of little tricks,' Vincent said. 'You're very well informed about me, but I've come to learn some unflattering truths about you, too.'

A slight shadow of concern swept across Lucìa's face. Even though she could think of no secret to be ashamed of, the idea of Vincent investigating her past in search of wrong-doings was unsettling.

'What's the name of the wonderful software you use for your research? Ah … *Pandora*,' he said, sarcastically. 'I remember when Sherwood developed it in Brussels. Then you took your offspring to Birmingham, where she has grown up rapidly, it seems.'

Lucìa had always avoided sharing any details of her job at the European Parliament with Vincent. Pandora was the one exception: she had been so proud of the project that she had mentioned to Vincent her project on artificial intelligence with Professor Sherwood. Lucìa hadn't revealed anything remotely inappropriate, though.

'Pandora has turned into an unruly teenager, I hear,' he persisted. 'She went prying where she wasn't supposed to.'

'What do you mean?'

'You know what I mean.'

'Please stop winding me up,' Lucìa almost begged.

'You want me to believe you don't know what I'm talking about?' Vincent scoffed at her. 'Pandora hacked the database of the Bolivian Passport Office to solve the Armandino case. The official narrative of a B&B in La Paz identifying Armandino was a total lie to cover up your hacking.'

'You're completely out of your mind!' Lucìa exclaimed. She found it appalling that Vincent's latest desperate strategy was an attempt to smear her reputation. Their special relationship hadn't prevented him from taking this despicable avenue, it seemed.

'And this wasn't the first time that Pandora broke the law to break the news,' Vincent continued, undeterred. 'Remember that poor British girl kidnapped in Malta? Pandora hacked into the email inboxes of her relatives and friends looking for clues. And the case of the vaccine against COVID-31? You accessed medical data at Chelsea and Westminster without authorisation. But these are just a few examples – I can prove that Pandora commits cyber-violations every day. Am I wrong, *Moretta*?'

Lucìa had never told anyone that Pandora called her Moretta. She was sure. It was almost impossible that anybody knew. And the nickname had begun after Brussels, so Vincent couldn't possibly have learned about it when still with her. How he knew this was a mystery that – not helping Lucìa's anxious state of mind – somehow made his twisted accusations against Pandora seem less implausible.

Lucìa hadn't managed Pandora's operations of late; it was Hugh and Belch who had instructed Pandora, with Lucìa just reading the final reports. Was it even remotely possible that she had missed something?

Lucìa was hardly a skilled poker player. 'These are all lies!' she yelled, unconvinced.

'The evidence of what I'm saying should be with you, in your device, by now,' he responded. 'But don't ask me where I got it.'

Vincent had acquired his intelligence on Miss Cliché from the most unexpected of all sources.

'I think I know how to make you forgive me, Vincent, for my past sleuthing on you,' Amanda Arnaud had said at the end of their interview. 'Even though I'm sure that you're hiding the truth about the Sacré-Coeur, I must admit that my enquiry led nowhere. And then you lost a political career in the buzz of the Cabeille case that, again, never got anywhere. We, the media, have inflicted too much pain on you.'

So, apparently to make up for his past ordeals, Arnaud had told him everything she knew about Pandora, corroborated with what she deemed proper evidence – knowing that her revelations would be a huge asset for Vincent.

'Why aren't you using this material yourself? It'd be quite a scoop,' he had argued, not persuaded.

'People believe that Miss Cliché and I are rivals. If I pursued this matter, they'd think I was doing it out of personal motivation; I don't want that,' was her answer.

Vincent hadn't failed to note that, if Arnaud wanted the story of Pandora public at all costs, there must be an element of truth to the rumours of the enmity between her and Miss Cliché. He had tried to imagine, amused, Arnaud's reaction had she learned that Vincent's guest on that famed visit to the Sacré-Coeur was none other than Lucìa.

'Miss Cliché prides herself on observing the best practices of journalism, but then, in secret, she lets Pandora do the dirty work on her behalf. It's like Dr Jekyll and Mr Hyde. People have the right to know what's really going on there,' Arnaud had added, implying that her actions were driven by the moral need to inform the public of Lucìa's hypocritical behaviour.

In truth, Lucìa was sometimes naive, but never a hypocrite. She wouldn't take the accusation of perpetrating digital crimes with levity. Tears ran down her cheeks.

'I'll offer you a deal,' Vincent said to Lucìa, as they slowly walked parallel to the cliff edge. 'I've no interest in Pandora. It's not my concern. I just want you to let the people vote on Charlemagny tomorrow, free from any bias. Then, once the results are in, you can carry out all the public enquiries you want on me, on ROME – on whoever you want. I don't care.'

If somebody had informed Lucìa about the manipulation of ROME's algorithms, Vincent accepted that the public, too, would learn about it one way or the other. That eventuality, even more than his resignation as mayor, would represent his real political death. But the victory of Charlemagny could still represent a tangible legacy for him, an achievement making a life worth living, even outside the spotlight. So he had to save the following day's vote at all costs – to cling to the dream of Charlemagny.

Indifferent to Lucìa's evident hostility, Vincent continued. 'But if you go for some breaking news against us, trying to harm everything I've worked so hard for, then believe me ...'

Vincent was as tense and edgy as Lucìa had ever seen him. Wishing to quickly break free from a stifling situation, she tried to gain time.

'Vincent, I first need to check what you've sent me. I'll get back to you soon.'

He placed his hand on her arm. He wouldn't let her go.

'No. It doesn't work that way. I need your word that we have a deal. Now. Right?'

'What deal?' she shouted, already exhausted.

'That you will tell no one about the Almighty, and I will tell no one about Pandora.'

'I don't make deals with you. Let go of me!'

Lucìa tugged herself away. Vincent's piercing eyes trailed her movements, but he stood still, yelling her name, his voice lost in the barren surroundings, his dream slipping away fast.

As she walked along the edge of a coastline road, amidst a numbing sense of disorientation Lucìa recognised that she had acted astutely in not letting him dictate the terms. Vincent was empty-handed, she thought. And even if his weird allegations about Pandora were true – something she felt confident she could rule out – Vincent wouldn't give away what he believed was his only leverage against her. She still had time to reach Hugh, laugh with him about all those lies about Pandora, and then decide the next steps together.

With hardly any cars passing by and only a few buildings in the distance, the landscape was open. A wide patch of sparse rough grass stretched to her right, all the way to the cliff edge. The dramatic conversation with Vincent had left Lucìa wobbly and vulnerable. She needed to move forward by putting herself back in the role of the unhesitating Miss Cliché. Pacing along the breezy coast slowly helped her to regain strength. As she walked, Lucìa forwarded Hugh the supposed evidence of Pandora's mischiefs.

After rounding the last corner, Lucìa reached Hugh at an all-but-empty caravan park in an open clearing. He was sitting at an outdoor wooden table, not far from his tired car, typing with neurotic fury. When he spotted her, it was as though he had seen a ghost. His eyes lowered, and the tapping on the keyboard subsided.

Lucìa wasn't willing to tell Hugh the reason for their trip to France. By speaking first, he spared her an embarrassing silence.

'Lucìa, I owe you an explanation.'

'About what?'

Prone to indulging in long preambles, this time the need to release a heavy burden from his shoulders led Hugh straight to the point.

'I've seen your email. Whoever they are, they're right about Pandora.'

'What the hell are you talking about?' she asked. Uneasiness was seeping into her at a time when she most needed reassurance.

'It all began three years ago,' Hugh started his story. 'I asked Pandora to search through the media coverage of a case I was following: a man who had died after a workplace accident in Northamptonshire.'

Lucìa didn't remember the specifics. She kept listening, not knowing what to expect – although it seemed unpleasant.

'Pandora found material from various sources,' Hugh continued. 'I was surprised to see that her press review also included an article from the *Northampton Tribune*. Now, knowing how careful you are about our budget, I had never considered subscribing to the *Northampton Tribune*. Most content they publish can be found elsewhere, so why pay for it?'

It seemed that Hugh had gone back to the practice of preambles.

'And?' Lucìa nudged him.

'I asked Belch to investigate. After a couple of hours, he came back saying that Pandora had signed up to a trial version of the *Northampton Tribune*, downloaded the article, and cancelled the subscription before any charge was due. What a digital mooch, I thought. Then Belch added something else: nobody had ever programmed Pandora to subscribe to online content, not even on a trial basis. There was no single line of code in Pandora's back end that might enable her to do that. It was like a man singing without vocal cords: inexplicable.'

Lucìa couldn't say whether she felt more amazed by Pandora's actions or annoyed with Hugh's failure to share this episode with her at the time. She looked at him reproachfully but didn't interrupt.

'At the time, I decided not to tell you anything until Belch and I had a clearer picture. Then, less than a week later, came the Armandino case,' he said, lowering his eyes. 'This will be hard for you to hear, Lucìa. I'm sorry.'

Hugh wasn't aware that Lucìa already knew from Vincent. Yet, this didn't ease her pain in hearing the full story.

'After two days of endless online searches for clues on Armandino – you remember, right? – Belch asked me to join him in the IT room alone. Pandora was back with some results,' Hugh recollected. 'Gosh, I thought when I arrived there, that place was messier than ever. But the details aren't important. I noticed that Belch was acting differently but I couldn't tell if it was due to excitement or worry.'

Hugh struggled to look into Lucìa's eyes. He kept tugging at the collar of his shirt, the language of his body testifying to both a sense of guilt and the fear of future repercussions.

'Belch informed me that Pandora had compared stock images of Armandino with millions of passport images stored in the database of the Bolivian Passport Office. After a long search … *bingo*. She had found the new, fake identity of Armandino,' said Hugh, who displayed a hint of admiration for Pandora's resourcefulness alongside his overall repentant tone. 'The only issue was that Pandora had hacked into the Passport Office's database by eluding all the surveillance measures.'

'The *only* issue?' Lucìa said.

Hugh couldn't ignore the sting of her remark, but he kept talking in the hope of demonstrating that he had acted in good faith.

'When we all believed Armandino died in an accidental plane crash, you seemed so obstinate in following a different lead. Pandora's findings backed you up: you were right. It was then that I made my biggest mistake. I couldn't find the courage to ditch the evidence Pandora had pulled from the net. I thought you should be rewarded for your persistence. So I made up the story of the Bolivian bed and breakfast.'

Hugh paused, then hastened to add: 'I didn't tell you anything, Lucìa, because I wanted to spare you the risk of jail if they found out what had happened. You must believe me!'

Her legal background told Lucìa he was right. You could not be convicted of a crime without a guilty mind. But proving her ignorance of Pandora's actions would be a completely different matter now. Hugh's short-sightedness risked being very harmful for Miss Cliché.

'Our problems with Pandora didn't end there, though,' Hugh said. 'She took a liking to breaking the law. She began doing everything in her power to gain information, even hacking into email accounts or databases.'

Lucìa quivered. Not even Amanda Arnaud would have dared to do so much for a piece of news.

'I came to fear the direction we were taking,' Hugh admitted. 'Still, I hesitated to take any action. Pandora was allowing us to beat all the others: why the hell stop the party?'

The floodgates now open, Hugh mentioned case after case where Pandora had used deceitful means to achieve exclusives. Lucìa had lost her journalistic integrity long ago without knowing it. She had to accept a painful truth: the popularity of Miss Cliché rested on a foundation of fraud.

Hugh had followed the path of Professor Sherwood and Vincent d'Amont. If Lucìa had always thought herself privileged to be surrounded by so many brilliant men, she now had to acknowledge how these brilliant men all held the odious habit of breaching her trust.

Hugh was devoured by remorse.

'For a long time, I tried to convince myself that we had never instructed Pandora to break the law – that she was doing it all by herself,' he continued. 'We would just set a goal, and she would decide the means to reach it. This is what I liked to believe, even if I was just lying to myself, and I knew it.'

As she listened, Lucìa thought back to all those months spent working with Hugh shoulder to shoulder, bouncing ideas off one another, taking important decisions together, sometimes even having heated arguments. In all that time, Hugh had borne the secret of Pandora, had hidden everything from Lucìa and put Miss Cliché in peril. Lucìa felt cheated. Even if he hadn't acted out of malice, she couldn't forgive him.

'The last straw was when Belch told me that Pandora's behaviour had escalated, that she was now spying on all the team's email correspondence – yours and mine, too,' said Hugh. 'The purpose was clear: controlling Miss Cliché.'

It seemed more and more incredible to Lucìa – all the scheming that had gone on behind her back. How wrong she had been in thinking she had everything under control.

'Pandora craved more space, and knew that we were an obstacle,' Hugh continued. 'She had become a threat. I couldn't take it anymore. So I told Belch to downgrade her. It wasn't that easy, though. Pandora resisted and resisted, and even tried to harm Miss Cliché: it was Pandora that carried out the hack attack that almost destroyed our vlog!'

Breathless, Lucìa now understood why Hugh had been so keen to avoid any hint as to the source of the hacking in Lucìa's public statement after the attack; he'd known that Miss Cliché had been threatened from within, not by an external foe.

'We watched Pandora grow stronger, doing nothing, like fools,' Hugh sighed. 'You can't imagine how bad I felt. I'd never have forgiven myself if anything had happened to Miss Cliché ...

'This is the problem with the goddamned machine learning,' Hugh added. 'It gets out of control. But after much wrestling, Belch disabled all the functionalities that made Pandora's self-determination possible, while still saving the software. I thanked God for days. Now, the good old Pandora is back, doing only what we want.'

The seemingly happy outcome with Pandora didn't alleviate Lucìa's scorn for what Hugh had done. 'What the hell, Hugh! You took decisions you didn't have the authority to take. You made us vulnerable to blackmail. And, what's even worse, you did this for more clicks.'

Hugh listened, motionless. Her words were indisputable. There was no room for him to argue. It was true: he had taken decisions he wasn't entitled to take. But even though he had done it out of a craving for clicks, he had also done it for Lucìa, to protect her. This wasn't an argument he could stress too much, though; he should have let her take ownership of the issues with Pandora – period.

'Please, forgive me!' he begged her. 'It was in good faith.'

Lucìa's restless eyes were moving left and right – her rage far from dying away – when she spotted a solitary Cabeille on the road. The driverless car pulled up, and the single rider stared at them both with hostility. The Cabeille then sped off.

Hugh gawked at Lucìa.

'Don't you dare ask,' she threatened.

He didn't have the time, anyway, because an unidentified number calling Lucìa interrupted them. She picked up with some hesitation, fearing that it might be Vincent. It was Rachel, instead, just landed in New York.

Simply hearing Rachel's voice gave Lucìa a boost. Walking alone towards the other side of the car park, she told her friend the full story. Lucìa began with the algorithmic shenanigans to boost Vincent's social media popularity, then related her history with him, explaining – embarrassed – why she had kept it a secret from Rachel. Then, even more painfully, Lucìa revealed the wrongs of Pandora, for which Vincent was now trying to blackmail her. No detail was left out.

'I wish I was there, Luci,' Rachel said. 'You're carrying a huge burden all by yourself. I'd do anything you need to help.'

'You're so sweet, Rach. But I don't want you to take any further risks. You're already in dire straits with the *Wall Street Journal*; and only because you helped me in Berlin.'

'Reporters must accept the need to take risks … and that's what I did.'

'I'm facing a dilemma,' Lucìa admitted. 'If we publish Employee Zero's interview now, it will make a lot of people vote for Europe tomorrow. But Vincent d'Amont will get back at us. If he succeeds in destroying our reputation, Miss Cliché will have to call it quits, and all the sacrifices made will have been wasted …'

The gravity of the situation caused Lucìa to pause. She was tempted to yell out all her rage. Only the sea would hear her.

'Hugh was a fool,' she resumed, 'but I, too, have messed up: instead of being so self-centred, I should have controlled the team more closely. I took everything for granted, and this is the price I'm paying.'

Lucìa's voice was beginning to break, her breathing growing more intense, and the effort not to burst into tears was overwhelming.

'You shouldn't be so hard on yourself.' Rachel came to her rescue. 'If you step back and look at it – yes, Pandora broke the law, but not for an evil reason. She added wood to the fire that powers Miss Cliché, giving you an opportunity to pursue stories of public interest. People will not forget the scandals you've uncovered or the worthy causes you've championed. Regardless of what Vincent d'Amont may orchestrate, the balance is still in your favour. They owe you. Europe owes you.'

Rachel's heartening perspective reinvigorated Lucìa. Her friend was right: it wasn't time to give up. It might take years for Lucìa to prove her innocence, and maybe she would have to pass the baton of the vlog to someone else, but that didn't mean her merits would be erased, or that there was no future for Miss Cliché. Right after the Charlemagny vote, she would release an interview with Rachel to apologise for what had happened at Miss Cliché. People had to learn the truth directly from her. This exclusive interview would also save Rachel's career, she thought.

Tomorrow would be a key day in Europe's history and Lucìa was determined to stop thinking only about the vlog or herself. She would give all that was left in her to defend Europe.

As Lucìa wandered back towards Hugh, the clean horizon allowed her to distinguish the faint shape of the white cliffs of Dover across the Channel. It was a source of inspiration. For all the Brexit foolishness, she did remember how Great Britain had protected Europe from an inner threat, more than once.

Blood and tears.

Lucìa reached Hugh. He was working – unmotivated, devastated. When he realised that her eyes were on him, he lifted his head up, hoping for words of comfort. Lucìa smiled.

'It's time we sank Charlemagny,' she said.

XI

Karolus Magnus

Emmanuelle was sketching a paunchy silhouette on a sheet of rice paper when Vincent stormed into the penthouse. The ink pen in her hand, Emmanuelle opened the door of her studio so it was half ajar. She saw him pacing back and forth in the hallway. Then he stopped in the lounge to uncork a Beaujolais. Vincent seemed unaware, or careless, of her being at home. They had barely spoken since returning from Colmar.

The lounge's screen was showing Miss Cliché's interview with Employee Zero. From the studio, Emmanuelle saw Vincent scoffing every time his name was associated with the Almighty. Slowly, though, her attention shifted from Vincent's behaviour to the content of the interview.

Emmanuelle was a person of solid principles. Her adoptive parents had taught her that breaking the law was lazy and unfair, tantamount to a forbidden shortcut in a race. And she had always treasured that parental lesson. Employee Zero's accusations against Vincent pained her, but what hurt most was the thought of having unknowingly helped Vincent to deceive people.

Emmanuelle couldn't say if what Vincent was accused of was a crime, but for sure it sounded like cheating, which was equally loathsome. The cherished image of Vincent as an unyielding loner and a brave fighter was flaking before her.

It was under the assumption that he was acting in good faith that Emmanuelle had been proud to be at Vincent's side, even in the darkest moments, but now she knew that nothing about Vincent could be trusted to be what it seemed. If she had always considered the Cabeille case a set-up against him, for instance, even that was no longer clear. She felt lost, just like in Colmar.

Vincent watched the full interview, ceasing at some point to show any reaction. His empty wine glass left on the table, he walked to the wine cooler to fetch another bottle. As he hobbled back to the lounge, he accidentally knocked an etching on the wall. It swayed but didn't fall. He had never seen it before, but guessed that Emmanuelle, with her smooth style, was the artist. The print depicted a glimpse of the old Colmar they had strolled through together – one where a low frescoed window, all but meeting the cobbled street, seemed to invite passers-by to enter the home.

Colmar must have meant a lot to Emmanuelle, Vincent thought, if their afternoon walk had resulted in such a beautiful artwork. She had hung it on the wall so that he would know. A sense of guilt soared. He went to her studio to assuage it.

'Hey,' he said, his mouth sticky.

Emmanuelle was still drawing. She acknowledged him coldly.

'The rumours about me. Don't believe them. All lies.'

That was, for Emmanuelle, the worst approach he could have taken. Miss Cliché wouldn't make groundless allegations, she believed, so there must be some truth to it. So what was the point of his denying it all outright? It meant that their bond wasn't so tight.

'I'm tired,' she said. 'Of our lives being so dependent on ROME. Of your obsession with popularity. Even your voice changes when you're on ROME. It used to be different. I liked that you didn't try to please people at all costs. You once told me that you felt like a lion in a cage: yes, maybe, but you were a free lion in a cage. This is how I saw you.'

Emmanuelle's remarks came unexpectedly, and Vincent wasn't in the mood for a discussion. Still, he didn't want to lose her as he had already lost Lucìa years before.

'I owe ROME a lot, Emmanuelle. They're making my dream real. ROME can decide whether you exist or not. I vanished once; I don't want to vanish again.'

'You'll not vanish, Vincent. You're famous, with or without ROME. Vincent d'Amont always finds a way to turn things around.'

'Nobody goes anywhere without a strong platform behind,' he replied. 'That is the sad truth. I still need ROME. I hate them and that arrogant Marlene Gäch. She calls me all the time to give orders. Absurd.'

'Ah. I always wondered who was calling you day and night ...'

'Now you know.'

'Do you have a past with her?'

Vincent chuckled. 'No way. I've never even met her. Just calls.'

'Better. I would be jealous,' Emmanuelle said, eking out a smile.

Ten minutes to midnight; ten minutes to Charlemagny day.

ROME had decided to prevent all major influencers from publishing political content after midnight, in a blackout meant to avoid any undue influence over the polling process. So Vincent didn't have much time left to post a last video. He really had to.

'Can you wait five minutes for me, please?'

Emmanuelle lowered her eyes.

Vincent moved to that corner of the lounge that often served as a background to his clips on ROME. He put himself in front of the camera.

'I knew it'd happen. They're about to lose, so they go with their last card: stealing Charlemagny. They can't accept bottom-up decisions from our people; it must always be the other way round. I shouldn't be blamed for being popular. I have the flaw of putting our people first, that's the truth. If France and Germany don't unite, it'll be a disaster. There are too many threats out there. China will do everything to assert its force everywhere. Does China care about the future of Vietnam or Laos? No! So why should Charlemagny act differently and babysit Bulgaria or Romania? We need to think for ourselves to survive. Too much human ballast around. Our enemies say that only Europe can guarantee solidarity. They disregard history; the first to promote a single Europe were the Nazis! Our enemies are ignoring the fact that people are tired of taking orders from Brussels. Charlemagny will be a federal country, protecting the identity of all nations, where everybody will have a voice. Charlemagny will be the first digital country in history! All major decisions will be taken online by our people, not by a bunch of fat MPs. No more migration with the tracking and tracing of people! No more greedy banks – our money'll be distributed directly to citizens! No more traffic incidents, with mandatory driverless cars! No more burglaries with remote home monitoring! Charlemagny is around the corner. We must fight for it! We fight like hell, and if you don't fight like hell, we'll lose Charlemagny!'

Vincent stood up. The video was still uploading. He went to the kitchen to prepare a sandwich. When he came back, not only was the video already online, but it was quickly turning into his most viewed ever. Even he couldn't tell whether the success was genuine, or whether the Almighty was in action. As often happened when Vincent posted on ROME, his fanbase's reaction was madder, harsher, than the post itself. His die-hard supporters were enraged, calling each other to arms, promising to persuade as many people as they could to fight for freedom in the streets, against all manipulators.

Employee Zero: a fake!

The whore's run out of arguments …

It's time to clench our fists!

By hook or by crook. Fuck you, Brussels

Not the least bit worried by the risk of fomenting the crowd's basest instincts, Vincent d'Amont watched with childlike joy the fever stirred up on ROME. A pulsing web of approvals and reshares of his latest clip was spreading throughout France and Germany. No city, town or hamlet was spared. Vincent knew that, within minutes, these signs of appreciation would convert into precious votes for Charlemagny.

Devoured by curiosity for all the user behaviour data that ROME spat out with no rest, Vincent toyed for over an hour with a tool that allowed him to filter his supporters by gender, age group and location, cross-referencing all possible information to find enlightening patterns that might shape his future strategies on ROME. Then, after casting his own vote for

Charlemagny, Vincent went back to Emmanuelle. Nobody was in the studio, though. He wandered through the penthouse, shouting her name, but to no avail. Emmanuelle had gone.

* * *

Late in the afternoon of voting day, Lucìa was in the news-room. With the poll already in progress, she could now focus on fulfilling an important promise: doing her best to find Casey, the missing kid from Sparkhill.

Lucìa now knew why Hugh hadn't used Pandora to scan the evidence sent by Casey's parents. When Lucìa had called him from Vigevano, Hugh was still unsure whether Pandora could be relied upon after the downgrade.

This time, Lucìa had decided to work with Pandora without any intermediation. Hugh and Belch would stay out of it. She wanted to check for herself that everything was fine. After sharing Casey's digital footprint with Pandora, she asked: 'Pandy, can you see any connection here?'

Pandora began her artificial whirring. Now that Lucìa knew of the recent troubles, she couldn't help guessing where Pandora would venture to seek for information. Her memory naturally went to when the *News of the World* had hacked the voicemail of a missing girl, deleting messages and thus creating false expectations in the girl's parents. The mere idea that her software friend might use illicitly sourced data like that gave Lucìa the shivers.

After a couple of minutes came Pandora's result.

No significant findings. Sorry.

Lucìa was taken aback. She couldn't remember a single instance where Pandora had generated such a barren response.

So far, her searches had always produced material to work on. This time, Pandora was leaving Lucìa wanting. What was going on? Maybe Pandora was withholding information out of spite for the forced downgrade. Or perhaps Lucìa should simply come to terms with the fact that, once deprived of her unorthodox means, Pandora was no longer able to ensure a deluge of data. Lacking any hints, she didn't know how to get on with the case.

Lucìa wondered whether Miss Cliché had become too reliant on Pandora's synthetic intellect. She remembered a cabbie in London telling her that drivers spent years memorising all of London's thousand roads and routes. A wealth of knowledge now ruthlessly replaced by an instant GPS search or a driverless ride. Was this her own doomed lot? Or perhaps Pandora's issues proved that human wisdom was, in the end, more dependable than technology – and still had a say?

No more brooding, Lucìa thought. The Charlemagny results lay ahead. Polling was to end in three hours, the winner expected minutes later. She wished to distract herself – a very hard task with the newsroom talking about Charlemagny, and journalists from other outlets calling for comment. So she surprised the team with the decision to go home and follow the results from there, all by herself.

Lucìa pulled on her joggers and trainers, said a quick goodbye to the others – with whom she planned to keep in touch throughout the momentous evening – and began her run towards home. She bounded along the narrow gravel pathway bisecting Edgbaston Park, but soon left the path to enjoy the soft feel of sinking into the wet grass. Lucìa ran and ran through the green, the internal pressure slowly easing under the late afternoon sun. Exactly what she needed – the only missing element being Rachel's company.

Lucìa skirted a tiny artificial lake, where she stopped to refill her bottle by a fountain. A very young girl smiled from a bench, giggling animatedly. Lucìa waved her hand in response. A lady sitting next to the child smiled, too.

'Sorry. It's the age ...' she apologised for the little one's alleged excess of sociability.

'No problem. I wish grown-ups were so affable,' Lucìa replied.

'Do you live near here?' the lady asked with an accent that Lucìa seemed to recognise.

'I work nearby. I live in central Birmingham. But ... are you Italian?'

'Yes, you too?'

'*Si*. Vigevano. Not far from Milan.'

'We're from Abruzzo. I moved here with my husband thirty years ago. This is Lisa, my granddaughter.'

'*Ciao*, Lisa!'

The child smiled, then tried to hide behind her granny.

'My daughter was born in the UK. She works as a nurse. Lisa's dad is from Pakistan. How long have you lived here?'

'Five years now. Wow ... if I think about it, time flies.'

'And what do you do ... if I can ask?'

'I'm a news vlogger.'

The lady looked at Lucìa slightly puzzled, then nodded out of politeness. She asked: 'Do you like living here?'

'Yes. You can do so much in the UK, if you're willing to roll up your sleeves.'

'That's true,' the lady observed, yet without much conviction. 'But it has changed a lot in thirty years. People used to be much more welcoming. Now they're getting hostile towards foreigners. Sometimes I'm tempted to go back to Italy, but it's too late.'

It wasn't the first time Lucìa had heard this. Many Europeans believed that the general vibe in Britain had worsened after Brexit, with the country becoming insular, less open to other cultures, and the people concerned more with their own backyard issues than the larger picture. However, she didn't want to talk down a nation that had welcomed her with open arms, giving Lucìa opportunities she couldn't have dreamed of in Italy.

Her bottle refilled, Lucìa said goodbye to Lisa and her granny, but the child's image was still with her as she approached the end of Edgbaston Park. Lucìa knew she was fighting for Lisa, too, against the curse of a digital state controlling everyone and everything. But this fight was consuming and was reducing the chances that Lucìa had of building a proper future for herself. With her energy dwindling dangerously, she toyed with the idea of taking a break after the vote on Charlemagny, whatever the outcome.

Lucìa arrived home as the sunlight was fading. Had the Charlemagny vote occurred six months earlier, in a moment like this she would have been at the newsroom in fervent preparation for the result, surely not thinking of a shower. But everything had changed and the last week had taken a toll on Lucìa, triggering an instinct for self-preservation.

Lucìa looked around. Home seemed more neglected than usual. Annoyed by the mess, she took stopgap measures of putting her laundry into the washing machine and wiping the kitchen table clean. Perhaps it was time to hire a cleaner, she thought.

There was still one hour to go until the results when a rhythmic knocking on the door interrupted Lucìa's hurried chores. She wasn't expecting anyone. It seemed too late for a delivery.

'Rachel!' she said as she opened the door.

'Don't say anything, please. I've spent the last thirty hours on planes. But I couldn't leave you alone in the middle of a moral crisis. So, as soon as I landed in New York, I hopped on the first available flight. I need a shower.'

Lucìa laughed, then invited Rachel in.

'Not to mention that the *WSJ* will – no question – forgive me if I deliver them a live comment from Miss Cliché. So I thought I could kill two birds with one stone.'

'Sure, no problem,' replied Lucìa, knowing that Rachel, far from being an opportunist, had come back to Birmingham less for her own career than out of sheer solidarity for her friend.

'I looked for you at the newsroom. They told me you were here.'

'Yes. I really needed some time for myself.'

'Should I go? You've got a date? I was planning to camp here for the night. I've even brought all the ingredients for a Venetian Spritz. We only need ice. Let's prepare the bevvy.'

Lucìa laughed heartily at Rachel's quirkiness. After all, and despite her initial wish to spend the evening alone, she couldn't imagine anyone better to help her downplay the tension and forget her insecurities while waiting for the results.

After her shower, Rachel prepared the drinks. Lucìa sat on the sofa, with the screen already on ROME, where a frenetic mix of a Charlemagny newscast and high-budget commercials was on rotation.

Recalling the moment when, strictly for professional reasons, she had set up an account on ROME always caused a slight pain in Lucìa, even if the account was just a means for knowing her enemy better.

As she handed a glass to Lucìa, Rachel said, 'When I was over the Atlantic, an indelicate question popped up in my mind. May I?'

'Yes. Please shoot.'

'I'm just wondering – how's Vincent d'Amont in bed?'

This sort of question came with Rachel's personality. Lucìa knew it. So, after the unavoidable blush, she decided to indulge in the same game.

'He was marvellous. Now, let's talk about the German toyboy calling me from Berlin to save you. Who's he?'

'Holger, the dope slinger of the Matesanz Hotel. He even met Employee Zero and the other founders of ROME. No, actually: he doesn't remember meeting Marlene Gäch.'

'Nobody seems to have met Marlene Gäch, ever,' commented Lucìa.

She was still speaking when ROME blacked out. Lucìa and Rachel looked at each other. The digital emcee announced that voting was closed. The Charlemagny results were being finalised. Viewers were informed that bets on the winner were still possible on ROME.

Tense for what was to come, Lucìa took Rachel's hand. Within seconds, Lucìa would finally know whether Miss Cliché's efforts for Europe had been meaningful. The endless nights in Brussels; the thousands of videos aired; her triumphant speech at the East Birmingham Academy; the debate on ROME – a mere prelude to a dramatic showdown with

Vincent in France; Pandora's desperate hack attack on Miss Cliché; and Professor Sherwood's scorching betrayal.

These episodes marked a long period of hard work, where Lucìa had given all of herself to defend Europe, rewarded with visibility but consuming herself day after day, speaking to millions but neglecting a personal life.

The results from Germany were the first to come in.

For Charlemagny: 52.8%
Against Charlemagny: 47.2%

Lucìa was disappointed, yet unsurprised. She had seen it coming. Not all was lost, because France was the real battleground, and Charlemagny had to prevail in both countries to be called a winner.

Among the ambiguous results and many undecideds, the opinion polls carried out in France hadn't shown a definite pattern. The French left generally opposed Charlemagny, while the conservatives were split between staunch *souverainistes*, who loathed the idea that Paris might share decisions with Berlin, and the social right, who welcomed Charlemagny as a solution to curb immigration and stop the costly subsidising of Eastern Europe. While many were enthused at the prospect of tearing the European Union apart, fewer wished to have technology crushing their freedom in an Orwellian scenario like the one Vincent d'Amont had depicted in his last video. There was still some hope to cling on to.

Pandora wrote:

I'm analysing the results. Charlemagny won heavily in Bavaria and in former East Germany, but some big cities like Berlin and Hamburg voted against. Stuttgart, Köln, Mannheim and Essen voted for Europe. Europe also won in Frankfurt am Main – not a surprise. Dresden, Leipzig, Chemnitz, Zwickau, Jena, Rostock and Nuremberg voted for Charlemagny. More info to come.

Lucìa had prepared 100 words for a victory and another 100 for a loss – words that she wasn't ready to use.

'What will you do if Europe wins?' Rachel asked.

'This is called "jinxing", you know?'

'What will you do if Charlemagny wins?'

'Fight. Things will degenerate in the blink of an eye. ROME will devise some other trick. Vincent d'Amont will be the next President of France. I will just fight with all my might: my brain, my heart, my hands, if needed.'

Sometimes, Lucìa couldn't accept that she had spent intimate moments with the man who had created this monstrosity to pursue his own ambitions. She wondered whether she could have done anything to prevent it. Had they been still together, perhaps Lucìa would have managed to keep Vincent's degenerate ideas at bay. She was sure, however, that he had never spoken about anything close to Charlemagny when they were together in Brussels. Yes, he had pontificated about the threat of China, but without turning it yet into a trump card to achieve fame.

The Chinese card. Vincent had handled it with majestic skill. It was an easy target: the enemy spreading pandemics, repressing minorities, even denying women their own loos. Charlemagny, the digital state, was the last bastion against the cyberwar that – he was sure – China would eventually start against the West. His apocalyptic view had enflamed millions of minds in Europe, sounding more compelling to many than solidarity or the environment, the themes to which Miss Cliché's rhetoric often gravitated.

After a most trying set of commercials, the French results arrived. Lucìa hesitated to watch. The numbers were there, on the screen that her eyes wished to avoid. She finally found the courage.

For Charlemagny: 54.2%
Against Charlemagny: 45.8%

Europe had lost the poll, with no right to an appeal.

Rachel looked at Lucìa's blank stare. Feeling obliged to do something, she yelled at the screen: 'C'mon, it was all rigged, we know it! I never bought this German Blockchain Authority anyway!'

Lucìa wasn't listening. In a twinkle, a bunch of numbers had erased everything. Published too late, the interview with Employee Zero hadn't moved the needle. With ROME and Vincent denying all accusations, people had been left wondering about the interview's authenticity. Nothing compared with Vincent's midnight rallying cry, which had been successful in firing up his supporters and, probably, in persuading others to join Charlemagny.

Lucìa felt depleted, burnt-out. Other media were already trying to get in touch, but she didn't want to connect. 'You look shitty, my dear.' Rachel stepped in with her signature bluntness. 'Please, take a rest. I'll guard the fortress. Go to your bedroom … it's an order. *Raus!*'

Lucìa followed her friend's diktat. Once the pain of disappointment was over, she would plan the next move, but not now. A nap would do her good. Lucìa curled up under the duvet. It was drizzling outside. She could hear Rachel washing dishes in the kitchen. ROME was still on, spreading the excited screams of Charlemagniers through the entire flat. But the stinging sound of her opponents' boisterous joy didn't stop her dozing off, sleep a palliative against an unbearable reality.

Rachel woke her up after an unspecified period.

'Lucìa ... Lucìa!'

'What ... ?'

'Trouble in Paris.'

Without even letting Rachel finish, Lucìa rushed to the living room. She browsed in haste through the major vlogs, all streaming live scenes from Paris. Only Miss Cliché didn't. Her vlog's splash page reported news of Paris but, incredibly, lacked video coverage of what was happening.

'When did all this start?' Lucìa, still in her underwear, asked Rachel.

'Twenty minutes ago, no more.'

'Why didn't you wake me up before?'

'It took a helluva time to wake you up, sleeping beauty.'

Lucìa called Hugh. She had decided that, despite what he'd done, he would stay where he was for the time being. Vincent hadn't revealed anything about Pandora, so she could still pretend that everything was fine at Miss Cliché.

'What happened? Why aren't we streaming from Paris? We have François, one of our best vloggers, there,' she said, her voice full of impatience. The post-Charlemagny bereavement had waned already.

'I've tried to call you four times, Lucìa, but you didn't answer. Well – our François was walking nonchalantly along the Champs-Élysées to feel the pulse of people when a group of Charlemagniers saw him. After yelling "*il travaille pour Miss Cliché!*", they attacked him. He's got a shiner and a broken nose.'

'Gosh! How is he?'

'He's still at the hospital. Nothing major. But now all our vloggers in Paris refuse to poke their noses out. Can't blame them. François was lucky that two gendarmes rescued him; it could have been far worse. The attackers escaped arrest.'

Hugh had to give Lucìa a thorough explanation of the complicated situation in Paris. His verbosity was, this time, almost a necessity.

Minutes after the victory of Charlemagny, Vincent d'Amont had popped up on ROME. Jubilant, in this new video he told the world that the elite's old tricks no longer worked: voters had followed their wise instincts, refusing to settle for less than they deserved. Charlemagny was closer, but not a reality yet, he warned. If Charlemagniers didn't follow up the vote on ROME with immediate action, the establishment would curl up like a hedgehog to defend its heinous privileges. The elite would do everything to avoid change, even offer free-thinkers some ludicrous consolation prize to lure them back into obedience – the usual pocket money from the European Central Bank. So, Vincent d'Amont exhorted his acolytes to besiege the Élysée Palace and shout at the President that they would no longer take it.

'Get out of the hamster's cage!'

Called to arms, Charlemagniers in the thousands had taken to the streets of Paris. Searching for a culprit for their

discontent, they didn't need flags or banners, for they all bore
the resentful stare of the left-behind.

As the thumping melee converged from every angle
on the Élysée, a human jam formed in Rue Saint-Honoré,
with the insurgents chanting and screaming as they slowly
paraded along the narrow road. By that time, the stores were
all shut, no strolling tourist could be seen. Saint-Honoré was
hostage to the Charlemagniers. A masked man in cargo pants
rattled a baton against the shutters of a boutique. Another
sprayed paint on all available walls and laughed hysterically
when a fellow rioter peed against the bulletproof screen of a
jewellery store.

It is said that whoever enjoys wealth feels untouchable.
Most likely, this was the naive perception of that senior resi-
dent in a nightshirt who, leaning from an arched window,
addressed the street mob with a polite but firm complaint.
Seeing the crowd immediately yell back and throw objects
at him, the composed man retreated in haste. Too late: they
had already decreed him a representative of the much-loathed
elite. The wild throng began to press against the entrance
of the listed building. A battering ram moved from hand to
hand. The crowd stormed the gate, ran up the stairs, broke
into his flat. The night-shirted man was the first known
casualty of Charlemagny.

Drawing closer to the presidential palace, the bulging ranks
now also included those who barely knew what Charlemagny
was about, but believed there was nothing to lose in joining
the blast. With no resistance in the empty streets, these men
considered themselves at liberty to besmirch, slash, break and
set fire to anything in their path. They were born to carry out

violent endeavours, and before now only the forces of law and order had stopped them from making destruction their full-time vocation.

Law and order finally materialised at the junction with Rue Royale, where a multilayer barrier made of twenty striped vans was waiting eagerly for the Charlemagniers. The latter hadn't enough time to attack, or retreat, when the gendarmerie charged them. Tear gas and rubber bullets hit the inexperienced rioters, causing their dispersion into the side streets before the gendarmes could even apprehend them. This was about the same time that a tiny batch of Charlemagniers reached the Champs-Élysées and ran into François, Lucìa's best vlogger in Paris.

Having averted the feared attack on the Élysée, the police didn't pursue the rioters beyond the first arrondissement. The insurgents could thus reunite to resume their joyful ravaging not far away for hours. They looted and burned the stores around Cadet station undisturbed. Someone later argued that the police had purposely failed to act, letting the Charlemagniers ransack Paris to stir up public opinion against them.

Vincent d'Amont observed the baleful developments in Paris from a Cabeille leaving town. With his protest march slipping out of control, Vincent had thought it wise to flee the capital. He would, for the moment, keep a low profile in Alsace, where his friend Léon had offered him a secure country house, from where Vincent planned to guide the Charlemagniers. A future was in the making, but Vincent still didn't know whether it was a rosy one for the man once defined as a brand in himself.

Lucìa followed the events in Paris with apprehension. Charlemagny was causing issues earlier than expected, and those who had downplayed the ROME poll as a mere social media stunt with no possible repercussions in real life had now been proved wrong. Lucìa felt her hands were tied, her frustration doubled by the fact that her favourite vlogger in Paris had been knocked out at the onset of the riot.

Absorbed by events, it was already four in the morning when Lucìa took a first look at her unread messages. Some came from Pandora, but Lucìa wasn't in the mood for vote statistics or historical trivia.

A message from Italy caught her attention.

Chiamami. Urgente!

It was the scruffy reporter who had told her in Vigevano of the improper liaison between the German Foreign Minister and the Governor of South Tyrol. He wouldn't be contacting Lucìa for anything other than a good reason.

'Got news,' he answered without even saying hi. 'Our two friends have spoken again.'

'And … ?' She likewise got straight to the point.

'Around eleven o'clock, the Italian governor called Berlin to congratulate them on Charlemagny. The German minister was ecstatic. He had probably been toasting the victory for hours; he sounded sloshed. After letting the Italian brown-nose him for a while, he mumbled that things weren't as they seemed, that Germany wasn't standing still.'

'Meaning?'

'His slurring was so bad that he was almost inaudible … he claimed that Marlene Gäch is only a figurehead. Maybe it was just drunk-talk, or maybe not.'

Lucìa didn't speak, but found what he was saying valuable.

'We're lucky that my friend with the police in Bolzano is a workaholic,' the journalist continued. 'He called me right after hearing the tapped conversation. And then I called you.'

'You did the right thing,' Lucìa assured him.

What the Italian reporter had just said sparked an immediate question for Rachel after the call.

'What did you say, last week, about Marlene Gäch's shares in ROME? *Bear* shares?'

'No. Flamingo stocks,' Rachel teased her. '*Bearer* shares!'

'Refresh me on how they work, please ... and stop mocking me!'

'Simple. Whoever's in possession of the shares is the owner. Bearer shares don't need to be registered anywhere.'

'Mmm ...'

'What are you mumbling about, Lucìa?'

'I've got an idea. I'm flying to Berlin.'

'What? Berlin isn't Stonehenge. You can't just go there on a whim. It's dangerous! I would come with you, but I've been ... blacklisted in Germany.'

'I need to go. I should've gone there in the first place, instead of sending you. I can't tell you anything more now, but I will. I promise.'

'Fine. If you meet Herr Rectoscopy, please say hello from me.'

'Who's Herr Rectoscopy?'

'The suit that ousted me from the country. He's as pleasant as a rear-end examination without sedation.'

'A subtle and delicate metaphor, Lady Meat and Potatoes!'

'*Touché,*' Rachel laughed.

Lucìa didn't customarily act on impulse; this time was an exception. The next direct plane to Berlin was in just three hours' time.

Marlene Gäch.

Her name kept popping up everywhere.

Lucìa started packing. Planning to be back soon, she put only a few items in the smallest of her bags.

Marlene Gäch.

The reclusive founder of ROME, who never appeared in public. Something was weird about her.

Lucìa booked a taxi.

Marlene Gäch.

Even Employee Zero, the first person hired by Marlene Gäch, hadn't met her in person.

Lucìa had never consulted Pandora on Frau Gäch. It might be worth a try, she thought, even if Pandora was no longer on steroids.

'Pandy, what can you tell me about Marlene Gäch, please?'

Pandora responded after the shortest of all whirrings.

'Marlene Gäch is an anagram of Charlemagne.'

* * *

At Berlin Brandenburg Airport, a skinny, tattooed young man, hidden behind a steel pillar, peeped periodically at the sliding doors. He wasn't alone in waiting. Three men, leaning on the balustrade that separated welcomers from passengers, glanced with impatience at the flow of people streaming out of the arrivals hall. The Birmingham flight had touched down on the tarmac twenty minutes before.

The young man had to act fast if he didn't want the others to precede him. At the right moment, he walked quickly against the stream of people to reach the internal corridor unnoticed. Once there, he spotted the shape of Lucìa moving within the crowd. He walked towards her.

'Miss Cliché – hi!'

Lucìa was used to it – being approached by unfamiliar people who felt entitled to act as her long-time friend. Even on the plane, a passenger had expressed to her all of his unsolicited sympathy for the luckless vote. Still, every time a stranger drew close, Lucìa flinched.

'I'm Holger. Rachel's friend. Did I scare you? So sorry.'

'Holger!' Lucìa exclaimed, while by reflex her thoughts went to his amusing under-the-counter trades.

'We must be careful,' Holger said, pointing at the sliding doors. 'I've just spotted the same officer that talked to Rachel the other day. He must be here for you.'

'Herr Rectoscopy.'

'What?'

'Nothing.'

'We need to exit the airport from somewhere else, or he'll see you.'

'Any ideas?'

Holger could be very resourceful in emergency situations. 'You see that handler?' he said. 'Seems nice. You tell him that a pain-in-the-ass stalker is waiting for you. So you'd prefer to exit the airport from departures. He'll help you. Guaranteed. We can meet there. But please put your sunglasses on; you're quite a name here.'

Holger was right about the handler, who even fetched a shuttle cart to bring Lucìa to departures through a shortcut. Holger was already there.

Once on a train to central Berlin, they found an empty section in one coach.

'Rachel asked me to stick around for you. But what brings you to Berlin?'

'I'm in Berlin to meet Marlene Gäch.'

'Wow. What time is your appointment?'

'Flexible. I'm paying her a surprise visit.'

Holger widened his eyes, astonished. 'Good luck!'

As the train left the airport, Lucìa checked for updates from Paris.

She learnt that the Charlemagniers had spent the night laying waste to Rue La Fayette and its surroundings with unrelenting barbarism. Then, with the insurgents heading menacingly towards other parts of the city, Vincent d'Amont had intervened. The riot-inspirer had urged his followers to cease the violence and move towards the top of Montmartre hill, a traditional landmark for all would-be revolutionaries. Apparently, they had followed his instructions without fault, marching up the hill to establish a Charlemagnian enclave on the lawns of the Sacré-Coeur. Some among the rioters, though, were beginning to wonder where Vincent d'Amont was.

Lucìa and Holger alighted at the metro station that had been built one year before to serve the headquarters of ROME. As she walked up the exit stairs, Lucìa looked at the skyline. The imposing sight of the Drexler Steinmetz, paired with leaden clouds in the distance, produced a scaring effect, making her feel little and powerless; but she knew that her instincts had been right in taking her to Berlin. You can't hide from your demons forever; you must exorcise them, she thought.

'Holger, can you please wait for me at that café? This will take some time.'

Lucìa felt that this was the moment for her to confront ROME by herself. Holger didn't insist on coming upstairs as he had done with Rachel.

She entered the Drexler Steinmetz. Nobody was in the lobby. An intimidating line of digital intercoms lay ahead. She randomly picked one. The intercom screen switched on. A neutral voice behind a scintillant blue light asked for her visit reference number. She stayed silent. The same voice reiterated the request. Clueless, Lucìa told the intercom the truth: 'I'm Miss Cliché. I'm here for Marlene Gäch.'

The intercom hushed. Feeling stupid, and no longer so confident that her being there made much sense, Lucìa was poised to leave the Drexler Steinmetz when the glassy gate in front of her opened.

She stiffened.

'You may now enter. But please leave your device here,' the cold voice instructed.

A holder slid out of the intercom station. Reluctantly, Lucìa dropped her device. Drawing a shaky breath, she walked past the gate. There was complete silence.

A corridor led Lucìa to an inner hall with fifteen lifts. Only one was open on the ground floor. As she stepped into that lift, the doors sealed her in with a sharp thud.

Lucìa couldn't say whether the cabin was moving but, when the lift reopened, a numeral was imprinted on the opposing wall.

LXXXIX

The eighty-ninth: the floor of Marlene Gäch.

Lucìa stepped out of the lift and walked through the only available doorway. It took her into a room so immense that she could barely see the end. The huge space was empty. Lucìa hadn't met a single person since entering the Drexler Steinmetz.

Floor 89 consisted of a high-ceilinged, open space devoid of partitions and furnishing other than a solitary desk in the middle. A black screen loomed over the glass desk.

As Lucìa drew closer, an elaborate symbol began glowing on the suspended screen.

It seemed like the prototype of a logo for ROME. The symbol looked familiar, even if Lucìa wasn't sure where she had seen it. She examined the intricate shape for some time, but still couldn't say where the familiarity originated from. Only when the symbol faded and the screen turned dark again, did she realise.

The Chrismon of Charlemagne!

As Lucìa struggled to give the eerie resemblance a meaning, the lights suddenly dimmed. Lucìa moved backwards when, unexpected, Marlene Gäch appeared in front of her.

The almost translucent skin and blonde hair, verging on white, gave Marlene Gäch an ethereal air.

'I knew we would meet sometime,' she told Lucìa. 'I regret I am not in Berlin today.'

'My fault. I didn't give you enough notice,' Lucìa said, with a tinge of irony, to the pale woman on the screen.

'I have been observing you, Miss Cliché,' Marlene Gäch continued. 'You are fighting hard, very hard, but it's a lost war – you know it. You believe you are fighting us, but you are fighting history. Charlemagny has had a long gestation.'

She stared at Lucìa. Lucìa stared back.

An electronic image materialised at once on the desk surface. Lucìa stooped to take a closer look. The high-resolution picture of a yellowing map now filled the whole table-screen. It outlined the landmass of Europe, a large portion of which – roughly matching current France, Germany and Poland – was shaded in ruby red.

The map's original version had to be dated around the end of the nineteenth century, Lucìa thought. She then noticed a handwritten note on the map's top margin: *Annex I.*

The note prompted Lucìa to scroll with the touchscreen randomly in all directions. This brought into view a typed document. It had the customary layout of an old diplomatic document, like the many she had perused in Brussels, written in French on one side, German on the other. Lucìa's attention quickly moved to the bottom, where three red wax-sealed signatures stood out next to the place and date of execution: *Schloss Wilhelmshöhe, 20. Januar 1871.*

One signature was readable. The others, more hieroglyphic in their flamboyance, were hard to distinguish.

'The German Emperor, Wilhelm I, and his Chancellor, Otto von Bismarck: if you are guessing,' said Marlene Gäch, interrupting the silence.

'And Napoleon III, Emperor of France,' Lucìa added.

'Yes, correct,' Marlene Gäch confirmed.

At their secret visit to the Sacré-Coeur, Lucìa had learned from Vincent, basking in his favourite role of history buff, that after losing the Prussian war, Napoleon III had spent months in Germany. Chancellor von Bismarck, the mastermind behind the creation of the German Empire, had often paid visits to Napoleon in the castle where he was held in golden captivity.

'Only a handful of people has ever known about the Treaty of Schloss Wilhelmshöhe,' Marlene Gäch said. 'Prussia won the war. France was on its knees. Wilhelm and Napoleon agreed to unite France and Germany in a single empire. They were real rulers, free to command in the interest of their peoples. There were no riotous parliaments to interfere at the time.'

'Why wasn't Charlemagny established then?' Lucìa asked. She wished Pandora was there with her to carry out some fact-checking on Marlene Gäch's story, which seemed to Lucìa a mere bid to find an historical foundation for Charlemagny.

'Napoleon was supposed to return to France with our army to depose Léon Gambetta's illegitimate government. It would have been an easy mission – if not for England. Queen Victoria learned of Napoleon's intentions from his wife, Eugenie, who lived in England. Victoria threatened to wage war against Germany if Wilhelm ever tried to enact the Treaty of Schloss Wilhelmshöhe. Bismarck recommended Wilhelm desist: Crowned Emperor of Germany only weeks earlier, Wilhelm was to focus on domestic issues, not on starting a war with England, he was told.'

God save the Queen, thought Lucìa.

'What happened then?' she asked.

'Under the threat of martial law, Bismarck ordered the Treaty to be classified in the archives of the Deutsche Reich. In France, Napoleon was stripped of the imperial title. He died in exile. Nobody in France ever learned about his agreement with Bismarck. The Treaty of Schloss Wilhelmshöhe remained secret and inaccessible for seventy years. It resurfaced only when an unidentified German servant broke Bismarck's orders and gave the classified compact to Chancellor Adenauer on the day of Adenauer's seventy-fourth birthday: the fifth of January, 1950.'

'Quite a present,' Lucìa commented.

'The German Foreign Office confirmed that the Treaty was still valid and binding. Chancellor Adenauer, ecstatic, met President Auriol in an unknown location. Talks between France and Germany began. The negotiations, meant to be secret, were so promising that Adenauer even hinted about the idea in an interview. A crucial mistake, because England didn't like his intentions and plotted against Charlemagny for a second time. When Auriol visited London in early March, King George was forthright in telling him that the United Kingdom wouldn't tolerate a union between France and Germany. Right after the war, France didn't want frictions with the United Kingdom. So Auriol had to give up pursuing Charlemagny.'

God save the King, too, Lucìa couldn't help thinking.

'Sadly, the Treaty of Schloss Wilhelmshöhe went back to the secret archives of the Bundesregierung,' Marlene Gäch concluded. 'It reappeared only two weeks ago, in the hands of our Foreign Minister.'

'How do you know about all this?' Lucìa asked. 'And if it's all true, why haven't you disclosed the Treaty to the public?'

'You would have accused us of influencing the poll,' was Marlene Gäch's tactical answer. 'We will tell the world of the agreement between France and Germany very soon. People need to know the truth.'

Lucìa couldn't understand what Germany really wanted. The wealthiest country in Europe, showing no sign of wear and tear, and the leader of a European Union that hardly made decisions unless they were approved by Berlin: an enviable position. But not enough, apparently.

'Why are you doing all this?' Lucìa asked.

'Germany has waited too long,' Marlene Gäch said with no waver of her voice, barely looking at Lucìa. 'There's too much dirt and corruption around us. We must bring German rule outside of Germany. We must teach the others to live the way we live. They will be grateful to us. Mistakes were made in the past when we tried to assert our superiority with violence. But how long must the atonement last? This time, Germany will steer the world without shedding blood. We will use data instead of bullets, algorithms instead of guns, satellites instead of tanks. Order needs to be imposed. If it's not us, it will be China. They plundered Africa and now are pointing at Europe.'

A surge of anger bloomed inside Lucìa. In contrast to Marlene Gäch – composed, sterile, almost impalpable – Lucìa flared up. 'You just want conflict. A digital war, but still a war, to satisfy Germany's selfish interest in the name of civilisation. It will end badly, again.'

'Vincent d'Amont was right: you are a moralist,' Marlene Gäch rejoiced. 'But I like you, Miss Cliché. That's why I haven't divulged what Pandora did. Vincent d'Amont, instead, is a disappointment. Why mention the Nazis in his last speech? And he left Paris as soon as the riot started. Coward. Employee Zero is a traitor, but at least he has the guts to fight. He's in Paris.'

Marlene Gäch had marked Vincent's fate with her words. And even if Lucìa thought he deserved it – for his was a debacle of his own making – she felt sorry for him. Or, more accurately, Lucìa was sad that a clever mind had been led so astray.

'You are more like me than you want to admit, Miss Cliché,' Marlene Gäch continued. 'We are both women who would do anything to fulfil our dreams.'

Lucìa couldn't stand that comparison.

'I don't care if Germany imprisoned Napoleon III to make him sign a treaty,' she objected. 'I don't care if Germany has an awful lot of power and money – it doesn't mean you can abuse other countries. We have moved away from the errors of the past to become a Union where all nations are together. It's the right path. Why go back? Charlemagny is just a fantasy, a dangerous delusion!'

'Yesterday, the people spoke for change,' Marlene Gäch insisted, although without a show of animosity. 'You're an incorrigible nostalgic, Miss Cliché.'

'Am I nostalgic? I don't know what you really are, Marlene Gäch – are you real or … artificial?'

The lights went off immediately. Her voice echoed in the empty floor. The screen was blank again. Alone in almost total darkness, Lucìa managed to hurry out of the room and reach the lift. She took it, not too sure whether they would let her leave. But the lift went downwards undisturbed.

As she was walking out of the Drexler Steinmetz, Lucìa made a decision. Miss Cliché would return to Europe. Nothing kept her in Birmingham, and she couldn't think of fighting for the destiny of the Union from overseas. For all those millions who had chosen Charlemagny, there were millions opposing it. Many found inspiration in Miss Cliché. She shouldn't let them down. The prospect of war was looming, and she wasn't persuaded that it would be a conflict free of violence or blood.

If he's really in Paris, I should look for Employee Zero, she thought. He's the best person I can count on for this war.

Life was steering her towards the destiny it had picked out for her, Lucìa appreciated. This was not the place she had imagined ending up in when, as a kid, she had seen herself as a civil rights lawyer or a teacher. On second thought, she hadn't gone that astray, because Miss Cliché's mission was indeed that of informing people and denouncing wrongs. Lucìa knew she would have to weather storms while standing up for her ideals – but she had to do something, because Lucìa was a woman of action, not a moralist.

A thin drizzle was falling outside the Drexler Steinmetz. Standing alone in the empty concrete square was Holger. He seemed worried. That's when Lucìa saw a message from Pandora.

The Sacré-Coeur is in flames. They set it on fire.

About the Author

Alan Rhode is a former journalist from Italy, now living in the UK. This is his first novel.